UNTIL THE LAST DOG DIES

a Joe Box mystery

UNTIL THE LAST DOG DIES

a Joe Box mystery

by
John Laurence Robinson

RiverOak®
Good News in Fiction

An Imprint of Cook Communications Ministries
COLORADO SPRINGS, COLORADO • PARIS, ONTARIO
KINGSWAY COMMUNICATIONS, EASTBOURNE, ENGLAND

RiverOak® is an imprint of
Cook Communications Ministries, Colorado Springs, CO 80918
Cook Communications, Paris, Ontario
Kingsway Communications, Eastbourne, England

UNTIL THE LAST DOG DIES
© 2004 by John Laurence Robinson

**Published in association with Hartline Literary Agency,
Attn: Janet Benrey, 123 Queenston Dr., Pittsburgh, PA
15235.**

First Printing, 2004
Printed in the United States of America
1 2 3 4 5 6 7 8 9 10 Printing/Year 08 07 06 05 04

ISBN: 1-589190-211

Dedication

For Barb,
All my love.
All my life.

"A question settled by force and violence remains forever unsettled and will rise again."

—Jefferson Davis

"When the truth is shown to be lies,
and all the joy within you dies,
don't you want somebody to love?"

—Jefferson Airplane

1

rite this down: Any phone call taken after 10:00 PM will be bad. I've never seen this rule fail in nearly fifty years, and it was proving itself again now. I'm not sure how long the ringing had been going on, but the insistent, intrusive clamor was dragging me inch by stubborn inch back from the sleep I'd so much needed. I'd only crawled into bed a scant hour before, having pulled a thirty-six-hour nonstop marathon working a child custody case, and I was wiped out. Still in a mental fog, I fumbled the receiver from its cradle. I rubbed a rough hand over gritty eyes as I mumbled my greeting.

"This had better be either a beautiful woman or someone who owes me money."

The voice was high. Tinny and nervous. "Joe Box?"

I slapped my jaws shut. It couldn't be. I sat up with a

frown. "Little Bit? Is that—"

"Joe!" The relief in the man's voice was pitiful. "I wasn't sure if I had the right guy or not, no."

"This *is* Little Bit, right? From Louisiana?"

"Saint Charles Parish. Yeah, it's me, Joe. We gotta talk."

Perfect. This guy, of all people. I hadn't seen or heard from Leo-Bob "Little Bit" Frontenau since the Vietnam War more than thirty years ago. Which I suppose was for the best; the memories from that time weren't good. Little Bit had been a lousy soldier, certainly the worst I'd ever served with. The man was lazy, incompetent, complaining, scheming, woman-crazy … and with all that probably the closest thing I'd had to a friend over there. What could he want now? I rotated my neck, listening to my vertebrae pop. Getting older stinks. But it beats the alternative. "Do you know what time it is? What in the world do you want?"

"I'm in trouble, Joe." I heard him swallow. "So are you."

I shook my head. "Bad time for jokes, Lit—"

"It's not a joke!" he broke in.

"Whatever it is, it can wait. I'm in bed. Call me tomorrow."

"It's only seven here in LA," he said. I heard the clink of a bottleneck against a glass. There's nothing else in the world that makes that noise. I should know. It was a sound I'd been intimately familiar with, until a midlife course change three months ago.

"Well, this isn't LA," I shot back. "It's Cincinnati, it's ten o'clock, and I'm beat. Like I said, call me back in the morning. At my office. We'll talk then. And Little Bit? Sober up before you do." I went to set the phone down, but as I pulled it away from my ear I heard his voice again, sounding even more frantic.

"Don't! Don't hang up!" I ignored him, my hand still moving the thing back to the nightstand when he shouted, "He's out, Joe."

Those words jerked me fully awake. I slowly pulled the receiver to my ear. "Say that again."

"You heard me right," Little Bit breathed. "God help us, it's true. I don't know when, no, and I don't know how, but he's out."

I scowled. "That's impossible."

"Says you. He called me." The man was almost sobbing with fear. "Just now. Not ten minutes ago." I heard him swallow. "And he soun' bad, Joe. Real bad."

"Little Bit." My words were slow and deliberate. "Listen to me. It's not him. It can't be. He was put in a prison for the criminally insane more than three decades ago. Remember? They practically welded the door shut on him. He's been in there ever since, cozy as a mouse. You should know that as well as anyone."

"But—"

"He's in there to be studied," I went on. "Probed. Guys like him they don't let out. Ever." I began rubbing the bridge of my nose. "Somebody's pulling your chain, pardner."

"Oh yeah?" Little Bit snapped. "Then listen to this. Here's the worst part." His voice dropped. "He knows about the cards, Joe. And what we did wit' them." His laugh was bitter. "Now who's chain gettin' pulled, huh?"

That stopped me. "Are you sure?"

"Yeah," he groaned. "Oh yeah. And nobody else knew about them, no. The Loot had told us we was the only unit using cards beside the Berets."

I remembered. Our platoon had taken to using a variation of an old psychological warfare trick the Special Forces had started. But instead of placing an ace of spades on a dead Cong's face, like they did, the lieutenant had decided to use a Tarot card. Specifically, Death—old Skinny Bones himself. He wanted to strike some terror into the Cong, secure a little payback.

The brass frowned on such practices, but we did it anyway. Lieutenant Calhoun figured, correctly in my thinking, those constipated monkey-runners could afford such niceties; they were in the rear with the gear. We were the ones humping it through the bush.

Little Bit rushed nervously on. "We always put a death card on the face of a Cong we killed. And he *knows* about that, man."

"Yeah, yeah, again assuming it's him." My voice was gruff. "Get to it already."

"He sent me one, Joe! A death card!" Little Bit swallowed again, a huge sound over the phone. "I got in from work late, and there it was, stuck in my door. When I saw it I almost croaked right on my gallery." For some reason Cajuns like Little Bit call the porches on their houses "galleries." I guess even in LA some things don't change.

He was shouting now. "I pulled the card off and stumbled inside, starin' at it, and not ten seconds after I did, he called me! It's the voodoo, Joe, the *gris-gris*. He's watchin' my house.

He knows where I live. He—"

I broke in on his ravings. "Calm down. Take a breath. Do you know how crazy you sound?"

But it was like Little Bit hadn't heard. "He told me his dead Cong brothers have voices, and he said they're callin' to him from the earth. I'm tellin' you it's the *gris-gris*, man! They said it was time for him to pay the debt, and he told me I was marked. I was goin' to be next."

"Next? Next for what?"

"I ain't sure, no," he moaned, "but it can't be good."

I really wasn't in the mood for this tonight. Was *not*. I lay back on the bed, phone still against my ear. "You know what, Little Bit? I'll tell you who's doing this. Ed Ralston. You remember him. You remember what a sick, twisted dude he was. And he was with the platoon quite awhile, so he'd know all about those cards. This is just the kind of stunt Ralston'd pull, especially on you. He knew how superstitious you were. And still are, I guess." I yawned. "See? Isn't that simple? Mystery solved."

Little Bit's voice went flat as he said the next. "That'd solve it, except for one t'ing. Ralston's dead."

I narrowed my eyes. "When?"

"A week ago," he answered, his speech shaky. "It was in the papers. Ran a bug up my back, that's for true. See, old Ralston only lived a couple of miles from me, and we got together a few times to have some drinks, but not much. I didn't like that man. He had mean eyes. But it don't matter, 'cause last Monday afternoon he croaked. His car went off the PCH, the Pacific Coast Highway. Right over a cliff, man.

It blew up when it hit the beach. Almost took out a bum lookin' for cans."

"Cars crash all the time," I said.

"But the timin'—"

"Doesn't matter," I broke in. "Ralston always was a jerk. You know he was. Especially when he'd had a few. I'd bet if you'd check with the cops they'd tell you he had a gutful of liquor in him when he went over."

"Maybe." Little Bit didn't sound convinced. "But—"

"You know, I'd love to keep talking to you," I said. "But I'm not going to. I've given this about all the attention I feel like giving it tonight. Call me back in the morning. Or not. Your choice. Hang tight, soldier." I hung up the phone.

But sleep was a long time coming.

Again, the phone was ringing. Again, it was pulling me back from my rest like an alligator dragging its prey into the swamp. I opened my bleary, sleep-encrusted eyes, glancing out my bedroom window at the slate-gray dawn, then I rolled over toward my clock. Five-thirty in the blessed AM I was going to kill Little Bit.

I snatched the phone up. "What now?"

"Is this Joe Box?" The voice was a woman's. She was crying.

"Yes," I said, squinting and calming my tone. "Who's this?"

"M-Melanie Frontenau—" The woman's voice caught on the last syllable. "I don't know if you remember—" Her voice snagged again. "It's Little Bit, Mr. Box. He's dead."

2

I hate going to the police station, any police station. Which makes it doubly bad for me, seeing as how I used to be a cop. But Jack Mulrooney—check that, make it Detective Jack Mulrooney, head man of the Cincinnati Police Department vice squad—had insisted I come down in person to ask him for the favor I needed. I suppose so he could look me in the eye when he said no.

I sighed in disgust as I headed down I-75. I also don't like going into town. With Cincinnati's riverfront revitalization in full cry, the city's pace had picked up, and the April riots that had put our town front and center on the world stage for a while were just a fading, and rotten, memory. So combine the usual big-city busy bustle with the pre-Thanksgiving, pre-Christmas buying rush, and downtown Cincy was a place I tended to avoid like the plague. The only good thing about the trip was that I knew I'd get free parking at the underground garage beneath the Whittaker Building.

I get that benefit there for life, thanks to Nick Castle. His company, Castle Industries, takes up the entire thirtieth floor of the Whittaker, and I'd done a good turn for one of Nick's directors back this past summer. The *gratis* parking was a perk in return. Not to mention Nick's been dogging me to take a position as his firm's corporate investigator. I'm still thinking it over.

I also thought about last night's phone call from Little Bit as I drove. And then the call this morning from his wife, Melanie. Was he really dead? If the grief I'd heard in her voice was real, he surely was. I'd only met Melanie the one time, the day I got back to the land of good 'n plenty after my tour in hell was done, but I remembered her well. Little Bit and I had been discharged the same day. In fact, we were supposed to be on the same 727 bringing us back to LAX, but the army being the army, I was put on one plane and Little Bit on the flight nine hours behind mine. At Phu Dhoc airbase, the first leg of our trip home, the land lines were once again out, and the smirking sergeant in the commo hut had refused to let Little Bit use the radio to put through a call. Melanie now had no way of knowing that her husband was going to be late. Little Bit desperately turned to me, eyes huge, and asked me to help. I said sure.

Now my plane had landed, and I'd disembarked straight into a mess. Somehow I was supposed to find Little Bit's wife in the airport snarl of garbled loudspeaker messages, blaring radios and TVs, anxious soldiers leaving, relieved soldiers arriving, tearful families for both, skycaps, ticket agents, cops, vendors, religious nuts, and utterly confused hippies staring around at it all.

I finally spotted Melanie in the mob, looking past me for a husband who wasn't there. Little Bit had given me her picture, but even if he hadn't, she wouldn't have been hard to miss; he'd described her to us all enough times. And had I seen them together; they would have made, as they say, a cute couple.

Little Bit was what was known in Louisiana as a redbone, an uncertain mix of black and Native American, with some white thrown in. The result, at least in his case, was a smallish, wiry, copper-colored man with red-tinted hair and turquoise eyes. His wife, Melanie, on the other hand, was an octaroon, a person only one-eighth black. Spying her, I saw she was nearly as small as he. And at first glance, Melanie, for some reason, struck me as a sad type, not so much one of life's victims as one of life's ignored ones. Her hair was thin and black, and hung straight down on either side of her olive-hued, flat-planed face, the part in that hair going down the center of her skull in a line so even it could have been cut in with a bandsaw. Her eyebrows were heavy but not unattractive, the eyes themselves liquid and dark-brown and melancholy.

When she saw me waving at her across the way, she frowned and looked away. But then something must have clicked, and she looked at me in the puzzled way people do when they see a face that should be familiar. At least I hoped that was true; Little Bit had told me that he had described me to Melanie in his letters.

He must have, because she smiled uncertainly at me and headed over at a trot, pushing her way through the press of bodies. That small smile did wonders for her.

"Melanie?" I asked her as she reached me.

"Yeah." She cocked her head. "Don't I know you or sumpin'?"

I smiled. "Maybe you do from Little Bit's letters. I'm Joe Box." I held my hand out, and she gripped it.

The woman's palm was rough, and I noticed the backs of both her hands were crisscrossed with small, white scars. I remembered now that Little Bit told me he'd met his wife at an oyster bar in the French Quarter in New Orleans, where she shucked the shellfish with a knife at ten cents a throw. Tough work even for a man; the bill-like edges on those shells are as sharp as razors.

"Woo, you a big one, Joe." Melanie's smile up at me was better now as we released hands. "Little Bit said you was. Said you a tough fighter, and that's a fac'." She rose up on her toes, peering past me. "So where is that man a' mine? Still on the plane with them flygirls? He surely like the wimmins, for true." She was cranking her head around when I told her.

"We got separated, Melanie. He'll be on the next plane, but it won't get here for another nine hours."

"Nine *hours*?" She looked back at me, shaking her head, the sadness seeming to settle back in. "Well, that's just fine. What'm I sp'osed to do for nine hours? We'll miss the Greyhound bus to Destrehan."

I smiled at her again. "We'll wait together. I'm sure there'll be another bus tomorrow."

She sighed. "I s'pose. I guess I ain't got a choice," then she cut her eyes my way. "Donchew be tryin' nothin' while we're waitin'. Little Bit might like lookin' at the wimmins, but I'm his woman, an' he knows it. He'd fight you for me, Joe. He would."

I wasn't about to tell her of her husband's visits to the Saigon cathouses, so I just said, "I'm your big brother, Melanie. For nine hours anyway. Okay?"

"Okay," she nodded, then said, "But what about your bus? Ainchew gonna miss it?"

"Yeah," I said. "It's no big deal. I've ridden the dog all over, and one thing I know: there's always a bus to Toad Lick."

Her eyes widened. "To *where?*"

I grinned. "The mighty village of Toad Lick, Kentucky. As they say in *The Music Man*, that's the town that knew me when."

"Toad Lick!" Melanie shouted. "And I thought Loo'zeana had some funny towns." The idiot name of my birthplace must have finally broken through Melanie's funk. She threw back her head and laughed.

She had a point. So did I.

3

*B*ut all that was more than thirty years gone. Now here I was facing another task of duty. Before I was sent to 'Nam I'd heard that combat bound you to others in a way nothing else could, that you'd find yourself doing hard things for men, men that in peacetime wouldn't even have appeared on the radar screen of your life. I found that to be true. Which by logical inference would have to include doing hard things for those men's widows.

Melanie had told me what had happened to Little Bit, how he'd been found. And in between her body-racking sobs she'd begged me, *begged* me, to find out who'd done this to him. But the entreaty wasn't needed. Little Bit and I, regardless of our differences, had fought a common enemy together. In my heritage, that counted as strong as blood. Duty and honor are inextricably bound to Dixie's sons.

And in spite of my all faults, I'm still a Southern man.

I'd parked my 1968 Junebug-green street-legal Cougar, which I affectionately called the Goddess, in the slot with my name stenciled on it in the Whittaker Building's underground garage. Now I was walking five blocks north, on Ezzard Charles Drive, toward District One headquarters. If the street sounds familiar, it's because it's named after one of Cincinnati's native sons from several decades past, a remarkably fierce prizefighter for his day.

I puffed slightly as I walked. I suppose I could have parked closer, but police station or not, I didn't put the Goddess in harm's way if I could help it. Sticky fingers and all that. Besides, now that I'm pushing fifty, the walk couldn't do me anything but good.

The day had grown as cold and overcast and gray as it had promised in the morning. The winds were blustery here a week before Thanksgiving, making me wonder if we were going to have a white Christmas in another month. That would suit me fine, something I couldn't have imagined not long ago.

I'd lost Linda, my wife of just a year, on a Christmas Eve nearly thirty years past. With her death, my own will to live had nearly vanished. But things are improving, little by little. Angela Swain, a kind and sweet woman I'd met through church just a few months back, is helping me get things back on track.

Step by step.

Finally I was there. Blowing out one last steamy breath, I walked inside the station lobby, where I knew the maintenance guys would have the furnace cranked up to one tick under a killing heat. They did.

I shook my head as I emptied my pockets, giving the contents to the bored, fat, old sergeant manning the security gate. The man was as much a fixture there as the grimy bricks out front. When I was a young cop back in the early seventies, I'd worked out of District Three over in Price Hill on Warsaw Avenue, but the few times I'd been sent to District One for one thing or another I'd found the lobby's temperature always the same eighty degrees, July or December, it didn't matter, and sitting behind the desk that same sergeant. I doubted he remembered me; I'd only been a cop for a year, and had quit the force two days after my wife's funeral.

I went through the gate, and the tired old man gave my stuff back to me with a visitor's pass and a noncommittal grunt, whether "thanks" or "move along," I couldn't tell. He never even looked at my face.

After taking the creaky elevator to the third floor, I got out and turned right, finally pausing at a well-used frosted glass door that read, simply, Vice Squad: Detective Jack Mulrooney, OIC. Officer in Charge to you. I knocked once and entered without being told.

Here we go.

◆ ◊ ◆

When I was a young police academy graduate, as fortune would have it, I was put under the mentoring of a remarkable partner by the name of Sergeant Tim Mulrooney. To me, Sarge was the quintessential cop. He was of Irish descent, in his late forties at the time, still ramrod straight, and blessed with ice-blue eyes that could twinkle with humor or grow flat in an instant with a seen-it-all world-weariness. Sarge told me he'd grown up fast as a young Marine Corps rifleman in the frozen hell of the Chosin Reservoir in Korea, but that was also where, facing the sixth Chinese assault in as many hours, he'd made a foxhole conversion to Jesus Christ. Usually those things don't hold; I had seen enough of that from my own time in combat. But in Sarge's case, the conversion had stuck. He and his wife Helen practically adopted me, and then did the same with Linda, showing us both the unconditional love that so marked their lives. Now Sarge and Helen were long since retired, enjoying the good life at a small beachfront condo in Florida. The man I was to see at the cop house was Sarge's son, and you couldn't have come up with a more different man from Sarge if you'd paid cash money.

Here's just one example of why I say that: this past summer, after the conclusion of the case that had so dramatically changed my life, Sarge and Helen had flown up for a visit. One evening while they were in town, Sarge suggested going out to dinner, the six of us—Sarge and Helen, Angela Swain and me, and the Mulrooneys' son Jack and his wife, Sharon— so I could finally meet them. It sounded good to me; after the awe I held regarding my old mentor, I was curious to see if his boy was cut out of the same cloth. Turned out the answer was, nope. The dinner started innocently enough. Sarge had left the restaurant location up to me, and since I knew he and Helen were now certified sunbirds, I'd picked a small, modestly priced seafood place over in Norwood. The Mulrooneys rode over with Angela and me in the Goddess, and as we pulled into the lot Sarge pointed out his son's car. I parked next to it, and we all got out.

Jack's handshake was cool as he gave an almost imperceptible shake of his head at what I was wearing. Big deal. I also noticed him giving the Goddess the fish-eye. That also really didn't bother me; classic muscle cars aren't everybody's cup of tea. But it was only after I saw him spit a loogie that nearly hit the old girl's left rear tire that I finally got it. You need to understand that not everyone in Cincinnati likes transplanted Kentucky folks. Shocking, I know, but true. So there was no easy way to put it: Sarge's son was a bigot. I smiled at Jack without humor. Skin color aside, I bet old Ezzard Charles and I could have found some common ground in Jack Mulrooney.

The evening ran downhill after that. Jack didn't like the restaurant's looks; he didn't care for the canned music; his salad was limp; his fish was undercooked; the lights were too bright; his dessert tasted old; etc., etc., etc. But that wasn't the worst. Mixed in with Jack's incessant carping was his endless bragging: I did this sting, I collared that guy, my crew was in the paper three times this month, the chief thinks I hung the moon. Jack's poor longsuffering wife Sharon got in maybe three words the whole evening, which I ended up cutting mercifully short, pleading an early start to the next day. And stupid me, I insisted on paying the tab for everyone. Take that, Jack Mulrooney, and the horse you rode in on. As I said, congenitally dumb.

It was while I was in the washroom after paying up that Sarge cornered me. The look in his eyes was the same as the one that had been in Sharon's.

"Sorry about tonight, Joe," he muttered as he dried his

hands. I just looked at him. I've known the man for many years. I've seen him happy, sad, introspective, worried, and red-dog mad with anger. But I'd never seen him embarrassed. Until now.

I cleared my throat as I checked my tie. "It's all right."

"No it isn't." Sarge pitched the paper towel into the bin and turned to face me. "Jack has his problems. I know that. Not the least of which is his refusal to get right with the Lord."

"Yeah. Plus Jack's a jerk." I gave my tie a final tug. "I'm not so sure that him getting saved would fix that."

"No, maybe not," Sarge allowed. "It sure couldn't hurt though. Thing is, I'd hoped he would be better tonight. I told him all about that last case, how proud I was of you, and how it had changed your life when you accepted the Lord for your own self." He sighed. "Guess it didn't mean much."

"Guess not," I said, leaning back in toward the mirror as I checked my teeth for crud. "But the good Lord willing, I doubt I'll ever have to deal with Jack again." Still checking my teeth I muttered, "That boy'll never know how close he came tonight to having a crab leg rammed down his throat." I glanced over at Sarge just in time to see him wince at that. Immediately I regretted my crack. "Sorry."

"No, you're right," he sighed again. "He's our cross to bear, Helen's and mine. All the prayers that have gone up for him ..." Sarge then gave me a wan smile. "But someday ..."

"Someday," I smiled back, and we left together.

4

oe Box." Jack was grinning nastily at me as I entered his office. "Been a while." Jack favored Helen more than Sarge. He was a few years younger than me, somewhere around his mid-forties, his curly brown hair showing silver on the sides, and his nondescript hazel eyes mirrored his mother's. About the only things Jack had gotten from his dad were Sarge's cussedness and his height; Jack topped by an inch my own six-foot-three frame.

"Been a couple of months anyway." I motioned to the wooden chair opposite his desk. "Do you mind?"

"Not at all." Jack's expansiveness was as phony as his grin. "As a taxpayer, you own it."

"Thanks," I said evenly as I sat down. "I'll try to make this brief."

He fanned the air. "Take all the time you need, Joe. After

all, you're a private citizen, and you pay me. I'm just a lowly civil servant."

I leaned back, examining him. "Good grief. Is that it? Is that what's kicked a board up your behind? That you're still a cop, and I'm not?"

Jack's *ersatz bonhomie* dropped off as he leaned across his desk. "Don't make yourself proud." The words were said through gritted teeth, eyes and voice gone flat. "I'm a blood-bought, dues-paying member of the brotherhood. You're a quitter. It's just as sad and as simple as that."

"So everyone who doesn't go a career path with the cops is less than human, huh?" I shook my head. "I bet you were a real treat on the street."

"Still am," Jack said. "Something you wouldn't know anything about."

I sighed at him. "You know what? We both have more important things to do with our day than screw around with each other. Jack, you were the one who insisted I come down here to ask you in person for a favor I know you could have given me over the phone." I spread my hands. "All right, you've won. I'm here. Now let me ask it and I'll leave."

"Ask away." He was grinning again. "That's doesn't necessarily mean I'll give you what you want."

I tried to keep my voice level, but inside I was seething. "I don't think you're as petty as that, to get me to drive all the way down here only to send me away empty-handed. Nobody gets to be head of detectives that way. So let me put it like this. As a nod to what we have in common, our respect for your father, will you give me the information I need?"

That finally nailed the boy. Sarge had told me he and Jack had their problems, but deep down there still must have been some sort of bond there. Jack blew out a breath, leaning back, then he tossed his pencil down on the desk blotter and gazed at me. "All right, ask. I'll do my best to answer. Then leave."

"Fair enough." I crossed my legs, pulling out a small spiral-bound notebook and a pen as I did. "Last night around ten I got a phone call from Los Angeles. It was from a guy I'd served with in Vietnam. Without going into the reasons why, he told me he thought his life was in danger. I blew it off." I smiled thinly at Jack. "And that's something I'm going to carry with me to the grave, because at five-thirty this morning his wife called me to tell me my friend was dead. Electrocuted. So what I need from you is the name of anyone on the Los Angele's cops that can help me out with this."

"The coroner ruled on it yet?"

"I haven't even asked. There's no point. I'm only licensed in Ohio, Kentucky, and Indiana. If a Cincinnati PI wants information from an LA cop on an open investigation, you and I both know how far I'll get. Without help, that is."

Jack picked his pencil back up off the blotter, grinning crookedly at me again. "So now we're there. You need me to front you the name of a contact on the LA force so you can get the skinny on this guy's death and give his widow closure." He shook his head, still grinning. "Awfully noble. Better than I'd expect of a PI. And in exchange for this I get … what, exactly?"

"Oh, I don't know," I said airily. "The beaming pride of

your wife? Wide-eyed glistening looks of adoration from your kids? The thanks of a grateful nation? The perks could be endless."

"Gosh, none of that moves me, Joe." That grin was really starting to grate on me. "Maybe I should just send you packing."

"Did I mention a heartfelt 'attaboy' from your dad?"

That wiped the smile off of Jack's puss. "Oh, all right," he growled. "I'm gonna give you this, then you're gone. When you call the main headquarters number there, ask for Alex Barber, Division Five. He's a lieutenant, homicide. Mention my name."

"How do you know him?"

"That's not important." I must have given Jack a look. He sighed. "Alex and I served on a federal drug-interdiction task force a few years back. He'll remember me."

I didn't doubt that. Preening martinets like Jack Mulrooney tended to stick in the mind. I smiled at him. "Will you give this Barber guy a call first? Clear the decks for me?"

Jack scowled. "Don't press your luck, Box."

"Just thought I'd ask," I smiled again, and got up to leave. "Jack, old buddy, you've been a brick. Really. Let's do lunch sometime."

He stood as well and pointed. "Get out."

Grinning, I got.

◆ ◊ ◆

"Hi, is this Lieutenant Barber?" I was back in my Mount Healthy office. (Don't ask. Cincinnati has a lot of oddly named neighborhoods. This, from a man whose hometown is called Toad Lick.) It was noon in Cincy, around midmorning in LA.

"Yeah. Who's this?"

"My name's Joe Box, Lieutenant. I'm a private investigator calling from Cincinnati. We have a mutual friend"—I almost gagged on that one—"Jack Mulrooney."

"Jack," Barber grunted. "Yeah, I know him. I also know how he feels about PIs. I somehow doubt you're friends."

"True," I allowed, "but his dad and I *are* friends, so I guess that would make me Jack's pal once removed."

I could hear Barber take a long slurping sip of something—coffee, I bet. "What do you want, Box?" he asked me tiredly.

The man had a point, and I got to it. I told him about Little Bit's phone call, and then the one from his wife. "So what I'm asking for is simply any information you have on this."

"Hold on a second," Barber sighed. Rough night, I guess. I heard him put something down. "Okay, let me check the system here. The dead guy's name is what?"

I told him, making sure I spelled Little Bit's last name carefully. Barber then put me on hold, presumably so he could hand the task off to an underling. I waited. Finally he came back on.

"Okay, I've got the preliminary coroner's report right here. Our new system just got up and running. Lemme see ..." I heard him muttering the words as he read, then his voice came back up. "Nope, looks pretty cut and dried. Seems your pal had been hitting the sauce quite a bit last night, according to his stomach contents ... sure you want to hear all this?"

"I've seen autopsies before, Lieutenant."

"Okay. It goes on to say he'd had pizza and beer—quite a lot of beer—earlier, before switching to whiskey."

"That tells me he was scared," I said. "Little Bit always drank whiskey when he was scared."

"I'll take your word for that. Anyway, according to the responding officer's report, the wife gets up around five this morning. Her husband's side of the bed isn't even mussed. She goes looking for him, finds him in the basement. He was lying on the floor in front of his workbench, in a pool of his own urine, the innards of a radio he must have been working on scattered around him. The radio was plugged in. The medical examiner figures he was liquored up and went to work on the thing without unplugging it first. The doc's ruling it accidental electrocution."

"No signs of a struggle?"

"Inconclusive. Why would there be? The facts are pretty simple. Your guy got drunk. Being in a state of intoxication and unable to reason it out, he tried to work on his radio while it was still connected to the wall. Bingo. The hot squat to heaven."

That was one way to put it. "Maybe. The urine bothers me, though."

Barber sighed again. "Why?"

"Did the M.E. say if the urine was released after death or before?"

His scowl came clearly over the phone. "Now why would that possibly be important?"

"Simple," I said. "If it was released after death, that would be consistent with what happens to some bodies then. You know that as well as me. If it was before, I believe it could be because somebody forced him to fool with that radio. See, I served for a year in Vietnam with the man. And I know Little Bit was terrified of electricity. He wouldn't even use our field telephone in the rain. He thought it would fry his head. So that's the reason I was asking if they could tell us more about that urine, because it's possible the electrocution occurred after the fact, after he'd piddled the floor. And if that's true, it might just mean that Little Bit was frightened to death."

5

O ver the years I've gotten to be a kind of gourmet of pencils. I like to gnaw up and down on 'em while I'm thinking, right down to the eraser. Eberhard Faber makes a good one, I've found. The wood has a rather sweet aftertaste, and the yellow paint on it doesn't flake too badly. Every year when school starts I load up on them, maybe twenty or thirty boxes. The kids look at me funny. I was chewing the life out of this one now, because this slight mission of mercy for Melanie Frontenau had taken a decidedly eerie turn.

Lieutenant Barber had reluctantly agreed to check with the M.E. regarding the question I had about Little Bit's urine—and I can assure you that's one subject I'd never concerned myself about. But Barber wasn't happy about sending me the report, and told me so.

"You got a fax machine, Box?" he sighed at me.

"No, but there's a place right around the corner from me." I gave him the number. "How long do you figure this will take?"

"You'll get it when you get it. And you know the only reason I'm doing this at all is because of your relationship with Jack. But you tell him this is it. You tell him this squares us for all favors, past or future."

"I'm sure he'll be grateful, Lieutenant. You know what a sweetheart old Jack is."

I heard Barber snort over the phone. "Yeah, Jack's a prince. And it's not like I don't have anything better to do."

"I have an inkling of that. I was a cop myself once, a long time ago."

That didn't seem to impress Barber much. He gave a noncommittal grunt. "In a town this size, we never get through the stacks of deaths we check into. And now you add this to my plate."

"Sorry."

"No you're not," he grunted again. "And your timing couldn't be worse, Box. Listen to this." I heard him rustle some papers near the phone. "Hear that? That's just a few of the open cases from the past week." He started reading them off to me. "We've got Yoshiro Mori, male Oriental, thirty-seven, hit-and-run. Bessie Stokes, female African-American, sixty-eight, poisoning. Lakeesha Tallin, female African-American, eighteen, blunt head-trauma. Vlad Przbasky, male Caucasian, forty-nine, GSW—"

"Wait," I said, standing. "Say that again."

"GSW. Gunshot wound. In this case self-inflicted." Barber

barked a derisive laugh. "You used to be a cop and didn't know that one?"

"Not GSW. The name. What was the victim's name again?"

"Vlad Prz—"

"—basky," I finished. The hair was rising on the nape of my neck, never a good sign. My Granny had told me as a kid that all the Box clan was subject to premonitions from time to time. She called it "being fey." My friend Nick Castle says it has another name in Christian circles: discernment. Whatever the name, I was feeling it, and I swallowed. Hard. "Oh boy," I said.

"You sound like you knew this guy." I could hear suspicion, every cop's companion, clearly coming to me from Barber over the phone.

"I did. From a long time back." A long time was right. More than thirty years ago.

Vlad Przbasky—and it had to be the same person, there couldn't be two men on the planet with a name like that—was with our platoon in Vietnam. We'd found Vlad to be a right enough guy, even though we all teased him unmercifully about his name. Vlad. As in Vlad, the Impaler. The real source for the Dracula legend. I was the one who had pointed that out. I've always been an inveterate reader, even as a kid, and the craziest things tend to lodge in your brain. So, of course, we called him Bela. The thing is, in spite of his name, Vlad was as American as Gene Kelly. He told us his unfortunate moniker came from a mom who'd been a fan of Gothic novels. But what was really weird was Vlad's job: he was one of our medics. So he was always around blood … I guess you had to be there. We thought it was funny.

And here he was gone. A suicide to boot.

Three dead soldiers, men I had known. Mentally I tallied it. Little Bit said that Ed Ralston's car had crashed a week ago, killing him. Then Little Bit himself died last night. And now Lieutenant Barber was telling me Vlad Przbasky had shot and killed himself sometime in the past few days.

Vlad, Ed, and Little Bit. Three members of the same platoon dying from what appeared to be random acts of violence inside ten days of each other. Things like that just didn't happen. Call it strange, call it a conundrum—or even, as we used to say in Kentucky, call it a "poser." It was simply beyond the bounds of probability.

And something else was bothering me about those deaths. What it was, I couldn't rightly say; like a squirming minnow in a streambed, it was tough to hang onto. I filed the thought away in my head to percolate for later. It would surface when it was ready and not before.

I told Barber about my connection with Vlad.

His response was laconic. "According to the M.E.'s report, this guy Przbasky shot himself three nights ago outside a bar on Sepulveda. You know any reason why he would do that?"

"I haven't seen the man since 1971, Lieutenant."

Barber ignored that. "Witnesses say he was shooting pool with some of the local denizens all evening, drinking nothing stronger than ginger ale, then he leaves the bar about eleven. Two minutes later there's a shot heard from the back alley. Przbasky's pool buddies rush outside to find him lying dead next to the dumpster. He'd placed a .38 in his mouth and pulled the trigger. The gun was a throwdown, serial number burned off. Przbasky's pals have no idea where he got it."

"And you're sure it was suicide?"

"Well, the angle of the shot fits, as well as nitrates on the shooting hand. What else could it be? What we don't know is the why. Sometimes you never do."

"What hand?"

"Left. Your guy a southpaw?"

"Yeah," I sighed. "He was."

Barber's voice softened a little. "You said you knew him. How well?"

"Not really well. But in another way, I knew him like a brother."

"That doesn't make any sense."

"I know. It's hard to explain unless you were there. Were you ever in combat, Lieutenant?"

"Nope. I was a swabbo on a minesweeper in Cam Ranh Bay. Closest I ever got to death was bar fights in Da Nang." He barked another laugh. "And now I'm working homicide. Go figure."

"There's no way I can relate the bonding to you then. You eat the same dirt with a group of men for a year, fight with them, laugh with them, listen to their stories; there's something unique there. Now it's more than thirty years after the fact, and I'm hearing that three of those men I served with have met violent deaths, all in the past ten days. That's hard to accept."

"Three?"

I told Barber about Ralston.

"How do you spell that?" he asked. "Like the hot cereal?" I said yes. "Hold on a sec," and the phone went dead. I waited for a bit before he came back on. "Okay, I had records pull the file. This is another one I can't get too cranked up about. Edgar James Ralston. Male Caucasian, age forty-eight. Itinerant laborer, heavy drinker, couple of minor busts for public intoxication and possession of marijuana. Seven days ago his 1994 Corolla takes a turn too fast on the PCH and goes through a guardrail on a three-hundred-foot swan dive to a beach below. The car explodes on impact, and the said Mister Ralston is identified through his dental records. His blood alcohol content was twice the legal limit. The end."

"Open and shut, is that it?"

"That's the way we see it," Barber said, then he sighed at me again. "Look, Box, I know it's tough to lose buddies. And to lose three in ten days must suck royally. But we've closed the files on both Ralston and Przbasky. And to tell you the truth I have the feeling we're gonna do the same on this Frontenau guy."

"And there's nothing I can say to change your mind?"

"Sure," he said. "Bring us evidence. Hard, credible evidence that we've missed something. But I don't think you can, because it doesn't exist. The fact is, you've lost three pals in the past week and a half through coincidence. If there wasn't any such thing, they never would have come up with a name for it."

I blew out a breath. "Well, thanks, Lieutenant. I guess."

"Don't take it so hard, Box," he admonished. "Maybe this'll end your string. Maybe you and all the rest of your army buds will live to ripe old ages."

There really wasn't a reply to that, so I thanked him as civilly as I could and hung up.

Okay, I was ramming a wall here. Time to bring in the heavy artillery.

6

I'd left my office then and hopped in my car, heading toward the one place I felt could do me some good—the library.

Libraries and I have been good friends ever since I was a kid. I took to reading early, and thankfully my dad and Granny didn't discourage it. It was almost as if they knew reading would be my passport out of our little town. They were right.

The library I frequented was near the corner of Galbraith and Colerain, not too far from my office. It had undergone a much-needed renovation a couple of years earlier and now was about as good as it could get. The reason I say that is my affection for the head person there, a small, elderly, birdlike woman named Mrs. Brake. From her thick glasses, blue-rinsed hair, and clear, unlined face you would expect her to be a shy, timid soul, unfamiliar with the world and its ways.

You would be wrong.

One rainy afternoon about three years ago I'd come in here to scout out something good to pop in the VCR that evening. This was well before I had met Angela, and most nights, when I wasn't staking out some place or another for a client, I would make a bowl of popcorn, grab a beer, stick in a movie, and then my cat Noodles and I would settle back and watch the flick together. Whoopee. I was scanning the shelves, unsuccessfully searching for a title I hadn't seen for the umpteenth time, when Mrs. Brake called out to me from behind the counter. "Mr. Box? Are you looking for something in particular?"

"Not really," I replied, turning to her. "I was just hoping for something new."

She furtively looked from side to side, then motioned me over with her finger. "Check this out," she grinned up at me with her store-bought teeth as I approached the counter, adding, "That's a little library humor, by the way." She reached under the counter and brought out a fistful of tapes still in their cases.

I leaned down and looked. What she was holding were all brand-new movies, just out that week in the video rental places. "Where did these come from?"

Mrs. Brake's grin grew wider. "It's a dirty little secret we librarians have. A lot of times we get movies here the same week they come out in the stores. The reason they take a while to show up on the shelves is we take them home and watch them first." With that confession she snorted a little laugh, which she then stifled by placing her gnarled fingers over her mouth.

I faked shock. "Why Mrs. Brake. I'll be hung. You're a sneak."

"True," she chuckled. "And worse. But I'd bet there's a lot about me you don't know, Mr. Box." Son of a gun. Was this old lady flirting with me? I looked into her eyes. Danged if she wasn't.

Right about then the thunder outside crashed, and the rain started coming down harder. I glanced around. We were the only two in the place. I've always been fascinated by people, one of the reasons I got into this profession, so I smiled at the woman. "You know, it's rotten outside, and I think most of your patrons are going to be staying home. Let's swap stories."

She nodded. "Sounds fine. You go first."

I did. I told her about what I did for a living, my hometown, my love of reading, my military service, my time as a cop … I even told her about Linda, and that was unusual. "Okay, your turn," I said as I finished.

Mrs. Brake then told me her story. And it was a tale worth hearing.

◆ ◊ ◆

These days most folks have never heard of barnstorming, but that's exactly what Mrs. Brake's husband Leonard did: he owned a one-man air circus. Len made the rounds of the Midwest back in the 1920s, using an old two-seater Jenny biplane he'd bought off a grizzled prospector in Billings,

Montana. Amazingly enough, the plane turned out to have been owned by a pilot in Captain Eddie Rickenbacker's Hat-in-the Ring squadron, the American air group that had lit up the skies over France in 1917. Len and his young wife brought the plane back to Ohio, where they took to the air. According to Mrs. Brake, Len could make the Jenny do everything but speak. Barrel rolls, Immelman turns, and harrowing stalls pulled out at the last second were all in a day's work for him. In between those thrills he'd take stouthearted but petrified farmers up for fifteen-minute flights at five dollars a head. But the most amazing thing about their air circus was Mrs. Brake's part: she was a wing-walker. I'm not kidding. She and Len would take the Jenny up to maybe two thousand feet, whereupon she would exit the cockpit and clamber around the struts and spars like a rhesus monkey. It was always a crowd-pleaser, she told me. But over the years people's tastes grew more jaded, and the couple at last sold the Jenny to a museum and retired to a small cottage up near Wilmington. Everything was idyllic. Then in the spring of 1957 Len discovered a small lump under his left armpit. He shrugged it off, said it was nothing, until the day it started to hurt, and his weight began to drop. By the time he got around to going to the doctor it was too late. Six weeks later the Hodgkin's disease had taken Len Brake.

Mrs. Brake told me she puttered around their place, lost in grief, for two more years, until one day she stirred herself. Anybody who could walk around two thousand feet off the ground on a biplane's wing could do anything, she reasoned with implacable Buckeye grit. So she applied for and received a full scholarship to Wilmington College, where she majored in library science. Then, upon graduation, of all things Mrs. Brake joined the Peace Corps. She spent the next ten years of her life helping build and stock small libraries in some of the most poverty-stricken little hamlets on the planet. She, like Granny, reasoned that education was the only surefire way out of grinding destitution. When at last her age caught up with her and her health began to wilt under bad water and worse food, Mrs. Brake moved back to Ohio and took over as head librarian at this branch.

"So what do you think of that, Mr. Box?" she asked me, her blue watery eyes twinkling hugely up beneath her thick glasses.

"I'm impressed," I said slowly. "And I don't impress easily."

From then on we were friends. At first I tried to get her to call me Joe, hoping she'd reciprocate and tell me her first name, but all she'd done was smile at me coquettishly. "Mr. Box, there's some things a girl keeps to herself."

Of course, I could have easily found out what her name was—I am a detective, after all—but I haven't. I figured at her age, let her have her secrets. A little mystery is always nice.

But not this particular mystery I was facing now, the one concerning my dead friends. And I knew if anyone in this town could help me, it was Mrs. Brake.

◆ ◊ ◆

She smiled at me as I entered her domain. "Mr. Box. It's been awhile. What brings you in today?"

"Computer help. Have you got a minute?"

Her voice lowered a bit. "Is it to solve a case?" The day

I'd told her I was a PI, Mrs. Brake had almost danced with joy, telling me she loved PI fiction. From then on she jumped at every chance to help me out with my work.

"A case? In a way," I said, and I told her the events of the last eighteen hours, and of the deaths of Ed, Vlad, and Little Bit. "So that's why I'm here," I concluded. "I'm still a total loss where the Web is concerned, and I need you to do a name search."

"Mr. Box, you're a young man," Mrs. Brake scolded, "in the prime of life. You really should master the basics of the Internet. If I can do it, you certainly can." We go through this act every time I needed her help with one of the infernal machines. Each time it ends with me promising to learn the ropes of the www.whatever.

"And I'll do just that, Mrs. Brake," I said, "at the earliest opportunity."

Of course I wouldn't. The Internet is composed of black magic and devil's work. Everybody knows that.

She didn't buy my line either. She fixed me with a withering look, then pointed to an empty terminal. We wandered over to it. There she sat down and readied her fingers over the keys, Elton John in drag—which wasn't that far off, come to think of it. I stood next to her, but two feet away from the screen. Radiation. At least.

She looked up at me expectantly. "I'm ready when you are."

"Okay." I handed her a piece of paper. "That's a list of six names. I'd like to see if you can do a search on each of them, and tell me where they're living now."

Mrs. Brake raised one eyebrow at me, like a Vulcan. "That's all? We're talking child's play, Mr. Box." I shuffled my feet in embarrassment.

"Of course, any other information would be good too."

"Very well," she sighed, "but before I start I noticed that each name on your list is a man's. By any chance, would these happen to be other soldiers you served with in Vietnam?"

I smiled at her. "That's awfully good, Mrs. Brake. You would have made a good detective."

"I *do* make a good detective," she retorted as she started to type. While she did her thing I wandered around the stacks, seeing what was what. Every now and then I'd spy a book that caught my attention. I'd pull it off the shelf, flip through the pages for a bit, and then carefully put it back exactly where I'd gotten it (Mrs. Brake is a fanatic about the Dewey Decimal System). After fifteen minutes of that I heard her gently call my name. Something in her tone caused me to move quickly.

"Look here," she said, pointing at the screen as I came up. "This is what I found. Can this possibly be right?" I bent over her shoulder and looked. What I saw froze my blood. The list I'd given Mrs. Brake contained the names of six of the men with whom I'd shared my ramshackle Vietnam hut, more than thirty years ago. Ten of us had called the place home, including Ed Ralston, Vlad Przbasky, and Little Bit Fontenau. I already knew where I lived now, and as far as Ed and Vlad and Little Bit ... well, they'd each moved on somewhere else.

The search engine—see, I do know a few computer

terms—Mrs. Brake used had listed those six remaining names alphabetically, along with each man's vital statistics and his location. That was all right, it was what I'd asked for. What made my mouth go dry was something else entirely. Three of the names on the screen had practically jumped out at me: Tobias Buntline, Robert Dagliesh, and Rafael Martinez. Beside each name was a big red *D*.

I pointed at the screen. "Does that mean what I think?"

"Yes, Mr. Box," Mrs. Brake answered slowly. She gazed up at me. "I am so sorry."

Not as sorry as I was. The program listed each man's date of birth, where he lived, his marriage status, employer, and other banalities. Pretty standard. But next to the Buntline, Dagliesh, and Martinez lines was another entry. The dates of their deaths.

My tally had just doubled. Little Bit, Ed, Vlad, and now Toby, Bobby, and Rafe—six men I'd served with, all dead in less than fourteen days. As much as my mind was fighting it, the evidence was undeniable. Something was killing my brothers.

And now there were just four of us left.

7

*S*o that explains my pencil chewing. I leaned back, my chair creaking in protest, as I stared up at a stain on my office ceiling. The wriggling minnow-thought about what had linked those deaths, beyond the obvious commonality of Vietnam, was still evading me, but it seemed if I sat quietly long enough I might grab it yet. Vietnam. Maybe that really was the common denominator. At least, it was where the thread started. But not only that. It's been said there's nothing worse than combat. That's mainly said by those who should know, men who've served time in that crucible. I count myself among them. Yet I'm also convinced there is something worse. I've experienced it.

And as I mused, my mind harked back to that time, and what I saw there. The thing I participated in, and the price I paid....

◆ ◇ ◆

Bobby Vinton did a song back in the early sixties about a lonely soldier who never gets any letters. I'd thought it was a pretty lame effort at the time, done as it was with Vinton's characteristic catch-in-the-throat weepiness and plenty of crying strings. But now it was 1970, and here I was an eighteen-year-old soldier myself, four months into a yearlong tour in Vietnam. Christmas was less than a week off, and I was convinced that a truer song had never been written.

A year earlier, 1969, had been a better time. A few days before Christmas Eve, Granny unexpectedly showed up at my high school and pulled me out for the day, ostensibly so I could help with a family crisis. The real reason was she wanted to go shopping at the Tri-County Mall. Granny was that way sometimes. Impetuous. Even her living with us in Cincinnati was proof of that.

Everyone has dreams. Somewhere along the way my dad had latched onto his, that of one day moving up to Cincinnati and working on the GM line in Norwood, building Pontiacs. He'd heard tell the money was there for the taking, and the hours had to be better than farming. I think the truth was simpler. Living in Toad Lick was like trying to cross quicksand; three steps in, and you realize you're doomed.

So at age thirty-five, and after years of rawboned pain, crushing poverty, and the disappearance of his wife when I was still a baby, my dad felt he had one last chance to break free. With lips pressed firmly together in hillbilly desperation he scrawled his name on a list the GM plant had sent him, mailed it in, and waited.

Five years later, the call came.

Granny hemmed and hawed around about leaving with us, but the day my dad and I were packing up our old Rambler to head north, she decided she had to come along. She said it was to save us from Cincinnati's heathen ways. Well, maybe it was that, but I'd bet our little clapboard farmhouse would have grown awfully huge with just her rattling around in there.

That's how three days after my fifteenth birthday the three of us made the five-hour haul from Toad Lick to Cincy up I-75. We finally crossed the Brent Spence Bridge into Cincinnati, Dad meticulously following the word-of-mouth instructions he'd been given on how to reach the neighborhood of lower Price Hill. What we discovered when we got there was a revelation. We found ourselves neck-deep among other dream-seizing hill-folk just like us.

Things went all right at first. Being in a community of people that spoke our dialect and held to the same memories and culture that we did helped. Our little rented house wasn't much, none of them in that neighborhood were, but we settled in as well as we could. It felt like home. And we were content.

"This is it," my dad would often tell Granny with a gap-toothed grin as he picked up his lunch pail, his graying hair hanging lank across his forehead. "I'm done with drinkin' and carousin' and whorin', Ma. Finished with it." Then he would look at me. "And no more beatin' on ya, Joe. I'm quits with all that stuff. I'm gonna make this family a good livin'. You just watch me and see if I don't."

And bless his simple heart, he did. For a while.

But then came the day a year later, a week before Christmas, when we got that awful call from the plant. My dad was dead. Just like that. It seemed he'd reached his hand inside a huge, supposedly stopped press to free something that was stuck, when the thing came alive and pulled him in. He never felt it, the floor superintendent told us. I wonder.

We buried him in the rain two days later, on the little family plot next to our Kentucky farm. Granny cried, but at sixteen, I didn't. Southern men don't cry. At least I didn't used to.

That's how a year to the day after my dad's funeral I ended up riding to the mall with her. There wasn't any emergency, as she'd told the principal. She simply wanted to be with me.

The shopping trip was all right, I suppose—as good as it could be, under the circumstances. But walking along between Granny and me, staring in the windows, was a third person, hanging around ghostlike—the unseen presence of my dad. Granny and I gawked as we strolled, listening to the mawkish Christmas music blaring down at us from the mall's loudspeakers high overhead, even stopping once to share a hot dough pretzel that didn't cost too much. She told me we had to make the money stretch; the proceeds from my dad's group life insurance from the plant and her dinky Social Security check were all the cash we had left to see us through. I tried to help out. The day of my dad's funeral I made a half-hearted attempt to tell Granny I was willing to quit school and go to work, but the glare she gave me was so murderous I just let it drop.

Our time at the mall ended with the two of us finally using a couple of dollars to buy some Christmas trinkets for one another. I bought Granny an imitation silk scarf at Sears, and she got me a gun magazine at the SuperX. It seemed she was holding up okay, better than I'd hoped. She even laughed now and then, but for the most part she gripped my hand tightly as we walked, shooting me glistening looks. Maybe that was how she handled the tragedy. Life had taken her son, but as long as she clutched my hand, it wouldn't take her grandson.

But take him it did, and with a vengeance. Now it was 1970, and I was celebrating the holidays in the undisputed armpit of the world, Vietnam. Granny, and my real life, seemed a world away.

◆ ◊ ◆

The monsoon season officially had been over for a month, not that it mattered. We had humidity in Kentucky, but I'd never seen the beat of this. You could almost drink the air, and the heat was beyond belief. Deck the halls. Let it snow. Please.

The little piece of heaven our platoon was assigned to cover was called the Ia Drang Valley. I know, I'd never heard of it either. Now, after four months here, it was like I'd never lived anywhere else. Somebody once said that war consists of long stretches of boredom interrupted by occasional flashes of terror. The boredom he maybe had right. I think he underestimated the terror.

The nightmare had begun simply enough. I was sitting in my hut—we called it a hootch—reading a tattered old Mickey

Spillane potboiler some previous grunt had left there (the juicy parts already underlined with a shaky pencil), when a shadow filled the doorway. It was one of my hootch-mates, Marcus Crowell, a large, thick-fingered farm boy from even farther south than me. Georgia. He just stood there for a moment, staring in.

"What do you want, Marcus?" I asked as I turned the page. I was getting to another good part.

"Mail call," he drawled. "Thought you'd wanna know."

"Mail? Why didn't you say so?" I jumped up, tossing the book on my cot, and headed for the door. Forget the good part. Mail call trumped all. Marcus and I trotted over to the commo hut, where Corporal Brooks already had a crowd gathered around him. He sat sprawled on his camp stool like a fat, grinning, simian-faced Buddha, our biweekly delivery of mail in an olive-drab ditty bag at his feet. Nobody much liked Brooks. He was a bit too shifty-eyed, always on the make and always, but always, looking out for number one. The fact his duties included that of being our company mailman didn't sit well with us either. Brooks had the unfortunate habit of holding your mail, and then watching you as you stared at the others getting packets and envelopes from home. Only later would he come to your hootch and tell you he'd "just found" your mail and would part with it. For a price.

He'd pulled that on me exactly once. I'd tried to give him the benefit of the doubt, wondering if the stories I'd heard about him were true. But my questions were soon answered.

◆ ◊ ◆

One day, an hour after mail call, Brooks showed up at the hootch, a letter in his hand. He said it was mine. Smiling, he gave me his spiel, all the while lazily flapping my mail back and forth. He then told me had a deal for me. His special delivery service today would only cost me ten dollars American.

Sighing, and feigning reluctance, I handed it over.

He tossed me my letter. Brooks was in the process of counting the money I'd given him, completely oblivious to anything but his greed, when I pivoted around and planted my right fist deep in his belly, aiming for his spine, from this side. He jackknifed forward, eyes bulging in panic as he tried to pull in a breath that seemed to have taken a vacation to Hawaii. Before he could recover, my left fist plowed into his jaw, cracking his head around like a man riding the Wild Mouse. Brooks crashed backward to the floor, still wheezing, his piggy eyes frantically searching mine for mercy. I squatted down and snatched my ten bucks from his trembling grip, my words to him low and even. "You won't pull this on me again, will you, Brooks?"

He moved his head jerkily from side to side, blood trickling down the corner of his mouth. His panic-stricken eyes still hadn't left mine, although it looked like he was finally starting to get some air in him.

"Good," I said. "Now get out, and let me read my mail."

He staggered to his feet, clutching his guts, and did just that. And I never had a further problem with him. Sometimes, I've found, if you just deal harshly with a problem at the start, it keeps you from having to mess with it later.

◆ ◊ ◆

But that was then. Brooks was calling out our names in that nasally voice he had, pitching each man his mail. It didn't take long. Within a few minutes he was done, and once again I'd gotten nothing. Yacking with each other, the men dispersed to private areas to read their letters and open their packages. I narrowed my eyes at him.

"Joe!" His grin was sickly. "I don't have anything for you! Really!" Sweat popping out on his brow, Brooks leaned over and snatched up the ditty bag, opening it to me. "See for yourself, man!" he babbled on. "It's the truth."

Shaking my head at him, I jammed my hands in my pockets and stalked off. "Letters … I get no letters …" Drop dead, Bobby Vinton. I hadn't gone twenty steps when I heard a voice call my name, and I looked up.

"Box!"

It was Sergeant Nickerson, yelling at me from across the compound.

"Stay close. We got a meeting at the Loot's hootch in ten."

I frowned. "What, just you and me?"

He put his fists on his hips. "Yeah. Us and Bob Hope. Whattya think, idiot? No, I mean you and those perverts you bunk with. You tell 'em, or I will." The sarge pulled back his sleeve and checked his watch. "Now we got nine minutes. Let's get it in motion, private." Nickerson dropped his hands and stomped off toward Lieutenant Calhoun's dwelling.

I went on inside our own hootch. The only ones in there

were Marcus, Ed, and Little Bit; I guessed the others had gone off to more secluded places to read their stuff. The three who were left were absorbed in their mail and didn't even hear me as I came in.

"Better put those away, guys," I said. "The Loot wants us."

Ed looked up from his letter with a scowl. "For what?"

"Well, now, Eddie, I wouldn't know," I replied. "I guess he'll fill us in when we get there." He returned to his reading.

"Forget it. I'm gonna stay here until Nickerson tells me himself."

"I'm telling you now." Ed's eyes were still glued to his letter.

"Beat it, Box." Marcus and Little Bit were already on their feet, trying to make themselves as presentable as they could. They both grinned at Ed.

"Hey, Marcus." Little Bit's tone was carrying. "Maybe the Loot's gonna tell us we all goin' home for Christmas. All 'cep' ol' Eddie. He been a bad boy this year. Gonna have to stay here an' get a claymore in his stockin'."

"Naw, not a claymore," Marcus drawled back. "A new buttstock for his blooker. I heard Ed keeps breakin' the things when he drops 'em while he's runnin' toward the rear."

"You know what?" I said over my shoulder as I turned to go. "I'm gone. You want me to give the Loot y'all's regards?"

"Hold on, hold on, we're comin'," Marcus chuckled. He and Little Bit joined me at the door, tucking in their shirttails and smoothing their hair as they came. Ed swore and threw his letter on his cot with a disgusted snarl. "Wait up, I'm comin' too. But this better be on the level." By the time we got to the Loot's hootch the others were already there, Nickerson having found them. I was the last one in, and I glanced around. This was the first time I'd been in there. It was fixed up about like I'd thought. No doubt about it, the Loot's place was a sight better kept than that sty we called home. For one thing, there weren't any nudie pictures on the walls, like Little Bit had insisted on decorating our place with. But that really shouldn't have been surprising: somebody had told me Lieutenant Calhoun's daddy was a Southern Baptist preacher; maybe that explained it. Or maybe the bare walls simply reflected Calhoun's standing as an officer. Not that that meant much in this outfit.

"Box, shut the door, and everybody grab a seat," the Loot commanded. We did, shoving each other around so we could all fit. That finally accomplished, he looked around at each of us. "All right, people, here's the deal. We've got a situation in this sector, a situation that battalion wants fixed ASAP. And since it's happening here, we pulled short straw. Sergeant?"

Nickerson stepped forward, scowling at us. "Battalion calls it a situation. That pretties it up. What it is, it's a sniper problem. But not any old sniper. Seems the VC have gone and got themselves a good one." He crossed his arms. "This guy first started his work here in the valley six weeks ago when he took out the leader of a group of PRU insurgents as the poor man was standing by the road relieving himself." A few of us snickered at that, but we shut up when Nickerson dropped his arms, cutting us with a glare. "It ain't funny, gents."

"No, it's not," the Loot said. "That shot was made from a thousand yards out at dusk in a high wind, and it caught our guy square in the back of his head. When the round was recovered, the armorer determined it was a 7.5 millimeter, probably from one of those old bolt-action French jobs the VC like so much. What kind of optics the guy is using, we don't have a clue. But I can tell you this: no natural eye could have made that shot unaided." Much later, I would remember that phrase: no natural eye. The Loot had no idea how right he was.

"That was just the start," Nickerson continued. "Since then Sammy's been a busy boy."

"*Sammy?*" Vlad piped up, a disbelieving grin on his face.

Nickerson grimaced. "Yeah, that's the handle the brass hung on him. Sammy the Sniper. Cute, ain't it?"

"How busy?" Bobby Dagliesh interjected.

"Real busy." The Loot answered, his tone grim. "In the past six weeks Sammy's killed twenty-two men."

"Twenty-two?" Marcus drawled in horror.

"Are dey sure it's the same guy?" Little Bit asked.

Calhoun nodded. "No question. Ballistics showed the rounds all came from the same weapon. But until recently Sammy stuck to only taking out South Vietnamese regulars or village chiefs friendly to us. And he's stayed true to form: all of the shots were technically impossible. Wind, rain, fog, poor light ... it didn't seem to matter. It was almost as if he was showing off." He frowned. "Then two days ago the guy decided to up the stakes. He went and shot a U.S. full-bird colonel in the throat as he and his party were on an inspection tour of a supposedly secure forward area. The bullet killed the colonel instantly, then it passed on through and took out his, ah, lady friend as well. She was a CBS reporter. That's all it took to move things up to the front burner."

"See, guys, it's okay to kill a few men, even if they're ours," Nickerson broke in. "But you croak a colonel and his squeeze, and well, that makes it personal."

We all laughed, but the Loot just glared. "That's right, yuck it up, people. But I doubt you'll think the next is funny." His voice went flat. "Counting that colonel and his lady friend, Sammy's tally is now twenty-four confirmed kills. Twenty-four. And I suppose somebody's decided that's enough, because we've been assigned to go get him."

8

The rest of the day I puttered around my office, trying to formulate what I was going to do next. I'd really wanted to check out the details on those three new deaths, but that would have to wait until tomorrow. The after-school crowd had thundered into the library about then, and Mrs. Brake had given me an apologetic smile. Customers. I'd left and come back here. I was deep in my pondering, the shadows of the late afternoon's twilight sliding silently across my carpet, when the phone rang. I picked it up.

"Joe?" the caller said. "Did you forget something?" I felt a smile break out. The voice was a woman's, and very sweet. Angela.

"Hey," I grinned.

"Hey yourself," she chuckled, "and the question stands."

I frowned. "What question?"

"Why do I have the feeling I don't have your full attention?" Angela murmured. "Joe," she said then, "I'm going to say four words to you. Tell me what they mean. Moo. Goo. Gai. Pan."

"Chinese?" I slammed my hand on my forehead. "Oh brother. I was supposed to take you out for Chinese tonight, wasn't I?"

"The operative word being 'was,'" Angela scolded, not really meaning it. I hoped.

"I'm sorry, Ange. Not that I'm making excuses, but I kind of got lost in some things today."

"Ah, that explains it." Now it seemed I could hear her amusement at me over the phone. That would be a good thing. "So you're saying it was a momentary lapse of reason?"

"Wow. The lady's not only kind and beautiful, she knows Pink Floyd as well. What more could a boy ask?"

"He could ask if the lady forgives him, and is willing to endure his company for supper, even now."

"Okay," I said. "He'll ask. Supper?"

"Charmer," Angela laughed again. "Supper it is, big fella. But let's do it at my house. I'll order us some Chinese takeout. In your frame of mind, I'd hate to see you embarrass yourself at a restaurant."

"That's the nicest thing anyone has said to me in hours."

"My place it is then. Forty-five minutes." Now her mock-warning tone was back. "So be there, or ..."

"Be square," I finished. "And she knows drag-racing lingo too. I think I'm in love."

♦ ◊ ♦

Fires can be nice, so they say. Angela and I were enjoying one now as we reposed on her newer beige sofa, facing her big stone fireplace. Somebody once said there's something primal about staring into flickering flames, an act that connects you with people long gone … Whoa boy. I shook that off with a barely concealed shudder. Thinking like that would lead me down dark paths I wasn't interested in walking just now. No, tonight was for better things.

"Penny for your thoughts," Angela smiled, breaking in on my reverie as she poured more coffee in my cup. Our dinner, which we'd eaten here in her den, had been good, as good as Chinese take-out can be. That den was tucked onto the rear part of her house, a modest, white-trimmed older two-story sitting at the end of a cul-de-sac, shoulder to shoulder with three other homes of equal vintage. All of the houses backed up to old-growth woods that were still miraculously undeveloped, which was an oddity here in Indian Springs, one of the most overbuilt parts of Butler County. To top it off, her house was also a stone's throw (if you were Nolan Ryan) from the church I now attended with her.

"A penny?" I smiled back. "Lady, you're in luck. It just so happens I'm running a two-for-one sale."

"Great," she grinned. "You know I'm a sucker for bargains."

"Well then, here they are." Suddenly my whimsy slipped away, and I found myself growing serious. "First off, I want you to know you're a special woman, Ange. Really special. These past three months … anyway. And two, after the day I've gone through, I was thinking that what we're doing right now, you and the fire and the soft music I mean, is exactly what I needed." I took a pull of coffee and smiled at her. "Now that I reflect on it, I'd say that all counts as a single thought. I owe you one."

Angela sipped from her own cup, looking over the rim at me with those incredible violet eyes. "I'll hold you to that," she smiled in return. Then she grew somber. "But there's something else going on here tonight, another dynamic. Your mind isn't in the game, as they say." She sipped again. "Would you care to talk about it?"

I shook my head resolutely, setting my cup down on the end table. Folding my hands in front of me, I leaned in closer to the fire. The wind outside was picking up, and for some reason the room seemed suddenly chillier. "Some other time maybe. Not now."

"All right." Angela set her cup down and placed her hands over mine, staring silently down at them. That small action was just one of the reasons I liked her so much. Angela never pushed me into saying more than I wanted to. Never. In the three months since we'd been seeing each other, she hadn't once probed or prodded me to tell her what particular demons I was battling that day. For her, it was enough to know I was in need. So much like Linda. And then quietly, and in her own way, I knew she would take those needs to God in prayer. Harvard Pike Church called her an intercessor. For me, it was simpler. Angela fit her namesake: she was the closest thing to an angel I knew.

A few moments passed. Still looking down then, she spoke. "Do they hurt you much?"

I blinked. "What?"

She met my eyes. "Your hands. The day we first met, they were so heavily bandaged. I was just wondering if they still hurt you." For a moment I couldn't answer. I remembered that day like it was this morning. I'd been seated at a large conference table in Harvard Pike's meeting room, giving a summary to everyone there, the principals who'd figured so strongly in that surrealistic case, the one that had very nearly cost me my life. But upon reflection, I reckoned that last part was true enough. In the final analysis I really had lost my life, my old way of living, during that week. I'd forfeited years, a good span of my adulthood, to drinking and despair and crushing loneliness, a nihilistic existence I knew now would never be revisited. Because in exchange, I'd found a new beginning in Jesus. And in that conference room, sitting quietly across the table from me that day, was this person, this ... compassionate one: Angela Swain. It was there I discovered that her prayers, and those of many like her, had been my only lifeline during the nightmare of that time. I was alive today because of them.

"No, they don't hurt," I finally managed to say, smiling at her. I cleared my throat. "I never did tell you the whole story of what happened, did I?"

She shook her head. "Just what you told the others."

I cleared my throat again. "Well—" but she placed her long, delicate index finger gently over my lips.

"Only if you want to, Joe." Her gaze at me went deep. I softly kissed her fingertip.

"I need to. It's time." So I told her all of it, every bit of that life-changing week this past August. I told Angela of Michael Taylor's visit to my office, and of his plea for me to help find his missing teenage daughter Francesca. I related the frustrations I'd encountered, and the strange occurrences that at the time seemed hell-bent—a good choice of a term, I was to find out later—on keeping me from locating the girl. I told her of where I'd finally found Francesca, held as a captive deep in an underground lab in eastern Indiana. There she, along with a dozen other young girls, had been unwittingly caught up in a weird, neo-Nazi superman scheme, forced to furnish their eggs to help launch a Fourth Reich.

Finally, to save Francesca and myself, I was forced to take the lives of those inhuman beings who had thought nothing of killing these girls. They were the first men I'd killed since Vietnam. At the inquest ordered by the state, the police ruled my actions to be self-defense. That's true, they were, no doubt. But still, those deaths went down hard. The tale at last told, I finally went silent, staring back into the fire. I couldn't really say I felt better in the telling. A few moments passed, then Angela spoke up, her eyes soft. "But, Joe. You've left out the best part."

I looked over at her. "What?"

She smiled. "Sarge." I felt a smile of my own growing in spite of myself.

"Sarge ..."

Sergeant Tim Mulrooney, my old friend and mentor from back in my rookie time as a cop, had showed up at my apartment door smack in the middle of that case, on a day when I was at my lowest ebb. With gentle persuasion and unassailable logic, he'd told me about Jesus Christ, and how he could help me. Sarge had talked on, and for the first time in thirty years I found myself listening. And what do you know? Two hours after he'd started, Sarge led me in a prayer. At its end, I was a Christian.

"So I guess that proves the old adage," I told Angela. "Something good can come out of even the worst of times."

She gave me an impish grin as she cocked her head. "Joseph Jebstuart Box. You're the master of understatement. I'd say to most people getting eternal life would qualify as a good thing."

"Yeah," I nodded. "Plus don't forget: I met you."

"And I met you. That's two more good things. See? They just keep piling up." Her grin widened. "So how about giving me a hug, you good thing?"

9

The next day dawned bright and clear, but still as cold, the gloom of yesterday gone. My frame of mind was better; I was finding that Angela seemed to have that effect on me. I entered my office building, pausing at the ground-floor business before mounting the stairs to my place one story up. I stuck my head in the door of Pronto Printing. "Yo, Mr. Yee," I called out. "Good morning. Are you here?"

An older, diminutive Chinese man came out from the back room, wiping ink from his hands as he did. "Mistah Box," he smiled. "Mawning to you. And the name is Lee."

We've gone through this more times than I can count. Mr. Yee/Lee runs the small print shop beneath my office, and has for longer than I've held a lease here. I've found he's a nice enough man and conscientious regarding his work. He also plays a mean ukulele, remarkable for a self-avowed communist such as he. But his politics don't really matter much; he's always given me a fair shake on any printing work I've needed. My main problem has been in understanding him. Not only is English far from the man's native tongue, Mr. Yee/Lee also possesses the worst harelip I've ever encountered. Hence my difficulty in ascertaining his true last name. It seems he likes to change it as the mood suits him ... inscrutable, I reckon. I smiled back at him.

"Well? Did it come yet?" I'd ordered a box of toys from American Science and Surplus, to give as Christmas gifts to the orphans at the homeless outreach our church runs. The holiday was fast approaching, and I was getting antsy about the shipment.

Mr. Yee/Lee shook his head. "Not yet. But I will ask you again. Why did you have the toys sent here? Why did you not have them sent to your home?"

"I've already told you, Mr. Lee—"

"Yee," he interrupted.

"Right." I started over. "My apartment complex isn't secure. Some punks would steal those toys, as sure as you're standing. Having them sent here makes more sense."

"Now I recall, yes," he nodded. "You must forgive me, please, Mistah Box." Mr. Yee/Lee tapped his head with his forefinger. "The mind. I am no longer a young man."

"Your mind is good enough to keep beating me at cards," I reminded him. He grinned, showing me a mouthful of tobacco-stained teeth.

"Against you, Mistah Box, that is no challenge." I laughed and went on upstairs to my office.

My phone was ringing as I opened the door, and I hurried over to pick it up. My answering machine, like Mr. Yee/Lee's mind, was showing its age, and the very time I would wait for the thing to kick on, that's when it would sulk and go silent.

The caller was Mrs. Brake. We exchanged greetings, then she said, "I know it's early, but you left yesterday before you had a chance to write down the information on those other men." *The three still alive,* I thought, my mood darkening once again. "So I took the liberty of printing out the sheet before I logged off," she went on. "I know you don't have a fax machine yet. Would you like me to read them off to you?"

"Please." I sat down behind my desk and flipped open a pad of paper, pen in hand.

"Let me see ..." I could imagine Mrs. Brake pushing her glasses more firmly against her nose as she began to read. "In no particular order, the first one is Delbert Haggin ..." Mrs. Brake gave me what she had. A few minutes more, and I had it all transcribed. Then I thanked her for her help and hung up.

I looked closer at the three names, along with their occupations, vitals, and addresses. Del Haggin was an auto parts dealer in Boise, Idaho; Greg Dapp had a job as a high-steel worker in Teaneck, New Jersey; and lastly the Georgia boy, Marcus Crowell, not surprisingly had gone back to his family farm in Waycross and taken up the plow. I read on. Del was married, wife's name Marjorie. No wife was listed for Greg. Marcus had been tabbed as a widower. And beyond that, zip. I sat back, clicking the pen against my teeth. Should I call those men? And say what? "Listen, guys, six of our bros are dead. You might be next. Film at eleven." I shook my head. Without concrete proof, as Lieutenant Barber had said, I would just be blowing moonshine. Del, Greg, and Marcus wouldn't buy it, any more than I would if I just up and said it like that.

On a whim, I picked up the phone to call Melanie Frontenau. Her line rang four times, then a machine, obviously better than the one I had, clicked on. The outgoing message was one of those electronic Robby-the-Robot-type things that came prerecorded, so when it had wound down and told me to speak after the beep, I did.

"Hi, Melanie, this is Joe Box. I guess you're not there." *She's probably out making funeral arrangements, dimwit,* my hindbrain called out nastily. She probably was at that. And having been through that process way yonder too many times for one lifetime, I wished her the best and was glad it wasn't me.

"Anyway," I went on, "I just wanted to tell you I'm still looking into Little Bit's ... accident." That word tasted wrong. "I'll keep you apprised," I finished lamely, and hung up.

With that done, the day stretched out before me. I leaned back and stared at the ceiling. I was sure an accident hadn't killed Little Bit, but I couldn't say what had. As I'd told Lieutenant Barber, I only knew one thing for lead-pipe certain: there was no way Little Bit would have been working on a radio, especially one still plugged in, drunk or not. But, flip the card, I was equally sure Little Bit's last frantic phone call had nothing to do with his death either. That was pure whiskey talk, nothing more; take it from someone who knows. The key to his deaths, and the others, lay elsewhere.

10

Snow. As a kid in the Kentucky hills we'd almost always had snow for Christmas. The first tentative flakes would sneak in unannounced right before Thanksgiving, their fellows slowly joining them one by one, until by the middle of December we'd have a foot of it on the ground. There it would stay until March. This Christmas was no different. I was standing in our kitchen looking through the spider-cracks in the window glass, out across the frosted meadow toward our ramshackle barn. It was shaping up to be a fine day. I'd already cut firewood, slopped the hogs, and filled the cow's trough with hay earlier in the morning. Now I had the day to myself and my family. The whole house smelled of baked gingerbread and wood smoke, the sounds of carols playing on our old Philco radio filling the living room, Granny humming along, the sky outside blue and clear. Perfect. I heard my dad come up behind me. I smelled the liquor on him even before he spoke.

"Merry Christmas, boy," he laughed, and slammed his fist deep in my side. My eyes jerked open.

"I said Merry Christmas, Joe."

Toby Buntline gently smacked my side again. "You plannin' on sleepin' in? Bet Nickerson won't like it."

I stared up into Toby's grinning black face.

"What?"

"Best get on your feet, my man. Rise'n'shine." Toby shot a look over his shoulder. "Give you a heads up. The sarge in a bad mood. Guess he wish he was home too." Toby trotted off to grab some coffee, and I shook my head to clear it as I raised myself off my poncho with a groan. The same old nightmare, only I knew it was real. It had happened to me too many times to count before we'd moved to Cincinnati.

The morning heat was already brutal, as it was every day, the humidity climbing. Christmas in Vietnam. Somehow it didn't sound like a holiday movie Bing and Danny would be making anytime soon. Somewhere in-country, Bob Hope and Joey Heatherton and Ann-Margret and Jerry Colonna and all the rest of the gang were giving our boys a bang-up Christmas show. But not here. I pulled my fingers through my hair. During the night a fine grit of leaf mold and general filth had settled deeper on my body. The last time any of us had washed was six days ago, right before we'd started this patrol. I'd long since stopped smelling myself or any of the others. I scraped my hand over my face, my eighteen-year-old's whiskers rough against my palm as I stumbled over to the cook fire. The rest of third squad didn't look any better. I shook my head again. Last night Lieutenant Calhoun had told us we had another two weeks of this nature walk before we could begin heading back to base. By then our own mothers wouldn't recognize us. And we'd still seen no sign of Sammy.

"Coffee, Joe," Bobby said to me, handing me a cup of it as I came up. "Get it while it's rancid." I took a cautious sip. My eyes nearly left my head at the taste. "Man!" I scowled. "You aren't kidding, Bobby." I pitched the brew out before thrusting the empty cup back at him. "You'd think somebody in the squad could make it right."

"Hey, man." It was Rafe calling out to me from the other side of the camp. "We've all took turns bein' cook. Tomorrow it's you. Then we'll see if you such a red-hot chef, *amigo*."

I ignored him as I squatted down by the fire, checking to see what was for breakfast. I frowned, then peered closer as I stirred the pot. Something gray, viscous, and definitely nasty swirled around in there. This wasn't like anything I'd ever seen. My voice cracked as I stared. "What is this?"

Bobby had a plateful of whatever it was. He sucked up another spoonful before answering. "C rations, man. What do you think?"

I ladled up a glop of the stuff, horrified. "No. I've seen C rations. I've also eaten C rations, and lived to tell it." I watched this obscenity as it dribbled down, plopping back into the pot like sewage. "This is C rations from hell. What did you *do*?"

Bobby slurped up another mouthful of the stuff with

relish. "Mixed a bunch of 'em together," he grinned. "Smells good, huh?" I stood and wiped my hands on my pants.

"Lord have mercy," I muttered.

Right about then Nickerson stomped up to us. "All right people, five more minutes, then we break camp and get after it." He sneered at me. "Good of you to join us this morning, Box. I trust you slept all right?"

I grinned back at him. "Like a baby, sarge, thanks for asking."

He put his hands on his hips and leaned in. "Well then. Are you ready to go out among 'em?"

I fastened my utility belt around me, snapping the alice clips to it. My grin grew wider. "I was born ready, sergeant."

Nickerson nodded. "Then pick up your weapon and let's rock." He turned away and called out the others. "Three minutes. Get it in gear, people. Don't forget to police the area." He walked off toward where Lieutenant Calhoun was standing. The Loot was checking a map. He looked lost. Vlad sidled up to me, shrugging into his medical gear and putting his red-cross-emblazoned pot on his head as he came.

"Nickerson says the same thing every time we break camp. 'Police the area.' Like we don't know that already."

"I guess he's just cautious," I replied as I pulled on my combat pack. "He knows we're pretty deep in Indian country now, and he wants to make sure we don't leave any clues for Charlie." I checked my M-16, making sure the safety was on before I popped out the clip and looked at it. Nineteen rounds. The thing held twenty, but as sure as you'd load in the regulation amount, it would jam on you when you needed it most. I stuck the clip back in, slamming it with the heel of my hand until it clicked home. Then I pulled back the weapon's charging handle, seating one of the rounds in the receiver. I nodded in satisfaction before I went on, "What's weird to me is he keeps reminding me to fieldstrip my cigarettes, and he knows I don't even smoke."

"Yeah, but if you start now you'll be ahead of the game," Vlad grinned.

I was about to reply when Nickerson called out, "Off and on, people. It's another lovely day with Mother Green's War Machine." He looked around, sniffing the air and grinning. "What a fine morning to kill us a sniper stone cold dead! Merry Christmas!"

With that we fell in line behind Lieutenant Calhoun and started walking, Greg Dapp squeaking out in a high falsetto as we went, "And God bless us all, every one."

We all laughed, moving along maybe ten yards when the Loot stopped suddenly. "Wait just a minute here. I must be crazy." Frowning, he turned to Nickerson. "Sergeant. Lieutenants don't normally walk point, do they?"

Nickerson shook his head. "No sir. They do not."

"Then why am I doing it?"

"Sir, only the lieutenant would know that," Nickerson replied with a straight face.

"Whose turn is it today?" the Loot asked.

"Sir, I believe that honor would fall to private Ralston."

The Loot nodded. "Make it so, sergeant."

Nickerson swiveled his large, square head at us, his gray

eyes crinkled up in fine humor as he screamed, "Ralston! Take the point!"

Grumbling under his breath, Ed did as he was told, with me falling in line behind him. Once again we all started moving down the trail, flanked on either side by waist-high sawgrass. I'd taken that position because Ed was our blooker man; in addition to my own gear, it was my job to carry a satchel full of his spare grenades.

A digression: a blooker, if you're unfamiliar with the term, was GI slang for the M-79 40-millimeter grenade launcher. Picture a single-barrel shotgun, hinged to open, but make the barrel eighteen inches long and widen it to the diameter of a paper towel tube. That was essentially it. You'd load in a grenade, which looked like a large, stubby .45 round, swing the gun closed, put it to your shoulder, and pull the trigger. A weapon doesn't come much less complicated than that. The "blook" sound the grenade makes as it leaves the barrel gives the gun its nickname. The effective range was around a hundred yards, and Ed Ralston, for all his lack of social skills, was simply fire on rails with the thing.

That didn't make him any sweeter to be around though.

"This really rags me off, Box," he groused as we walked. "I coulda sworn today was your day to take point."

"Maybe you're right, Eddie," I replied as I cranked my head from side to side. Experience had taught us that sawgrass could hold an uncomfortably large amount of Vietcong. The only warning a squad like ours would usually get was when our point man would drop dead, stitched by an AK-47. "But so what?" I went on. "Even if I took the lead, it wouldn't matter, because the Loot says we have to stay together. So what's the difference? You'd be the one that's second in line instead of me, and still not end up a whole lot safer than you are right now."

"College boy," he muttered.

"I'm not. Like I've told you already, I'm barely out of high school, just like you."

"Yeah, well you talk like a college boy," Ed spat.

"You ladies want to shut up?" Nickerson called out from two spaces back. "I'd just as soon finish this patrol alive, thank you very much."

Little Bit laughed uproariously at that. Little Bit thought Nickerson was a hoot. The day trudged on, the tropical sun climbing higher and hotter. As it did, I found my mind wandering back to our farm. What would Granny and her sisters be doing about now? Yes, I knew Vietnam was on the other side of the dateline, so back home it was either the day before or the day after Christmas (I never could figure that one out). But it helped me pass the time to imagine them sitting down to a fine tom turkey or a pot of savory rabbit stew, complete with side dishes of cathead biscuits (generously topped by churned butter from Regina, our cow), pawpaw jelly, tart fried apples, green beans with fatback, and round white new potatoes, all pushed aside on the plate by a big triangular slab of cornbread that had been baked in Granny's huge black cast-iron skillet, the bread golden yellow on top and crispy brown underneath and slathered stem to stern with more of that good churned butter. By then my mouth was fair watering at it all. Bitterly I thought back to Bobby's

C ration surprise he'd fixed for breakfast. I was so hungry by then I would have tried it—at least a bite. Noontime came, and we'd still seen neither hide nor hair of Sammy or his VC friends. That suited me fine. I'd been in seven firefights since I'd arrived in-country, and wouldn't shed a tear if I never again heard a shot fired in anger.

We all groaned with relief when Lieutenant Calhoun finally called a break for lunch. "Take twenty, people," he said. We dropped our gear as we flopped down next to the trail. "And eat your C rats cold. We won't be here long enough to warm them up."

That made my empty stomach knot up like a cat's cradle. C rats were bad enough hot; cold, they were one step up from bathtub grout. My only consolation was that I'd be eating them before Bobby could mess them up even worse. As we dug in our packs to pull out the meal boxes, the Loot said to Marcus, "Crowell, before you eat, get HQ on the radio." Marcus, who was our radioman, did as he was told and shrugged the box off his back, setting it down before him. He rapidly rotated a hand crank several times, then flipped a switch and held the handset to his ear. "Kingfish callin' Sapphire, Kingfish callin' Sapphire," he droned. "Come in." Base must have responded right away as Marcus nodded and said, "Kingfish here. Wait one." He handed the receiver to Lieutenant Calhoun. "I got 'em sir, but it's a little crackly."

"Thanks, Crowell." The Loot put the receiver up to his head. "Kingfish here, making sit-rep as ordered," he said loudly. "Still no contact, awaiting further instructions." There was a long pause as Sapphire answered, then the Loot's eyes bugged out. "What? But sir—Yes, but—I understand that, sir, but we—" With a visible effort the Loot got himself under control. You could make out a large vein pulsing on the side of his neck. "Understood, sir," he said stiffly. "We'll hold here until they arrive. Kingfish out." Calhoun practically threw the handset back at Marcus. "Put that away, Crowell, and grab some chow. I need a smoke." Muttering oaths, the Loot stomped several feet back down the trail from us before he angrily squatted down and drew a pack of butts out of his blouse pocket. Nickerson went and put a commiserating hand on Calhoun's shoulder. I cautiously went and stood by Marcus. The rest of third squad stared at the Loot. None of us had ever seen him so upset. "What was all that about?" I mumbled.

"I couldn't help but hear it, Joe," Marcus answered equally softly. "'Cause they was yellin' so loud at each other with the static and all." He leaned in toward me. "Seems Colonel Embry is mighty ticked at the Loot. Said we're doin' no good out here at all, so Embry's fixin' to bring the rest of the platoon out here to help find this guy."

Now it was my turn to bug my eyes. "First and second squads? To come here?" Marcus nodded. "That's over thirty guys, just to search for one," I said. "That's crazy."

"Guess so, but it's done," he shrugged. "Embry said they was comin' in on two slicks sometime later today, and he was gonna be leadin' 'em."

"Meanwhile the Loot looks incompetent," I said, staring over at him. Calhoun's head was wreathed in clouds of angry gray smoke as he puffed away. "Talk about a bad career move."

"Maybe he is—whatever that word you said, Joe," Marcus said. "I mean, I like Calhoun, even if he is just a fool Yankee. But if the man can't cut the mustard, I guess he can't. I'm sure tired of stompin' around out here for nothin'."

Suddenly Lieutenant Calhoun shrugged Nickerson's hand away. Ignoring his own rule regarding fieldstripping, the Loot threw his cigarette down and stood, grinding it out in the dust under his boot heel. "All right, people, that was Colonel Embry on the horn. He's bringing the rest of the platoon out here later to help us with our search. I for one will be glad to see them, and for their help." The Loot folded his arms across his chest, as if daring us to contradict him. None of us did, but then none of us believed him either.

11

The ringing phone jerked me out of my reverie. I snatched it up, momentarily disoriented. "Box, uh, Box Investigations," I stammered, hating myself for it. Ever since I was a young boy (hadn't a Who song started out like that?), I've tended to stammer when I get rattled. At age ten it was charming; at nearly fifty it was something less than that. "May I help you?" I went on, more slowly.

"Mr. Box? This is Melanie. You know. Frontenau." Not surprisingly she sounded lousy. "I'm callin' you back 'cause you called me."

"Hi, Melanie." I stopped myself at the last instant from asking her, how are you doing? I knew full well how. "And Mr. Box was my father," I went on with a scold, but not unkindly. "I'm just Joe. Remember?"

"Yeah." Her voice was listless. "I was gon' ask you if

you had come up wit' sumpin' yet."

"Not yet," I said gently. "These things take their own time. But I can tell you that I'm working on it."

"Well, dat's another thing I was callin' about." Melanie's tone turned tentative. "I was jus' wond'rin' how much all this is gon' set us—me—back." I heard a catch in her throat. "I ain't got all dat much. Little Bit's job at the weldin' shop wasn't dat good, and I'm still shuckin' oysters. It's all I know how to do, and it don't pay a lot." Now the catch was gone, replaced by a steely resolve. I could imagine her sitting straighter as she said the rest. "But what I got is yours, Joe. I want dat man a' mine revenged. You hear me?" Little Bit had once told me that Melanie had grown up hard and tough; she was showing that now. "I don' care how much it costs."

I gave my answer in a term she would understand. "Forget it, Mel. It's *lagniappe.*"

◆ ◇ ◆

Lagniappe, pronounced "lahn-YAHP," is a Cajun word I'd never come across until I heard Little Bit say it for the first time in-country. Third squad had been slowly moving through a friendly village one day in our search for Sammy when Little Bit stopped and sniffed.

"Smell dat, Joe?" he smiled. "Somebody's cookin' wit' dem hot Vietnam peppers. I heard dey was good. Reckon we could hook us some?"

Lieutenant Calhoun must have read our minds as he called a lunch break for us. Little Bit and I used that as an excuse to see where that intoxicating smell was coming from. It turned out to be emanating from a miserable hut so rickety a good sneeze could have toppled it. Inside we found an old mamma-san stirring a medium-sized black kettle, surrounded by a half-dozen young women and their children. They all looked at us with enormous eyes. Little Bit and I smiled at the old lady, making eating motions with our hands. She returned a toothless smile. By then the rest of the squad had crowded in, and as they did the old lady began ladling out generous helpings of whatever it was she'd been cooking into small wooden bowls. She handed them to us one by one, all but Ed. He refused his with a shake of his head and a scowl.

"Not me, man. God knows what that meat is. I ain't eatin' that swill."

"Eddie," I said, "you're being a jerk. And I know for you that's not a stretch, but look at her. That old mamma-san's hardly got enough for her own kin, but yet she's willing to share. Now quit making like the Ugly American and eat it."

He frowned. "The what?"

About then Nickerson stepped forward, clapping an avuncular hand on Ed's shoulder. "Box is right," the sarge said. "Remember those talks you got when you arrived in-country about 'winning the hearts and minds of the people'?" Nickerson's hand was now squeezing down, and Ed's face grew white. "You're making this woman look bad before her family," the sarge went on, "and that I will not abide. So private Ralston, you will eat this chow, now, and do it gratefully, or I'll take you outside and get it into you another way." Nickerson grinned, "And believe me, if I do, those peppers are gonna feel even hotter."

Ed nodded once without another word and dug in. So did the rest of us. Like Ed, I had no idea what the meat we were eating was—probably dog—but the stew was great, jammed full of potatoes and greens, and the tiny Vietnamese peppers dotting it throughout packed a punch that stayed with you. Little Bit grinned at me after a few spoons of the stuff, sweat running down his face.

"Not as hot as Cajun," he said, fanning his mouth. "But respectable."

At last we stood to go. The Loot pulled out some scrip, handing it out to the old lady with a smile. "That was mighty tasty, ma'am. Thank you." But she didn't take it. Instead she rapidly waved both hands at us and started jabbering away in her native dialect. The Loot frowned and turned to Del Haggin.

"What's she saying, private?"

Del, who'd proved to be a quick study in Vietnamese, translated the words. "Well, basically it seems she's telling us our money's no good, Loot."

"What?" Calhoun examined it. "It's army-issue scrip. Of course it's good. It's backed by the U.S. government." The Loot really had led a sheltered life.

"No sir," Del said. "That's not what she means. She's just saying it's been her pleasure to serve us." The old lady talked on, Del translating. "It seems the VC did a sweep through here last week, snatching the young guys as conscripts." The old lady finally finished, and Del's face blanched. "Her son was a cripple, so they shot him." She bobbed her head grimly, looking a thousand years old.

"I see," the Loot nodded. "Well, thank her, Haggin. Tell her we appreciate ... all her sacrifices."

Del did, and the old lady nodded again. We began filing out, Little Bit and I the last ones to leave the hut, when suddenly he reached into his pants pocket. Turning, he thrust his nearly new lighter into the woman's hands. She looked up at him, puzzled. Little Bit just closed one eye, touched his nose with the side of his finger, and smiled. A second later she returned the smile, and we left.

"What was all that about?" I asked him as we fell into line. "How did you know she'd take it?"

"People are the same all over," Little Bit answered. "I knew she wouldn' take the scrip, but a lighter, now dat's sumpin' she can use." He grinned. "*Lagniappe.* Dat's all it was."

"What did you say?"

"*Lagniappe.* It's a Cajun word. It means ... aw, it's hard to say. It means, like you din't expect it. Like a bonus. Like if you was to go into a bakery and order six donuts and the man gives you seven, just because. It's *lagniappe,* is all." I rolled the word around in my mind, savoring it like a ripe cherry. "*Lagniappe.* An unexpected blessing. I like it."

"Hang around wit' me, Joe," Little Bit grinned, "an' I'll do you some good." We laughed and moved on down the trail.

◆ ◊ ◆

"That's what my work for you is, Melanie," I said. "*Lagniappe.* Okay?" I heard her sniff. She wasn't as tough as she made out.

"Okay, Joe. And t'ank you."

12

I fooled around for a while longer at the office before I finally conceded that it was no use. Mrs. Brake had done her part in getting me the names and addresses of Del and Greg and Marcus, but that still left me the job of calling those men and warning them. And that I simply wasn't ready to do. Not that I was shirking the duty, far from it. It was just that I was trying to put myself in their shoes and imagining how my words would sound. There had to be a way to do it, and in the natural scheme of things I couldn't come up with a single one.

So that left the supernatural.

I picked up the phone and called my church.

It rang a couple of times before a cheery, feminine voice came on the line. "God bless you, Harvard Pike."

"Hey, Zoe. It's Joe Box."

"Joe!" the young girl said, her voice growing even brighter. "Hi!"

Zoe Gennaro was the bubbly twenty-something who answered the phones at the Pike, which was what we members—and that still felt strange, me numbering myself among those, even after all these months—call our church. She was one of the nicest people I'd ever met.

"Who do you need to talk to today, Joe?" Zoe asked. "Angela's not here, at least I haven't seen her yet."

"Pastor Franklin, if he's around."

"I'm not really sure where he is. I can connect you to Dotty, if you'd like."

Dotty was Dotty Leland, the pastor's secretary. A tall, older woman with a regal bearing, Dotty kept things in balance at our church. Harvard Pike had been undergoing a growth spurt, having surpassed the four thousand member mark just last month, and without Dotty's administrative gifts, Luke would have found his head sliding under the waves in short order.

I guess if you looked at it in business terms, and if you're running a four-thousand-member church you'd darn well better, Dotty served as the gatekeeper to the CEO.

But right now I needed an appointment with that CEO, something I don't often ask for. Luke's time is as valuable as mine—more so.

"That'd be fine, Zoe," I said. "Connect away."

She did, and few seconds later Dotty came on the line. "Hello, may I help you?"

"Hi, Dotty, it's Joe Box. Is Luke around?"

"Mr. Box, hello," she said. I like Dotty, but I haven't yet

been able to get her to loosen up around me. Maybe it goes with her job. "No, I'm sorry, he's not," she went on. "He's in the gymnasium, talking with the flooring man." The Pike had moved into a brand-new sanctuary two months earlier, built to handle the increasing crowds, and unfortunately the flooring contractor who had been hired to do the work in the gym had used substandard wood. Now a new guy had been hired to undo all that, and I understood the job was taking longer than it was supposed to. The problem had gotten handed off until it had finally landed on Luke's desk. So instead of him reading the Bible or getting his sermon ready for Sunday, he was having to mess around with a gym floor. I shook my head. And people think all a pastor has to do is to give a talk a couple of times a week.

"I can page him, if you wish," Dotty added.

I heard her key the intercom. In August, when I'd first met Luke Franklin, the Pike was still meeting in the old sanctuary, and the intercom system there was iffy at best. I hoped that the contractor for the new system wasn't a brother of the flooring man. A few seconds later my apprehension was relieved when Luke came on.

"I've got it Dotty." I heard her hang up. "Hello, Pastor Franklin here."

"Hey, Luke. It's Joe Box."

"Joe! What's the haps, bro?"

"'What's the haps?'" I laughed. "I think you've been hanging around Pastor Tony's youth group too much lately."

"Maybe I have at that," he chuckled. "Think I'm too old for that kind of slang, huh?"

"Only if you want to sound like a Las Vegas lounge lizard."

"God forbid. So what can I help you with? Does that sound better?"

"Yep. Have you got a minute? I know you're still messing around with that flooring guy."

"I was hoping to have the gym ready for our homeless banquet this Thanksgiving," Luke sighed, "but it looks like that's not going to happen. Maybe by Christmas."

"Well, I hate to add to your troubles, but I was calling to see if I could set up a appointment to talk sometime today."

"Trouble? You're no trouble," Luke said. "Truth to tell, I could use a break. These nit-picky details are making my eyes cross. And we really haven't gotten to chew the fat much, one on one, since the close of that big case of yours in August. How about, say, one o'clock?"

"That'll work. By the way, skip lunch. It'll be my treat. I'll bring us a bag of sliders and fries from White Castle."

"Then we really can chew the fat," the pastor laughed. "Don't breathe a word of this to Donna though. She may be a sweet wife, but that woman would have your head on a plate if she knew you were pumping this aging carcass full of oily food."

"I'm a private eye, Luke," I said. "Discretion is my watchword."

◆ ◊ ◆

It was about one when I pulled into the Pike's brand-new parking lot. As I got out of my car, I looked around. The lot was huge, encompassing nearly five acres, and I harked back to when I was over here last summer, the week the contractor was blacktopping the thing. It was a scorching day, and the stench from the hot asphalt had nearly run me off. As a kid, I'd found out the hard way the stuff had that effect on me.

Back when I was fourteen, my cousin Ray had gotten us summer jobs with the county, working on the road crew. The first day they set me to filling potholes, a really brainless task. But brains didn't enter into the equation; stamina did. The temperature that day set an all-time record for June 15, nearly 110 degrees, and the cloying animal smell of the hot pitch, combined with the dead air and the killing heat, almost laid me out. Somehow I put in my ten hours, but at quitting time when I drew my pay I told the road boss that was it for me. I braced myself, expecting the man to ream me good for being eight kinds of a wiener, but instead he merely nodded as he handed me my money.

"They ain't many a boy that would've stuck it out for the day like you," the young supervisor said, taking off his old felt hat and wiping his face with a yellow-stained handkerchief as he talked. I noticed his forehead was bisected by a line that stretched from temple to temple. North of it, where he wore his hat, his skin was bone-white; south to his neck he was the color of brick. A farmer's face. "Fact is, I near keeled over myself twice after lunch," he went on. "They ain't no shame in it." With that he shook my hand.

I was starting the long walk home when I passed Ray.

"Did I hear right, Joe? Did you really quit?" Ray's voice dripped with derision; although he was only a year older than me, he acted like he was thirty. He went on with a sneer, "You might be my cousin, but I'm glad I'm a Wilson and not a Box. What a sissy."

My ears burned like fire as I kept walking. I was afraid my voice would break if I answered him. The road boss was nice in what he'd said to me, but I still couldn't help the feeling that I'd somehow let down the male gender in general, and the Box side of the family in particular. In my mind I began working on the scathing reply I was going to give to Cousin Ray when our families next got together over the upcoming Fourth of July weekend.

But I never got the chance. Ten days later, Ray was dead. He'd been running across the road to retrieve the supervisor's hat when he was accidentally run over and crushed by a Caterpillar D-7 heavy dozer.

I was shaking my head as I entered the office side of the church, the bag of hamburgers clutched in my hand. *Crushed by a bulldozer.* Memories can be activated by the simplest things.

And with that I stopped short, my mouth involuntarily dropping open.

I'd caught the minnow. I knew what was killing my friends.

13

---

*T*he clue was found in the remembrance of that first day on the road crew. Ray and I had just arrived at the job site when we saw the supervisor motioning to us from across the road. I started toward him, but Ray hung back, looking from side to side.

"You'd better come on," I called. "We don't wanna get fired before we even start."

A moment later he caught up with me, and we started moving again. "I was just bein' careful," he said, "'cause I'm older, and Ma said I had to watch out for you. You're still a kid, see, and I know all about roadwork. Them big ol' dozers can run a feller down and the driver not feel it. The guy'd never even stop, but just keep on goin', and then there you'd be, boy, flatter'n a skunk."

"Aw, I ain't scared of 'em," I said.

"Well, I ain't either," Ray blustered, but I didn't believe him. He was still looking up and down the road as we went. "I'm just careful, like I told you. If you was to get run over and squashed, don't expect me to tell your Granny about it."

I didn't bother pointing out to Ray that if I was to get run over and squashed, I wouldn't be expecting anything from anybody. And as clear as a penny in the well water, there was the thread I'd been after.

Fear.

That was the key I'd been missing, the common denominator that had been eluding me. Ray had dreaded being killed by a bulldozer; it was in his voice. And in a macabre irony, he was.

I began running the deaths of the men from third squad, Bravo platoon, company C, through my mind, heedless of the hamburgers cooling and congealing in their paper sack. A few moments more, and there it was. It had started with an offhand remark by Rafe Martinez more than three decades past.

Once again I was back in Vietnam.

Third squad was now seven days into its patrol, on our endless search for the elusive killer. Vlad thought the fruitlessness of what we were doing would qualify as a good title for a tear-jerker movie: *Searching for Sammy*.

"Can't you picture it, guys?" he said as we trudged along the trail. *"Searching for Sammy*: the heartwarming story of a boy who's lost his collie."

"It beats losing a sniper," Sergeant Nickerson muttered,

but I don't think the Loot caught it. He had his own problems. Just after breakfast Colonel Embry had, as promised, arrived with the first and second squads, and then had taken, without ceremony, the reins of the operation from the lieutenant. You could tell the Loot was chapped about it, but was bearing it like a Spartan.

"Naw, don't make it a collie," Marcus said after a moment. "Make it a mean dog. Mean and big."

"Nobody would buy it," I said, wiping the sweat out of my eyes. "I say make it a scruffy mutt. Everybody likes those."

"Hokay, but then you'd hafta get a real good movie star to play the kid," Rafe said. "Hey, I got it. Maybe that one off of *I Love Lucy.*"

"You mean Little Ricky?" Del asked. "Isn't he like, I dunno, thirty or something by now?"

"Maybe, but at leas' he's Hispanic," Rafe said, "an' I think a Hispanic would be good." He nodded, for him the question settled. "That's what the kid should be. Hispanic."

"Little Ricky ain't Hispanic," Bobby panted. His right knee was giving him trouble. He'd twisted the thing pretty badly when we crossed that stream yesterday, and by now it had puffed up like a roll of toilet paper. "Little Ricky's a white kid. Or was. I guess he's a white man by now."

"Yeah, who says?" Rafe argued. "That ain't right, man. Can't be. Little Ricky's a Hispanic kid. I mean, dig it, Ricky Ricardo is Little Ricky's dad, right? An' he's Cuban."

"His dad?" Ed Ralston snarled. "How stupid can one guy get? Rafe, I know you're dumb, but you don't really believe Little Ricky is Ricky Ricardo's son, do ya?"

"Sure he is!" Rafe shot back. "I've seen it on the TV! You're the dumb one, man!"

"TV's not real, Rafe," I broke in. "Bobby's right. Little Ricky was played by a white kid."

"Huh?" Rafe appeared genuinely puzzled. "Izzat right? But—"

"You have to learn to separate what's real from what's fake," I said. "Life is full of that sort of stuff."

"College boy," Ed muttered.

I ignored the slur. I'd given up trying to correct him of that.

"Well, looks like we've got a casting problem for who's going to play the part of the kid," Vlad said. "We'll fix that later, when the money starts rolling in. So who are we going to get to play Sammy, the scruffy, useless mutt?"

Little Bit snapped his fingers. "Hey, I got jus' the one." His eyes were dancing as his lips turned up in a grin. "How 'bout Eddie Ralston?"

We all nearly fell down laughing. All but Ed.

The day wore on as we moved along the trail. At last we fell silent, the heat and humidity sapping our strength as surely as if our veins had been sliced. At noon Colonel Embry passed the word down the line for us to break for chow. We did, but I couldn't help noticing the Loot had planted himself a ways off from the rest of us before he started digging into his C rats. I felt for him. Calhoun considered himself shamed, and as a Southerner I can tell you there's nothing that'll send a fellow down quicker than knowing people think of him as less than a man. I briefly wondered if I should move myself closer to him, show him there were no hard feelings, but quickly discarded that idea. The Loot was an officer, and I was a private; the gulf of rank isn't easily breached. I kept my plan to myself and let it slide.

Lunch finally over, the colonel surprised us by giving us a few more minutes to smoke and yack before we saddled up again. I don't think Embry was being overly considerate to his troops; I think the truth of the matter was he was finding that leading thirty men on a forced march through heat like this was really a job for a younger man. The extra time of rest was more for him than for us. But I kept that to myself as well.

We were stretching out along the trail's edge, staring up through the leafy jungle canopy into the unforgiving whiteness of the sky, when Rafe finally spoke aloud the thought I'm sure we'd all been having. "So what're we gonna do when we find him?"

"Who, Sammy?" I asked.

"I ain' talkin' about the pope," he grinned.

Toby's ebony face was grim. "I say we kill him slow, baby. Real slow, a piece at a time, an' send the boy back to his mamma-san in ha'f a dozen shoeboxes."

"Yeah!" Little Bit jumped in. "Crab bait!"

"I wouldn't," Marcus drawled. "Here's why. I heard somethin' on the radio this mornin', while the colonel was givin' HQ a sit-rep. Seems ol' Sammy's on a roll. Just this week, he took out four more men. Dude's a regular Wyatt Earp. So you want my vote on a feller that dangerous?" He shrugged.

"I say we croak him just as soon as we see him. I wouldn't mind doin' it myself. Croak him quick and get me a medal."

Ed cut a glance Marcus's way. "Why, so you could hang it in your outhouse?"

The Georgia man's answer was placid. "I just think that a man that good with a gun you don't wanna give no quarter to."

"So what are you sayin', Crowell, that you're scared of him?" Ed sneered in disbelief. "Big strappin' farm boy like you?"

"Dang straight I'm skeered of him," Marcus replied. "I ain't ashamed to say it neither." He rolled over, his eyebrows rising in amazement. "You sayin' you ain't skeered of him, Eddie?"

Ed curled a lip as he tucked his arm under his head and resumed looking back up at the sky. "I ain't scared of nothin', boy."

"That's stupid," Rafe said. "Ev'rybody's scared of somethin'."

"Not me," Ed said simply.

"I gotta go with Rafe on this one," Del said. "Every man in the world has one thing that he's scared of. One thing that just thinking about it, gives him cold sweats at night."

After a moment Vlad spoke up in a sad half-laugh. "I know I do."

"Yeah?" I sat up and looked over at him. "What?"

He sat up as well and pulled a piece of grass from between his feet. Systematically he started stripping it. It was a moment longer before he answered. "Getting shot."

"Man, we've all got that," Greg said.

"No, I mean really," Vlad replied. "Why do you think I became a medic? Because I get off on the smell of a gut wound? Because I enjoy slapping field bandages on screaming men?" He shook his head and pointed down at the helmet lying on the dirt next to him. "No, because deep down I thought that red cross painted on my pot would make some slope think twice before drilling me."

"Good idea, but the VC don't abide by the same rules we do," Del pointed out. "A lot of times a slope'll drill a medic just because they know he's unarmed."

Vlad's laugh was bitter. "I know that *now*. Too bad I didn't know it before I agreed to wear the stupid thing." He picked up his pot and held it out. "Anybody want to trade?"

Our laughs in reply didn't carry any more humor than Vlad's. We all knew Del was speaking the truth.

"So anyway, that's what causes Mrs. Przbasky's boy to have nightmares." Vlad dropped his helmet back in the dirt. He was trying to lighten his tone and not doing a very good job of it. "Let's hear from the rest of you."

Nobody said anything for a minute. None of us was as willing as Vlad to bare his soul before the others. Finally Ed spoke up. "Forget it, Bela. Maybe the rest of us ain't as gutless as you."

His smile was still sad. "Maybe not, Eddie."

I was about to jump in and take the scorn off Vlad when Little Bit, of all people, beat me to it.

"All right, I'll fess up," he said. "Wit' me it's 'lectricity. Maybe ya'll noticed I don't mess much with dat radio."

"I think we all noticed that," Bobby said, "especially when it's raining."

"When ain't it rainin'?" Toby asked, and we all laughed.

"Ya'll laugh if you want," Little Bit said, "but I ain't been zapped by the t'ing yet, no." We laughed harder, and he went on, "When I was a boy I seen a man killed at a diner jus' by stickin' his fork in a toaster. Now ain't dat a hellacious t'ing? Man goes to get himself a piece a' toast and next t'ing he's wit' God. So it ain't gonna happen to me, no." Little Bit folded his scrawny arms over his narrow chest and shot out his lower lip. "And dat's what scares me. Who else gonna fess up?"

There was another long pause. Then slowly, almost like a catharsis, our laughing faded as we each began telling what terrified us most.

Bobby Dagliesh led off by saying he was afraid of drowning; as he did I wondered if maybe that's why he'd tried crossing that stream so fast, to get it past him. He'd only succeeded in slipping on a mossy rock and going completely under, coming back up spluttering foul water and with his knee wrenched. Rafe said with him it was the fear of being crushed; I involuntarily harked back to my cousin's Ray's closed casket. Toby Buntline was terrified of heights and falling, Marcus Crowell of suffocation, Del Haggin of stabbing, Greg Dapp of dying in a plane crash. Even Ed Ralston finally "fessed up," but he did it in true Ed fashion.

"I don't like to drive," he said. "Not that I ain't a great driver, 'cause I am, but there's too many nuts on the road. I live just outside of LA, and some of those dopers out there would run ya off the highway and never even stop. So I don't drive much." Then he leered, "But then I don't have to. I let my lady friends with their fancy sports cars drive me wherever I want."

That was met by the jeers and catcalls you'd expect.

Then Ed turned his head toward me. "So what about you, Box? We all told. Now it's your turn."

It was my turn, all right. But I didn't want to say. Did *not*. With me, my deepest fear was about as elemental as it gets.

Fire.

14

*S*omething this good ought to be sinful," I said around another bite of hamburger. I swallowed it before going on, "You're the preacher, Luke. Does the Bible have anything to say about eating sliders?"

He reached for the last of the cardboard boxes containing the small burgers. "Well, the Word says something about the three Hebrew children not eating the king's delicacies." The pastor grabbed the sandwich out of its box, devouring half of it in one bite. He went on with a grin, blowing onion fumes at me. "I think if the king had served those boys sliders, they just might not have been able to resist."

"And the church said amen," I said, scarfing the last bite of mine. At final count we'd had seven each, plus fries and Cokes. Gluttony on parade. I gave a slight belch. "Look at us.

Two guys eating belly bombers and burping at each other. Aren't men gross?"

"Donna would agree," Luke replied, wiping his mouth and leaning back in his chair. "I'm holding you to your promise to keep your trap shut to her about this." We were sitting at a small round table in the corner of his new office. I was pretty sure it was the same little table he'd brought over from the old place, the table where we'd first talked, more than three months earlier. A lot had happened to me since that day.

"The three Hebrew children," I said meditatively. "I've been reading the Bible whenever I get the chance, but I'm still having trouble keeping everything straight. They were the ones with those tongue-twister names, right?"

"Shadrach, Meshach, and Abednego," Luke said.

"And aren't they also the ones who went into the fiery furnace because they wouldn't bow down to the king's statue?"

"You mean King Nebuchadnezzer."

"Lord have mercy." I shook my head. "How would you like to have to sign that for the rest of your life?"

Luke grinned. "Maybe his pals just called him Neb."

I leaned back myself and stared at a point on the far wall past his left ear. "The fiery furnace ..." I muttered. It was starting to come back to me.

Luke's grin faded, replaced by a kindly smile. "Something tells me this is what brought you here today."

"I think it ties into it, yeah," I said. "But believe it or not, fire didn't even enter my mind until I thought of something else as I was coming into the building."

Luke pushed his lunch mess to the side before folding his hands and leaning in. "Tell me."

I did. I started with Little Bit's late-night phone call and went from there. With my Vietnam side trips down memory lane, the telling took longer than I'd thought it would. But Luke acted as if he had all the time in the world to listen. Finally I was done.

"There's something I'm missing here," the pastor said. "You said at first you discounted your friend Little Bit's fear of who's been doing all this as the ravings of an alcoholic. But now you think he was right after all. What changed your mind?"

"Simple," I said. "The word is fear."

"I still don't understand."

"I know." I felt cold sweat beginning to bloom on the roots of my hair. "I'm not so sure I understand it myself. But it's the only thing that makes sense." I swallowed. "You need to stay with me on this, because the next part of what I'm about to tell you is going to sound fantastic." And then I told Luke of that day.

The day we found Sammy.

15

wenty-one days." Greg Dapp shook his head as he fieldstripped his Lucky. "Feels more like twenty-one years."

"I heard that," Toby agreed in a low voice. "What's Embry tryin' to prove anyway, marchin' us this hard?"

Marcus shrugged as he prized open his C rat can. "Maybe he's buckin' for brigadier, and figures gettin' Sammy'd do the trick." He dug a round, flat, cello-wrapped hunk of grayish chocolate out of the can with a sigh. "I sure hope the Hershey folks never find out what the army's done to their candy bars."

"Brigadier," Toby snorted in derision. "That ofay sucker best be real glad nobody's fragged his butt yet."

I didn't join in the banter, even though I agreed with the sentiment. Crabbing is part and parcel of army life, but it was just too stinking hot.

"Here's what I think," Bobby said, but we never got to find out what it was, because right about then Colonel Embry blew his whistle to let us know break time was over.

"I wish I knew where Embry keeps dat stupid whistle," Little Bit muttered to me as we all pulled our gear back on. "'Cause I'd take it from him some dark night, for true." Cursing softly, we fell into line and started walking again.

It was sundown that evening when we got the news. Colonel Embry hung up the receiver on the field telephone and called us to gather around. His stern features looked nearly happy for once.

"Men, we've caught a break. HQ has it on good authority that Sammy was spotted in this sector night before last." We didn't cheer, so he went on. "Here's the deal. There's a village five klicks south of our position that we're going to be paying a visit to tomorrow. When we get there, a fellow named Tran is supposed to fill us in on Mr. Sammy's whereabouts. Then all that's left for us to do is verify that information, call it in to the 105s, and level the area where he's hiding. By this time tomorrow night we'll have that sniper's dead carcass tied to the skid of a slick." Smiling, Embry spread his hands, like he was expecting us to give him a round of applause. When we didn't, his smile faded. "Well. Sleep soundly, men. Tomorrow we hunt."

As we crawled into our bedrolls, Little Bit whispered coarsely at me, "Hunt? Ain't dat what we been doin'?"

I was too tired to answer. Moments later I was asleep.

◆ ◊ ◆

It was going on noon the next day when we approached the outskirts of the village. I surprised everyone, myself most of all, when I stopped dead in my tracks.

"Wait!" My voice was as shaky as I've ever heard it.

The platoon raggedly came to a puzzled halt. Embry trotted up to me, a scowl twisting his harshly handsome features.

"Box," he snapped, "just when did I lose command of this troop? You'd better explain yourself." In his mind I imagine he was already fingering his new general's insignia, and I was messing up his plans.

The problem was, I couldn't explain myself, at least not in a way he could understand. As I've said before, I come from poor mountain stock, and we hill-folk have ways and beliefs that, to a flatlander, seem almost to come from another time.

Being fey, for instance.

Now before you start sniggering, the word "fey" is an old English term that could best be translated "foreknowledge." Granny explained it to me when as a child one night I'd stumbled into her bedroom, finding myself crying uncontrollably.

"Oh Lord, Lord," she moaned, holding my trembling body close, "don't let it be this, please Lord. Let this cup pass." Still moaning, she gently rocked me as I sobbed.

Beneath my tears, I had no idea what she was talking about. All I know is somehow Granny knew I hadn't had a nightmare. I'd had those before, plenty of times, and how she held me then was ... different. Now it was as if Granny was doing her best to shield me from a terrible knowledge, but knew in her heart that she couldn't. Later the next morning we found out something awful had happened. My best friend, Harley Draper's dad had drowned, trapped beneath an overturned johnboat during a duck hunt, his lungs filling with fetid swamp water as his waders dragged him down.

And what had awakened me screaming was that I'd seen his death five hours *before* it occurred.

That's when Granny told me about the Box clan being *fey*.

Like any other eight-year-old boy, to me the word sounded weird, almost sissified. But she'd patiently told me that sometimes a Box would know something bad was coming, just from a feeling. The sensation, at least in my case, was an unpleasant one, like a fluttering running up and down my spine. It wasn't psychic, exactly, and it sure wasn't foolproof, but it had happened enough times during my life to give it credence.

Much later, when I became a Christian, my friend Nick Castle told me the Christian equivalent of fey was something called discernment. Discernment is given by God, he said, to certain individuals at certain times either to confirm something good or to stave off something bad. In my case, fey came along only to do the latter. So did that mean it was satanic, and not from God? To this day I don't know. All I can say is that since I asked Jesus to take the train wreck I'd made of my life and do something with it, I've never had that awful feeling again.

But I also can say that I was experiencing it strongly as we all stood outside that thatch-hut village on that hot January morning in 1971.

Embry was still glaring at me. "Well, Box? Are you going

to stand there blinking, or are you going to tell me why I shouldn't have you hauled up on charges?"

"It's just …" My mouth felt strange, like I was using someone else's. "not safe," I finished lamely.

Third squad heard that and passed it down. In seconds all three squads, the whole platoon, was roaring with laughter at me.

Like magic, Nickerson was suddenly by Embry's side. With the *de facto* demotion of Lieutenant Calhoun, the sergeant was now effectively the colonel's adjutant. "Do we have a problem, sir?" Nickerson said flatly, his gray eyes not leaving mine.

Embry's voice carried an edge. "It seems your man feels the village isn't safe, sergeant." I wasn't Nickerson's man any more than I was the Loot's; I was just me, trying to get home with my skin intact. But that was Embry's way, I was finding out, of letting us all know he was above this ratty command.

Nickerson spit into the dust by my left boot, his voice heavy with sarcasm. "Box, you moron, we're in South Vietnam, over seventy-five miles deep in Indian country. Of course it isn't safe." He jerked his thumb back over his shoulder, toward the settlement. "But the colonel has it on good authority that village has been secured, and as friendly to us as it's likely to get. So unless you're really a G-10 government spook, and you know something we don't, I'd suggest you get your sorry butt back in line and help us find this guy Tran." Then Nickerson grinned at me, and it wasn't pretty. "Or you can consider yourself under arrest, and when this is all over, and we're all getting our pictures in the paper, you can read about it while you break rocks in Leavenworth. Your choice, son."

I knew I was outgunned. With a small groan of dread I did as the sergeant said and resumed my place behind Eddie. Embry tooted his whistle, and we all started up again.

"Box, are you nuts or what?" Eddie mumbled back at me after a few steps. "I know we ain't pals, but I've seen you in firefights, and you ain't yellow. What's the matter with you?"

There was no way of explaining it to him, so I simply said, "I've got a bad feeling about that place."

Now he half turned to me as we walked. "What, like a superstition? One of them hillbilly things?"

I just shook my head and didn't answer. It was no use.

A few minutes later we entered the village compound. And stopped. That spinal tingling of mine doubled. It was all I could do to keep from dropping my rifle and running.

There was no one there. Not a soul. No cooking fires, no children, no dogs. The entire place was as deserted as a music hall three hours after the concert was done.

All conversation ceased, the thirty of us fallen completely silent at the same time. Then Embry gave us the look only a bird colonel can. Warily we started trudging down the main path again, our weapons swinging this way and that as we went, nerves taut. We were all well seasoned, and knew anything could happen.

Did I say the village was deserted? Not quite. Approaching the middle, we saw there was *something* folded up right in the center of it.

Nickerson walked up to the thing. As he did, his face

paled. "What's going on here?" The words hung in his throat.

We all crowded around to see. Then we started muttering, our silence broken, the horror as thick as paint.

The *something* before us was a Vietnamese man, or what was left of him. He was wadded up in a fetal position, his hands wired tightly behind him. The back of the man's skull was gone, his face a ruin. Somebody had wired this guy up, forced him to kneel, and then put a bullet in his head.

Execution.

The Loot spoke up, his voice thin and reedy. "Anybody want to bet this is Tran?"

He had no takers on that one. The muttering grew louder.

We were all a long way from home.

16

"All right, people, shut up!" Nickerson barked. I guess he was trying to tamp down his own fear. "We're gonna do this by the numbers. See what we've got here. First and second squads, secure the perimeter. Third—"

"Sarge," I broke in, not much caring how he felt about that. "It's a trap. We gotta leave. Now." My throat was gummy with the knowledge that what I was saying was the truth.

Embry by now was standing next to Nickerson. The colonel spun toward me, his visage grim as his eyes locked on mine. "Crowell and Ralston. Remove private Box's weapon from his possession and secure his hands. As of this second, he is under arrest."

Ed and Marcus looked at each other, unsure.

Embry turned from me to them. "Do it or share his fate. I—"

The colonel's head exploded. With it his lifeless body dropped to the ground, his right leg twitching and hammering the dirt.

Sammy.

For a moment we all stood shocked, unmoving, rooted to the ground like trees. That's when the mortar shells started falling, and the village became a pretty fair approximation of hell.

The first one struck with a horrendous explosion right in the middle of second squad, who'd unwisely stayed clumped together. It was a mistake none of them would repeat. The shrieks of the wounded and the silence of the dead were overshadowed by the sound of the next three shells landing almost simultaneously.

"Incoming! Take cover!" Nickerson screamed. His warning was unnecessary. Those of us still alive and moving were doing just that, each trying to find something, anything to crawl under or duck behind.

It seemed as if the barrage lasted for hours, even though that was impossible: obviously Sammy had hooked up with either an NVA or VC escort, and they were as far from their supply lines as we were. At best they couldn't have dropped more than a dozen shells on us, but right then it felt like they'd bought out the store.

Finally it was over. But what was next?

We found out a second later as a couple of heavy machine guns opened up on us. The rounds those things unleashed were as big as a man's thumb, and the straw bales first squad had cowered behind gave them no more protection than a wet Kleenex. One by one each man grunted or screamed as the bullets found their marks. The sounds the rounds made as they hit were the same as if you'd tied a steak to your hand and slammed it into a heavy bag at the gym.

We in third squad were luckier. The fifty-five gallon metal drums in front of us gave us at least the impression of safety.

But then, at long last, that assault too was over. The sounds filling the air now were only those of frightened monkeys and alarmed birds, and the moans of the dying.

I peeked my head over the drum for a cautious look. People never said I was smart, only pretty. A hundred yards off, a group of men were beating their way through the sawgrass, heading away from our position. It was too far to tell if they were regular North Vietnamese troops or their VC brothers. I didn't care; I just wanted them dead. I was sure the rest of the platoon would agree. The platoon ... I looked around.

What a mess. What a sad and sorry mess. To a man, second squad was gone. Completely wiped out. Of first squad, I only counted three up and moving. Vlad was attending the rest, doing what he could. It didn't seem to be all that much.

Those of us in third squad were the only ones untouched. Granny had told me before I shipped out she was going to be praying for me daily. Thanks, Granny, and what's left of our troop says thanks as well. What the dead of first and second squads had to offer, I couldn't say.

Nickerson and the Loot stood. Calhoun looked like he'd aged years in the last few minutes. Nickerson's voice was blistered with anger. "Boys, we've just been sucker-punched.

Right in the guts. I'd say it's payback time." He pointed toward the running men. "Nobody goes home until the last of those slopes are dead."

That did it. As one, what was left of Bravo platoon rose up with a roar. Heedless of what awaited us, we vaulted over our barricades and started running toward the fleeing enemy.

Looking back now, it was a pretty pitiful effort. Counting Nickerson and the Loot, there were only fifteen of us who could fight out of our original thirty-plus. If the moving grass ahead was any indication, we were going up against at least a platoon-strength enemy troop and possibly more.

We didn't care. We'd just been bloodied badly, and as Nickerson said, it was payback time.

Eddie Ralston unslung his blooker as we ran. I reached into the satchel that was bouncing against my leg and handed him a grenade. Then I squinted. Ahead, the enemy troops, which I now saw were NVA, had leaped over something. For just a second I saw a figure in the middle, the only one dressed in black VC pajamas, lift his weapon high to clear the obstacle. Even at this distance I could tell he was carrying some sort of heavy hunting rifle.

Our boy.

"The range has gotta be eighty yards, Eddie," I panted as we ran. "Can you do it?"

"Watch me," he said. With that he yanked the butt-stock of his blooker tight against his shoulder and pulled the trigger.

The blooker made its characteristic sound, as if you'd slammed your hand down over the end of an open metal pipe, and the grenade was on its way. We and our guys didn't stop, but ran all the harder. We were closing the distance.

I looked up as I ran, watching the grenade's trajectory as it fell. Eddie's aim was right on the money. The thing seemed to be heading straight for Sammy's head.

And then the impossible happened.

I saw that grenade come within a foot of Sammy's cranium when it seemed to hit an invisible barrier. It skittered off to Sammy's left and exploded a split second later, shredding two of the NVA next to him.

The sniper didn't stop. He ran on, untouched.

But Eddie and I stopped in amazement. What we'd just seen simply didn't occur. I mean, come on. What could have done *that?*

That was about all the thinking I was able to do on it as Nickerson pounded up behind us, slamming Eddie and me hard with his hands as he did. "Gawk later!" he yelled, not stopping. "After 'em!"

He had a point. Provided I survived this day, I could ponder later what I'd seen. Right now there was an enemy to kill.

We closed the gap to fifty yards, firing wildly in three-round bursts as we ran. I saw maybe six or eight of the enemy fall dead. I'd like to think at least one of them was mine. Unfortunately not all of them were dead, and they fired back just as wildly. Two more of first squad went tumbling down. Then the last of the first squad men, a guy named Perelli running next to me, dropped and rolled, his chest blown out. Nickerson stopped to help him; why, I don't know. As the sergeant reached down, an AK-47 burst caught him in the face. Nickerson's body fell next to Perelli's.

But there was no time to grieve, as now we had a complication. Sammy and his troops were heading into a dense copse of trees, one I'm sure they knew well. Another trap? As they disappeared into the foliage the Loot held up his hand. "Hold your fire! Take up defensive positions!"

We did, each of us sliding behind a grassy hummock or rotten stump. I pulled my M-16 tight against my shoulder as I squinted down the sights toward the trees. For the first time in my life I knew what it was like to have an itchy trigger finger, but I did as the Loot commanded and held off. Eddie crouched to my right, maybe five yards away. To my left, another ten feet or so, was Little Bit. All of us in third squad had our guns trained downrange. I'd be willing to bet we all had the same expressions on our faces.

"Crowell!" the Loot barked. "Are you still alive?"

"Right here, sir," came Marcus's laconic reply.

"Get over here with that radio."

Marcus did, duck-waddling his way as he came. A sudden burst of AK-47 fire from the tree line caused him to attempt to become one with the dirt. We returned fire, and Marcus used that cover to crawl the last few feet over to where the Loot was crouching. I was close enough to them to hear what was said.

Calhoun yanked the handset off the radio with his right hand, whipping the crank around with his left as he did, then he flipped the transmit switch and started yelling. "Break, break! Kingfish calling Sapphire, Kingfish calling Sapphire, emergency break, over!" The NVA must have seen the antenna from the radio swaying. Again they opened fire, trying to knock it out.

I got off three more rounds before I went dry. In one continuous motion I ejected the spent clip, pulled another one off my belt, knocked it against my pot to seat the bullets firmly, then slammed it home in my rifle, pulling back on the charging handle as I did. Five seconds after I'd run out of ammo I was back in business again. I hadn't learned all my gun skills in basic, but it hadn't hurt.

The enemy guns fell silent once more.

The Loot was still yelling. "Sapphire, we need an emergency patch to the *Kitty Hawk*, come in, over!" We waited. It must have worked. A few seconds later he hollered into the handset, "*Kitty Hawk*, this is Lieutenant Calhoun, Ninth Corps, Charlie Company! We've got a situation here, a bad one. Can you spare us a couple of fast movers?" The answer must have been in the affirmative. We saw him nod. "Very good. Here's where we are, and here's where we need them. It'll be tight." The Loot read off a string of numbers, showing the swabbos our position on their map. I was beginning to give him a grudging respect; for being a shavetail, he wasn't doing a bad job with the way this goat-grab of a mission was turning out. "Excellent," he said. "*Kitty Hawk*, you've just made our day. Out." His grin dark, Calhoun handed the handset back to Marcus, who hung it back in its place on the radio.

The Loot raised his voice, so we all could hear. "Men, we're going to call it a day and let the Navy finish this job.

The *Kitty Hawk* has two F-4s on patrol near this sector. Furthermore, those Phantoms happen to be loaded to the gills with nape. In the interests of better inter-service relations, the Navy flyboys have agreed to help us out."

Little Bit spoke up from his position. "Sir, what 'zackly does all dat mean?"

"It means we're gon' see some barbecue, *cholo*," Rafe laughed.

He wasn't wrong. Three minutes later a thunderous sound approached from the east. We all looked.

The twin F-4s came screaming in low, nearly at treetop level, their ungodly roar as they flashed overhead loud enough to suck the air from your lungs. The Phantoms seemed to be terrifyingly close to our position, nearly on top of us, when their pilots released their dark, bulky packages from the hard points under the wings. Shooting the machines nearly vertical, they then turned for home. A second later the far tree line holding Sammy and his friends erupted in six, seven, *eight* huge, rolling orange balls of hellfire, orange balls shot through with black. Halloween comes to the Valley.

"Ain't dat pretty!" Little Bit breathed, eyes dancing. He grinned over at me. "Napalm's a mother. Dat'd be the job, Joe, five minutes of work and then back to the ship for beer and steaks."

Eddie shook his head, giving him a withering look. "How do you know what those pilot boys eat, swamp rat? You ever been on a carrier?"

Before Little Bit could answer, Rafe did. "Man, why don'chew quit raggin' the little guy, huh?"

Eddie's blood must have still been up from the fighting. "You want some of me, beaner? You Mexican mutt—"

"Everybody be quiet!" the Loot said. "Listen."

We did. And as we did I swallowed, hard. There was a sound coming from the treeline I'd heard before, one I'd hoped never to hear again in this lifetime.

The screams of people burning alive.

Out of the flaming trees three of the NVA, no more than that, came staggering toward us, but it was no use. They were nothing more than shuddering, twitching, shrieking human candles. Without being told we opened up on them, all of us, and cut them down.

The rest of the burning men were too far away, still back in the trees, wailing like the damned.

Beyond our mercy.

17

I tipped my paper Coke cup up to my mouth, letting the watery dregs wash down my throat. I was bone dry from the telling. But not just that. In the telling, I was reliving it.

The look on Luke's face was compassionate. "Maybe you need to finish this some other time, Joe."

"Time." I shook my head, hoping I hadn't sounded too despairing as I'd said the word. "That's just it. I'm out of time, and so are Del and Marcus and Greg. If I'm right about who's doing this, all four of us are in this guy's sights." I peered into my cup at the brownish ice cubes, then set it down. "No, I need to tell you the rest, get your take on it. If I'm crazy, let me know. But I don't think I am. Like I said, it's the only thing that makes sense." My smile now was sad and rueful. "I think it was Sherlock Holmes who said that when you've eliminated everything else, whatever remains, however improbable, must be the truth."

Luke's smile was just as sad. "Wasn't that Churchill?"

"Whoever." My smile faded as I tilted my head back at his office ceiling, its off-white swirls like a drive-in movie screen.

And the mad projectionist popped in reel two.

◆ ◇ ◆

The ground beneath our feet was smoldering. Around us a few flickering flames still remained, but the jungle, being moist, puts out its own fires pretty quickly. The Loot had ordered us into the copse as soon as it was safe.

We were looking for Sammy's body.

The smell around us was sickeningly sweet, like roast pork gone bad. Not a few of us had puked, me included. That was weird, considering I'd smelled that odor before, as a boy. Maybe that's why it had hit me the way it did.

Around us lay the bodies of a score or more of smallish men, their corpses charred and shriveled, limbs drawn up as if they wanted to fight us. But their fighting days were past. Intermixed with them were the bodies of jungle creatures too slow to have outrun the nape.

Vlad, who'd joined us when it became evident that the rest of the men of first squad lying back in the village were beyond help, picked something up. It was small, black, and very crisp. "What in the world is this?"

"A monkey," Bobby answered, swallowing his bile. "What's left of one anyway."

Curling his lip in disgust, Vlad dropped the thing. He wiped his hands on his pants, looking around at the

Phantoms' work. "Not much here for me to do." Then he added, "Thank God."

"You've done enough for one day, Przbasky." The Loot's voice was shaky. He was looking around too. "I had no idea …"

I did, but said nothing.

Toby blew out a disgusted breath. "How we gonna tell which one be Sammy? 'Scuse me for sayin' it, but these boys all look alike."

"That'll be easy," I said, trying to get my roiling gut under control.

Del stared at me. "Yeah? How?"

I motioned at the corpses. "None of these guys are armed, not anymore. They all dropped their AKs when they started burning. Sammy'll still have his hunting rifle with him, probably strapped to his back."

Ed cursed at me, sneering. "Now how would you know that, Box?"

"Joe's right," Marcus jumped in. "Me'n him's Southern boys, an' we know huntin'. An' hunters." He nodded at me. "What Joe's sayin' is that Sammy's a hunter before anything else. He woulda slung that piece of his across his back right before him an' his boys went into these woods. In case he needed it later. Like to shoot us."

"Well, none of these guys are gonna be shootin' anybody, not anymore," Greg said grimly.

"I guess we listen to Box and Crowell," the Loot said. "We need to check these bodies and see if one of them has a rifle on its back." That was just about as appealing as it sounds, and none of us made a move to be first. The Loot shook his head at us. "Oh, for God's sake. It's not hard." He used the toe of his boot to roll the body at his feet over so its back was exposed. "See? You don't even have to touch them. This one isn't him, by the way." He swept his arm out over the area. "Don't just stand there, people. Let's get it done so we can go home."

We did, tackling the grisly task with something less than relish. If you didn't think of them as men, but only husks, it made it easier. So we told ourselves. Some of the bodies were so charred they broke apart on rolling over, as brittle as the ash from one of those black snake things they sell on the Fourth of July. Thankfully, with all of us working, it didn't take too long to check them.

Sammy wasn't there.

The Loot pulled off his pot, wiping his face with a filthy handkerchief and shaking his head. "This is crazy," he said, almost to himself. "Where could he have gone? He has to be here. No human could have lived through this."

"Maybe he's charmed," Rafe said with a shudder. "My mama used to tell us of the *bruja,* this witch, back in her village—"

"Witches?" the Loot snapped. "What do witches have to do with it? There's a logical explanation for this. We just haven't looked hard enough for him, that's all."

But Calhoun seemed to be disregarding what had happened to that grenade that should have taken Sammy's head off. Maybe Rafe wasn't too far off at that.

"Could be sumpin' else, sir," Little Bit said. "Could be the *gris-gris.*"

The Loot frowned. "The what?"

Little Bit gulped. "Voodoo, sir."

Calhoun threw his helmet on the ground. A swirl of ashes rose almost to his knees. "Now that's enough." His voice was low and full of menace. "The quickest way to send us all into a panic is to try to put a supernatural spin on this. I don't want any more talk of witches, or voodoo, or your Uncle Harry's magic hat. I'm telling you Sammy is here. He has to be. We'll search for him until next week if we have to." The Loot bent low and picked up his pot, slamming it down on his head in defiance. "Have I made myself clear?" We all nodded. "Excellent," he said. "Now—"

I held up a hand, cutting him off. Calhoun stared at me, like he couldn't believe I'd just done that. I didn't care; it seemed this was my day to upset officers. He opened his mouth to speak again, but I frantically waved at him to keep quiet. I'd seen something a few feet off to my left, something that didn't fit in with this dead and scorched landscape.

A puff of ash rising a couple of inches off the forest floor in regular intervals.

I leveled my gun at it. "Spider hole," I said in wonder.

And with that the camouflaged cover of Sammy's hideout exploded up as he made a mad dash out of there.

For a split second we all stood flatfooted, the second time this day for that. Then we took off after him, firing as we ran.

Surprise is not the infantryman's friend. Due to our shock at Sammy's jack-in-the-box trick, most of our shots went wild. But not all. We saw him stumble and fall as a round from somebody's gun clipped his shoulder. Del Haggin was the first to reach the sniper, landing hard on him, then they were rolling across the dirt and ash, fists and elbows flying as they pounded each other.

Three seconds later the rest of us got there and pulled the men apart. Del got his first good look at his catch. Standing and dropping his fists, his mouth then fell open in shock. So did mine. So did all of ours.

It was Marcus who broke the stunned silence. "Sweet 'tater pie," he whispered. "He's *white.*"

And so he was.

The sniper—Sammy—was small, lithe, and dark-haired. His skin, what we could see of it beneath the dirt, was fish-belly pale. Above a long, straight nose, he was the proud possessor of a high, bony, patrician forehead. Sammy's hands were outsized, as if they'd been grafted on from a larger man, and his fingers seemed to flex in and out of their own accord as he stood there glaring ropes at us. Deep down, nearly beyond perception, a hot mad light gleamed in his eyes as we kept his arms pinned. Those eyes were a pretty, almost womanly, dark blue, and were flecked with gold. I'd heard of such eyes, but had never before seen them.

Until now.

It seemed to me Sammy was memorizing our faces, for a later date and a better time; I guess he'd heard about payback too. Then he spit blood out of his mouth and spoke.

"My name is Martin ten Eyck." Crimson dribbled down his chin. "And I'm looking at a flock of dead men."

His attitude, his accent, the very way he held his body, was undeniable.

Sammy was an American.

18

The roar of chopper blades overhead caused us all to look up. The Loot had called for them an hour ago, after we'd bandaged Sammy's—Martin's—shoulder and then trussed him up like a game hen. During that hour the Loot had tried interrogating the sniper, but other than the words he'd said when we'd caught him, Martin didn't utter a sound. And the longer he sat and stared at us, the weirder the light gleamed in his eyes.

Marcus nudged me. "They used to be an old lady what lived down the road from us," he said in a low voice. "Ma said the lady had witchy ways. Told us stories about her. Said she could blow in a baby's mouth and cure the thrush. Or rub a wart off with her hands. But Ma also said that just by speakin' a word that old woman could blight a man's crops for a year. She didn't even have to do nothin' but stand there and look at a feller, and he'd start shakin'. I seen it happen. You could tell by her eyes she was a different breed a' cat from you and me." Marcus swallowed. "That there boy has them same eyes."

The noise grew louder. Two slicks the Loot had asked for, and two of them he'd gotten. But it wasn't until the slicks had set down in the sawgrass outside the burned trees that we realized they were something more than just our ride home.

The slicks' rotors had barely slowed before a civilian exited the first one, ducking his head under the blades as he trotted out from under them.

"Lieutenant Calhoun?" the man shouted as he approached, hand extended. The Loot nodded. The questioner was dressed in a dark expensive suit, foolish and stupid in this heat, and even though his mouth was full of costly dental work, to me his grin looked as fake as a chorus girl's. The man was stocky, with reddish hair and a freckled face, but his eyes were dark brown, revealing nothing. Howdy Doody takes the Fifth. As he spoke, he gripped the Loot's hand like they were long lost pals. From the expression on Calhoun's face you could tell the friendship went only one way.

"I'm John Baumgartner," the man went on. "I need to speak with you, with all of you." Without waiting to see if he agreed, Baumgartner released the Loot's hand and nodded toward the slicks. Inside the first one, another man, dressed much as Baumgartner was and with the same coloration, nodded back. He turned and said something to the pilot. Then he exited the slick and started coming in our direction, his steps mincing as he wordlessly worked his way across the grass. We all stared at him as he reached us and took our prisoner by the arm. Then before the Loot could say a peep, the man produced a small knife. Wielding it skillfully, he cut the nylon rope we'd tied Martin's hands with. He then turned and escorted the sniper back across the grass to the waiting slick, whispering something in Martin's ear as they walked. Whatever was said, Martin nodded and grinned like he'd won the lottery. They climbed inside, and the door slid closed.

What was happening here?

There was no time to ask. Baumgartner gripped the Loot's elbow, guiding him with us following, away from the slicks with their noise. We'd walked maybe thirty yards further when he muttered, "I suppose this is far enough." For what?

Then he told us for what.

"Please, gentlemen, gather around," the man began, his diction perfect. "As I said earlier, my name is John Baumgartner. But that's not important. What is, is that I'm special assistant to Senator Henrik ten Eyck." We looked at each other. Baumgartner nodded. "That's correct. *The* Henrik ten Eyck, five-time legislator from Ohio and head of the Senate Appropriations Committee." His smile was condescending. He was enjoying our discomfort. "In a way, you might say Senator ten Eyck is the man who signs your paychecks." Baumgartner's smile left just as fast as it had come. "Gentlemen, the senator needs your help. The young man you've just seen escorted into that helicopter, Martin ten Eyck, is the senator's son." He let that sink in.

"Hold on," the Loot said, his voice found at last. "Do all of ten Eyck's aides ride around Vietnam in slicks at taxpayers' expense, or just you?"

Now Baumgartner's smirking smile was back. "A very good question, Lieutenant. Pithy. I like that. So does the senator. He appreciates sharp men."

"Fine, but you didn't answer me," the Loot said.

"That's true, I didn't." Baumgartner sighed companionably. "All right. I suppose it's too hot to bandy words." He craned his neck around. "Terrible weather here, just awful," he said, then he raised his voice. "Allow me to explain things to you as succinctly as I can, gentlemen, then we can all get on with our affairs."

Today my affairs included killing people, but I kept quiet.

Baumgartner said, "Martin is AWOL, absent without official leave, from the United States Marine Corps, and has been for a year." We didn't gasp or fall over in a faint at that—all of us knowing what AWOL meant of course—so he continued, "But it gets a bit more complicated. Martin is, or was, known as a LURP, or LRP, for long-range patrol."

"Snake eater," Vlad muttered to me. I nodded. We'd all heard of LURPs. Their fame, as they say, preceded them. LURPs were the true wild men of the war. It went with their territory. A LURP's job classification, his M.O.S., was simple.

He was an assassin.

To a LURP's way of thinking, a really good time would consist of being airdropped deep behind enemy lines, where he'd stay for weeks at a stretch, living by his wits in the most basic, solitary existence imaginable, all for the express purpose of taking out a high-ranking NVA or VC officer. LURPs could go anywhere, stay anytime, eat anything, kill everything. They were either revered or hated, depending on who it was you were asking. To be a LURP was to be a full-bore, razor-honed, mad monk of the U.S. armed forces.

Which explained Martin's prowess with a rifle. His size too. LURPs, contrary to what you might think, as a rule weren't beefy lifeguard types. Mostly they were smallish, quick, and agile as cats, able to shinny up a tree or crawl in a hole no wider than a trashcan. And every one of them was as deadly a shot as you'd ever pray not to run across.

But even saying all that, Martin's expertise with his shooting was something extra-special. Weeks ago, though now it seemed years, the Loot had told us that no one knew what kind of optics the sniper had been using to such killing effect. And the answer, as far as we could uncover, was none. There was no scope attached to Martin's rifle, none in his spider hole, zip to be found in the surrounding area. As incredible as it was to think about it, he'd made all those technically impossible shots without help.

None, that is, that we could see.

"All right, Baumgartner, so he's a LURP," Calhoun said. "That still doesn't explain why you've taken him out of our hands and into yours."

His answer was an oblique question of his own. "Lieutenant. Let me ask you. How goes the war?"

Calhoun frowned. "Sir?"

Baumgartner motioned around at the area with his hand. "The war. How is it treating you?"

"What kind of a fool question is that?" Bobby jumped in with some heat.

"The only kind that matters, private," the flack replied. "Because I'll tell how it's going at home. Badly."

"It's been going badly for years," the Loot said flatly. "So what. It's likely to continue that way."

"You don't seem to get it, Lieutenant," Baumgartner snapped, the final semblance of friendliness gone. "Public opinion has turned. The last 'victory' the U.S. enjoyed of any military consequence was the Tet offensive in 1968. We won that one, but if you take the media as your guide, it was the worst defeat since Wellington smashed Napoleon."

"Sir," the Loot sighed then, "it's hot. We're tired. And bloody. And, truth be told, a bit sad for our losses. As far as history lessons, I learned all I cared to about the Tet campaign back at the Point. So no offense, but I really hope there is one to this. A point, I mean. Because as near as I can see, what's happened here is fairly straightforward. Your traveling buddy took a prisoner from us, a trophy rightfully ours, without our permission, for reasons that I'm sure you're about to tell us are outstandingly fine." The Loot's voice went even flatter. "But here's what *you* don't understand, Baumgartner. You and your twin are way out here in the boonies, surrounded by a bunch of armed men who've done a fair share of killing today. Men who wouldn't mind adding another couple of scalps to their total. Red ones. Like yours."

With that Calhoun pulled his .45 ACP handgun out of its holster hanging on his Sam Browne belt. In one smooth, almost casual motion he chambered a round, thumbed off the safety, and then pointed the gun at Baumgartner's midsection.

The flack turned pale beneath his freckles. My estimate of the Loot had just gone up 1,000 percent.

Greg Dapp laughed at Baumgartner's discomfort. "Whoa baby. Like John Wayne says in the movies, I think it's about time for a little beggin' our pardon, mister."

We all joined in the laughter, all but Baumgartner. His paleness was now supplanted with a crimson rage. "Lieutenant, you're messing with forces you can't begin to comprehend."

The Loot shrugged. "Maybe. But notice which one of us is looking down the barrel."

The two men glared at each other, the tension tightening. Then I saw something strange. Baumgartner, who a second earlier appeared to be moving into apoplexy, seemed to soften. His redness faded, his features eased, and his fiery rage banked down like a man putting away a suit of clothes that wasn't needed just then. "Lieutenant," he said. "You're right. I believe we've all gotten off on the wrong foot here. Let's begin anew." He smiled. "I have an offer for you, for all of you."

For a second longer Calhoun kept his piece trained on Baumgartner, then he sighed and flipped the .45's safety back on. "I thought you might," he said as he slid the pistol back into its holster.

Baumgartner's smile grew crafty, as if the Loot had just passed some sort of a test. "Indeed I do. But first, a bit of background." He sighed amiably, his anger of just moments earlier now seemingly gone. "As you can well imagine, the senator was less than pleased when his only son refused his help in avoiding military service. But Martin was insistent on going." Baumgartner chuckled. "The boy always was strong-willed. Not to mention a bit of an odd sort. While other twelve-year-olds were building model planes in the basement or playing sports on the field, Martin would spend hours on the family shooting range.

"But after a while shooting paper targets wasn't enough to satisfy him. He began asking if his bodyguards could start taking him on hunting expeditions during the summer and on school vacations. The senator, of course, was much too busy to go himself, but thought the idea sound. He felt the trips would harden the boy, toughen him."

Baumgartner's smile faded. "Toughen him they did. Martin loved the outdoors, the camping, the hiking. And the killing." He swallowed. "Especially the killing. By now the boy had become quite proficient with the rifle. He began bringing back trophies."

The flack shuddered at the memory. "Ears. Heads. Tongues. Ghastly stuff. Martin had grown obsessed with the hunt, with the act itself. It became his life." Baumgartner's voice darkened even more. "But one day it all came to a halt. The day Martin shot one of his bodyguards."

"*Shot* him?" Little Bit squeaked.

Baumgartner nodded. "The events remain unclear. Martin and the guards were on an elk hunt in the Rockies. The hunt was in a remote area, as they tend to be. The guard was scaling a rock escarpment when Martin's rifle somehow discharged, striking the man in the back. He had to be air-lifted out. Today he remains a paraplegic. Of course, the senator paid all the guard's bills, along with a handsome monthly ongoing stipend, assuring the man stays quite comfortable." Baumgartner paused. "As comfortable as one can be with a severed spine. During the police investigation that followed, Martin remained calm, insisting the rifle must have gone off as he was stepping over a log. The senator intervened. Donations were made. The charges were dropped." Baumgartner paused again. "Martin was fourteen years old."

"He got the taste early," I said. "For blood."

Baumgartner nodded. "That he did, private. And so the senator stopped the hunts. But instead of growing angry, as he matured Martin instead began spending even more time on the range and in the deep backwoods. Honing his marksmanship. Biding his time. During this period he also started reading books on psychic phenomena. He became obsessed with the occult, with mind-control. He studied Indian *fakirs* and snake charmers. Soon he began to believe those techniques could be used on larger game." Baumgartner licked his lips. "Perhaps even on men."

We all shuffled nervously at that, the day's heat beating down on us. I wished he'd get to it. I had an idea where this was going.

"The senator thought the two, firearms and the occult, an unhealthy mix," Baumgartner said, "but felt it was a phase that would pass as Martin grew older. It didn't. The senator's displeasure worsened when Martin became of age and enlisted in the Marines. Shunning his father's offer of intervention for stateside duty, Martin instead requested a billet in Vietnam."

"So he could use here what he'd learned at home," I said.

Baumgartner nodded. "Yes. But even though Martin couldn't be dissuaded from such dangerous duty, the senator could arrange that an eye be kept on him."

"And that's where you and your partner come in," the Loot said.

The flack nodded again. "Mr. Carlton and I have served Senator ten Eyck for many years. He asked us to monitor any news of Martin's activities. To step in and restrain the boy from getting into anything really stupid, if at all possible. To keep the senator's name unsullied."

"Somethin' stupid like killin' friendly troops?" Toby snapped.

The man winced. "That came later, private. Much later, after Martin had vanished."

"I'd like to hear more of that," the Loot said.

"There's not much to it, really," Baumgartner replied. "A year ago Martin left for leave in Saigon, and simply never returned. Upon the senator's insistence Martin's CO tried to work with us, even going so far as paying for off-duty Saigon police to try and locate the boy. After seventy-two hours with no success Martin was listed as AWOL." He then said, "That all changed two months ago. Our sources on the ground began hearing stories. Stories of a sniper better than any ever seen. Unnaturally good. One making his bones by killing South Vietnamese officers and friendly village chiefs." He paused. "A slayer rumored to be an American."

"Messy," the Loot said. "For the senator."

"To say the least. Now do you see our dilemma?"

"I think so," Calhoun said. "Senator ten Eyck is a force, a powerful man. And unfortunately, powerful men sometimes have weak sons." He pointed. "You're the fixer."

"That's quite astute, Lieutenant."

"So why us?" Calhoun said. "Why our unit?"

"It was simply a matter of pragmatism. Our sources had alerted us that Martin was possibly operating in this sector. Mr. Carlton and I did some checking and found your unit to be closest to the area in question. Plus we'd heard your men had a reputation for tenacity. Doggedness. We felt the fit would be good." Baumgartner smiled. "I also understand, Lieutenant, that you've taken a page from the Special Forces, and you, too, put a card on a dead Vietcong's face. But instead of an ace of spades, you use Tarot. The Death card. That shows a certain … panache."

"Heck, yeah," Marcus nodded. "We're lousy with it."

"We've closely monitored this unit's radio reports these past weeks, especially these past few days," Baumgartner said. "We knew you were getting close to Martin. It was a near thing, but Mr. Carlton and I were able to persuade the pilots to do some fancy flying today to reach you before the boy could be harmed."

"Harmed." Calhoun pulled his sleeve over his face. It came away dark with sweat and grime. "No, he hasn't been harmed. Not much, anyway. Not yet."

"For which you and your men have the senator's thanks."

Vlad cleared his throat. "You said something about an offer?"

Baumgartner's sly look was back. "Yes. The offer." He pointed back to where the two slicks waited, their rotors slowly turning. "Private, in that first helicopter is a briefcase. It contains a tangible display of the senator's gratitude."

Little Bit narrowed his eyes. "What's in it?"

Baumgartner slowly rubbed his hands together, his dry skin rasping like straw on paving stones. "Money. One thousand dollars, for each of you. That, plus a week's R and R in Saigon's finest hotel, all expenses paid." He again paused. "For your silence."

We looked at each other. Oddly, none of us seemed surprised at the bribe. I think somehow we all knew what was coming the second we saw the man step out of the slick.

"A thousand dollars apiece." Calhoun bit off each word as he said it. "You think you can buy my platoon mighty cheap, Baumgartner."

"Of course, Lieutenant, as group leader your share would be larger," the flack said, smiling now.

"Excellent. Money for lives." The heat snapped in Calhoun's voice. "I lost over twenty men today going after your boy. Good men. Not to mention the people Martin killed himself. How much for them?"

"Regrettable deaths, all," Baumgartner soothed. "But let's make sure those deaths were not in vain." His voice hardened. "Because I can assure you, Lieutenant, that's exactly what will happen should the news surface that the son of Senator Henrik ten Eyck is a traitor. The senator would be disgraced. Forced to resign. It's well known that Washington, like nature, abhors a vacuum. The next man to head the appropriations committee would not be nearly so fine a champion to the needs of the military."

"*Son of a ...*" Rafe breathed. "You got it all covered, man."

Baumgartner spread his hands. "If that's a compliment, I accept. But I'm merely the senator's messenger. You, all of you, must make the decision to take his offer."

"Yeah? And what if we don't?" Bobby asked guardedly.

"Why, nothing," Baumgartner murmured. "Gentlemen, it's a simple thing. I'm appealing to your sense of patriotism, and honoring your valor, while at the same time giving you all a taste of the good life you've so richly earned."

I don't think any of us believed him. But I also knew that with stakes this high, we'd end up taking his deal anyway.

Because my feeling had come roaring back, rearing up on its hind legs. Regardless of his bland face, John Baumgartner scared me. A lot. Somehow I knew that if we refused his offer, he'd make the calls and take whatever steps necessary to assure none of us lived out the week.

The Loot looked at us, the question dark on his face. As one, we all nodded at him. You didn't have to be a Mensa member to see how stark our choices were.

Another second, then Calhoun sighed and nodded back. He turned to the flack. "All right, Baumgartner, you win. But now you listen to me."

The Loot pointed his long, aristocratic finger in the flack's face. "I can't speak for the rest of the men, but I'm refusing your money. I don't want it. And I don't want your trip to Saigon. I don't want your whores or your gambling or your booze. You keep it. There are only two reasons I'm agreeing to this at all." Calhoun's voice shook with barely controlled rage. "For the good of the unit, and for the country. Are we fairly clear on that?"

Baumgartner smiled again, the deal done. It was the smile of a shady used-car man who'd just unloaded his worst clunker on a rube. "Of course, Lieutenant. If that's what you wish."

"So what's gonna happen to the guy?" Toby broke in. "To Martin?"

"A fair question," Baumgartner said. "There'll be treatment for him, of course. Counseling. Medication. Study. Martin will be placed in the most secure mental institution the government can find, to be held safely there for the rest of his life. Because of your men's actions today, never again will he be released to wreak his personal madness upon the world." Baumgartner nodded. "You've all done a fine, noble thing here today, gentlemen. You should feel proud."

I felt like I needed a bath. In a bucket of lye.

A few moments passed, then the Loot spoke up pensively. "I'm thinking something here, Baumgartner." Calhoun was staring at the smoldering forest, as if he was seeing the rest of his life lying there in the ashes. "I'm thinking it would have been better all around if we'd killed Martin back in those trees."

The flack shook his head. "No, Lieutenant," he sighed. "I've known Martin all his life. The better thing would have been had the senator reached down early and strangled the boy in his crib."

19

So you took the money," Luke said. There wasn't any condemnation in his words. But I felt condemned all the same.

"Yeah, I took the money." I glanced into my empty cup, then tossed it into the can next to the table. "I took the money and the Saigon hotel key, and I went there and stayed drunk for a week. I partied and fought and messed around with painted women and did my level best to shut my Granny's face out of my mind while I did." I looked at the pastor. "I'd never felt less honorable in my life, Luke. I felt like scum, like a ..." I tried to think of the worst thing I could. "A carpetbagger," I said then. Being a fellow Southerner, I knew he'd understand that. "If I'd been sober enough, I probably would have blown my head off. Joined my dead bros." My laugh held no humor. "You sure you want a guy like me in your church?"

Luke's smile was compassion itself. "It's not my church, Joe. You ought to know that by now. It's God's. There's only one standard for membership here, and you made it last August. The man who did those things in Vietnam is more than thirty years gone."

"Then why do I feel like I've still got him strapped to my back, like Martin's rifle?" My throat felt rough, as if I had been crying. Or screaming. "It's like I'm dragging around a dead man. I thought that stuff was supposed to be over with."

"The Bible talks about working out our salvation," Luke said. "It's a difficult saying, but I take it to mean that we all have issues we're going to have to face in our walk with the Lord. In your case, this killer's surfacing has simply brought what you did all those years ago back up to the top."

"Like sewage in a sinkhole," I said. Then I sighed. "So now what do I do?"

"Crack open the Word when you get home," Luke answered at once. "Fall on your knees and confess out all your inner feelings of guilt and shame. Lance the boil and let the healing in."

"You make it sound simple."

"Simple?" He shook his head. "No. Necessary? Oh yeah." He leaned in toward me. "Joe, none of this shocks God. He's shockproof. And he knows all about your actions then. Did you do wrong in taking Baumgartner's offer?" Luke shook his head again. "I don't know. If your feelings were right about the man, maybe he would have had you killed if you didn't. Or maybe the truth is, you were hip-deep in a nightmare situation, and your imagination was running wild. But the fact is, *you* feel like you did wrong. How did you put it? Like instead of taking the money you should have joined your dead friends. That's a pretty strong burden to cart around for three decades." Then he smiled. "You want my advice? Do like I said before. Take it to the Lord and leave it there. He's big enough to tote the weight."

"Then what? Martin's out, and he's killing every man who had a part in putting him away. What do I do with that?"

Luke's smile faded. "I think you know. You contact Del and Marcus and Greg and tell them who's back in your lives. Then you do whatever it takes to shut that madman down."

20

Whatever it takes." That covers a lot of ground. I was home, sitting in my cat-chewed easy chair in my living room at the Agnes, considering my options. Agnes Apartments, that is. Cincinnati has an abundance of old residential buildings, and an inordinate number of them carry the names of women. Why? I don't know. But the names aren't like those you hear anymore, at least not up north; they're names like Mildred, Dorothy, Mabel, Inez. And Agnes. They reflect the era when those buildings went up, many decades ago.

The Agnes dated her birth to the art-deco thirties, and in her prime I hear tell she was something to see: three stories of shiny red brick, fronted by a pillared portico, and flanked with imported Florida palms in big pots, pots the maintenance crew would bring inside in the winter. In the center of the front circular driveway, a huge fountain, graced by a sculpted swan, completed the overall effect of grace and elegance.

The brick now was faded, those once-mighty pillars pitted and darkened by seventy years of neglect. Of the palms, only memories remained. And the fountain, now dry and cracked, was filled with fast-food trash and dried leaves that never seemed to decompose. So why did I choose to live in such a place? Good question. Until a few months ago the Agnes had fit me like an old sweat suit, a crumbling building reflecting the lives inside it. But I'd been sensing for a while that the time had come to move into something better. My spirit had already left; my body needed to follow.

The TV was on, but I had no idea what the show was. If you'd told me it was Lithuanian midget tossing I couldn't have said you were wrong. I was deep in thought about the Sammy/Martin problem, and the set was only on out of habit.

Then something interrupted my musings, a rustling down by my feet, and I looked to see. It was my cat, Noodles, head-bumping the chair.

Noodles. To the uninitiated, he's a tough cat to look at. That's true, he is. His body is missing huge patches of fur, revealing instead wrinkled red scar tissue. His right ear is a stump, and his twisted, hairless tail sticks straight out off his fanny like an accusing finger. But his scars come honorably. I won him in single combat.

His appearance is a testament to the heartlessness of man.

One night, after coming home from a late stakeout, I'd heard a loud, tremulous screaming coming from the back of the apartment house. Being the curious sort, I got out of my car and trotted around to investigate. What I saw when I got there stopped me in cold shock. The commotion I'd heard was a couple of drunks squatting deep in the dumpster's shadow, doing something unconscionable to a stray cat. With strong, dirty hands they were holding it down as they burned its fur and skin off with butane lighters.

I suppose the men thought their cruelty was a lot of fun. I convinced them otherwise. Taking some time with the two, I reasoned with them, showed them the light as it were, and when I was done, I'd encouraged them to try something less strenuous, like crochet.

But seeing as how I'd left them in a pile with bloody faces and broken hands, that may have been tough to do.

Did I return a cruelty for a cruelty? Maybe. I'm not that deep. All I know is, I inherited a new friend that night.

And I'll bet those guys never burned another cat.

A few seconds more of head-bumping and pathetic mewling—from him, not me—told me Noodles wasn't going to let me alone until I got up and gave him a treat. He's tried them all, from national names on down, but the little beggar's favorite kind were some off-brand, crunchy-on-the-outside-chewy-on-the inside jobs I bought at Wal-Mart whenever they had them in stock, which wasn't often. So when they did get some in, I'd buy the stuff by the case and stick it in my cupboard. I often had the thought that if I was ever found dead in my apartment, the coroner would have some things to ponder concerning my eating habits.

I shuffled from my living room into the kitchen, grabbing

the first canister my hand closed on; chicken or tuna, I didn't look, and it didn't even matter. To Noodles either qualified as ambrosia. Which is good. I love cats but cannot abide a finicky one. He and I had reached an agreement on that subject years ago.

As I started prying the lid off the can, Noodles looked up at me placidly and said, "Naow?"

"In a minute," I answered. "I think it's stuck. You and your cut-rate snacks." A few more tugs, and the lid pulled free. I examined the label before pouring a handful of treats in his bowl. "Chicken this time, same as last. I hope that's all right."

In response he piddled the floor; he's getting older.

"Now look what you've done," I scolded, lightly, as he dug in. I pulled a paper towel from its holder above the sink, bent back down, and starting wiping up the mess. "One of these days I'm going to train you how to do this for yourself. Clean up your own stuff." Still holding the soiled towel in my left hand, I reached over and scratched my cat's ear-stump with my right. "Maybe I'll even teach you to start emptying your own litter box. Police the area, as poor old dead Nickerson used to say. How would that be?" Before Noodles could answer, the phone rang.

I threw the used towel in the sink—to be retrieved later—and walked back into the living room. The phone was on its third ring as I picked it up. "Hello?"

"Joe, it's Angela."

Dread gripped my heart. "Don't tell me I missed a supper date again."

She laughed heartily at that. "And what would you do if I said yes?"

"Grab a quick shower, the keys to the car, and some take-out Chinese, in that order," I answered without hesitation.

"You can relax," she laughed again. "You're safe. For now."

Good thing too. After being a widower for nearly three decades, with this woman I now was officially back in the game. Older of course, doubtless more beat up, and certainly no wiser, but still back in the game.

And with Angela as the prize, I knew this was one game I wasn't going to muff.

"No," she went on, her light mood falling away, "I just got done with some prayer. As I finished up, I felt a strong urge to give you a call. So I did."

Still holding the phone to my ear, I sat back down in my easy chair. "I'm glad. We left some unfinished business back at your place the other night, didn't we?"

"Yes. But as I've said, Joe, whenever you're ready to bring me in, I'm here. Whenever. All you have to do is ask."

"I'd like to ask," I said. Then I said, "I need to ask. Now. Right now, tonight. Can I come over?"

"I had a feeling you'd say that," she said, and I again heard her smile over the phone. "That's why I put on a pot of coffee before I called. Plus I got out those cookies you like." She chuckled. "Am I good or what?"

Dating an intercessor is not for the faint of heart.

21

*T*he telling of the day's events done, and the coffee in my cup long since turned cold, I leaned back, my weight sinking deeper into Angela's sofa. "That's thirty, as the newspaper guys say. The end."

"Maybe." She sounded doubtful as she sipped her coffee. "Have you warned those other men yet?"

"No."

"What? Why ever not?" There was no accusation in her tone, only startled curiosity.

My laugh was brittle. "I'm still working on how it's gonna sound, Ange. I ignored Little Bit's call as the ravings of a drunk. How do I know those guys won't think the same about me?"

Angela took a small nibble of her Pepperidge Farm Milano cookie—she's right, I do go weak in the knees for them—before answering. "Because you have prayer working in your favor." She wasn't aware she had a small crumb of cookie stuck to the corner of her mouth as she talked. It looked adorable as all get-out. "Prayer. That's your hole card," she went on. "Just ask God to prepare their hearts before you call them ... What?"

"Here." I leaned over and wiped the crumb off with the corner of my napkin.

"Thanks. You can't take me anywhere. Even my own den."

I leaned back and wadded the napkin into a tight ball in my fist, still not convinced of her argument. "But what if Little Bit did the same thing before he called me? Prayed, I mean. If he did, it didn't work. He's in the ground, while I'm still up and moving."

A sad smile played around Angela's mouth. "Yeah, I wondered if that was it." She set her own cup down as well before going on. "Joe, you're having a classic attack of the galloping guilts. Even though you and I both know it's not true, in your heart you feel you let your friend down. That Little Bit's dead because of what you did. Or failed to do." Her gaze at me was rock-steady. "Right?"

"Well, of course!" I said, jumping up. My nerves were raw from strain, and I stalked the five feet over to her fireplace, tossing in the crumpled napkin. I watched it burn for a moment before turning around and facing her. "Ange, Little Bit's gone. Fried like a fish, because of me. You weren't there; you didn't hear how scared he was. But I was there. I heard. And I blew him off. I wouldn't believe him when he needed me the most. Now his widow is staring at her walls, trying to understand how it came to be that her world's fallen in. She's wondering what she's supposed to do next. How to make all that pain go away." My voice thickened. "What do I say to the woman? How do I answer her?"

Angela stood as well. Then she came over, taking my right hand in both of hers, her tone even as she said, "You tell Melanie her husband didn't die in vain. You tell her that you're going to do everything in your power to make sure some other man's wife doesn't wake up a widow. You tell her that's how you honor Little Bit's memory, and that this isn't over until God says it is. You tell her that, Joe, and then you stop shilly-shallying and do it."

"Easy to say," I muttered as I dropped her hand. I turned away, again staring back into the flickering flames. Still not looking at her, I said, "This guy scares me, Ange. Like nothing else ever has." I shook my head, barely able to get the words out. "I'm not a coward, but there's something—"

"I'll tell you exactly what it is," she interrupted. "Oppression. It feeds on Martin's involvement with the occult." She laid her hand lightly on my shoulder. "Joe, what you're feeling is satanic influence. It's like a dark weight pressing down on you, a heavy thing with a gravity all its own. I've seen it before."

I didn't answer as I continued staring at the fire, then I felt her fingers lightly caressing mine.

"Martin is a twisted, evil man," Angela said. "That's a sad fact, but a true one. Maybe he's that way from birth, like Baumgartner told you all. I don't know. But I can tell you this. Martin's voluntary dabbling with forbidden things has shifted his naturally bent impulses into something far worse. It's no wonder you're scared." Then I heard a smile come into her voice. "But you don't have to be. You have God's power on your side, and nothing in hell can stand up to that."

Her hand now was gently squeezing my own. "Joe, God didn't let you down when you went up against that nightmare in Indiana, did he? He won't let you down here either."

A few seconds passed, then I said, "I'd told you before how Martin wasted those other guys, killing them with the thing that had scared them the most." I was still staring at the fire. "But I really didn't break it down for you. Mrs. Brake's detective work contained all the lurid details." I swallowed. "Little Bit you already know about. You need to know about the men behind those other names."

I turned back around, facing Angela squarely now, my eyes burning, fear gumming up my words.

"Vlad Przbasky," I said. "Vlad hated guns. That's why he became our medic. Now Ange, why would a man who's afraid of guns shoot himself in the mouth outside a bar? The answer is Martin. Somehow, God alone knows how, he did that and made it look like a suicide."

"Then there's Ed Ralston. Eddie was scared of driving. He hated telling us that, and made like it wasn't really so, but we all knew. Why would a guy that afraid of cars take one for a drive up on a cliffside road? Martin again. Somehow he lured Eddie up there, then caused his car to go through that guardrail. Nobody on the cops'll buy it, but it's the truth."

The words were rushing out now.

"Bobby Dagliesh went into a motel swimming pool one

night a week and a half ago while he was in Amarillo on business. Bobby was petrified of water. Martin drowned him. Toby Buntline fell over the railing of an observation deck at a downtown New York bank, even though he'd always said he'd never climbed anything higher than his head. Martin again. And Rafe Martinez. Rafe had said that his greatest fear was of being crushed to death. Yet last Friday afternoon, on a perfectly fine sunny Miami day, he fell, or was pushed in front of a road grader. It squashed him like a bug, just like my cousin Ray. Even their names sound alike."

I clenched my hands so tight I felt my nails digging in. "You're the expert, Ange. How do I handle all that? How do I keep Martin from using our worst fears, mine included, and taking out what's left of the rest of the squad? And how did he know what our worst fears even were?" I shook my head. "That's what's driving me crazy. How does he *know?*" Angela opened her mouth to answer, but I cut her off.

"I'm not like you," I said, "I haven't done this religious stuff for twenty years. I'm too new at it. That Indiana case nearly killed me, and now you're telling me this one is worse. That somehow Martin is hooked into hell itself." I squeezed my fists tighter, a parody of her caress of moments earlier. "How do I fight that, Ange? How in God's name do I fight it?"

"If you'll quit doing that, I'll tell you," she said calmly. She looked down at my knuckles, now white and trembling, then back up at me. "Well?"

I had to will my hands to disengage. Flexing my fingers, I shook my head and said, "I didn't mean to lose it, babe." It took a second for me to realize the last person I'd called "babe" was Linda.

Angela's grin was small but kind. "No problem. But I've got to get you off of red meat, Joe. Soon. It's making you too snarly." She motioned to the sofa. "Can we sit back down?"

My breathing was easier now. I hoped my answering smile of apology was as kind as hers. "Sure."

Back on her sofa, Angela tucked one leg up underneath herself, turning to me. "Now. I'll answer your last question, but first let me ask you one. You'd mentioned your own greatest fear a moment ago. I wonder if you'd mind telling me what it is."

"Why?" I said, my defenses beginning to rise again.

Her smile now had whimsy in it as well as a bit of something else. "I guess I'd like to know more about the man I'm falling in love with."

That sounded like good news, but still I guarded my words. "That's a dark place in my life, Ange. Is it important?"

"It might be," she replied. "But if you can't—"

"No, it's all right," I said. "If I could tell a bunch of raggedy troops in a jungle about it, I can sure tell you." I sighed. "Maybe I need to." I cleared my throat and leaned back deeper in her sofa, staring once again into the flames.

For what I was about to relate, it seemed appropriate.

22

Yoshiko Suto was her name, and to a nine-year-old hillbilly kid like me, she was mystery personified. Yoshiko, along with her little brother and their parents, had moved into the old Dillon place a half-mile down the road from ours only a week earlier, after her dad had gotten a job as bookkeeper at one of the Peabody mines. In retrospect, I can only marvel at their courage. Eastern Kentucky in the early sixties was less than cordial to immigrants of any race, especially Japanese; the county had lost more than a dozen of her sons to the war in the South Pacific twenty years earlier. Memories, and prejudices, ran deep.

Yoshiko's dad, Mr. Suto, was a short man with an acne-scarred face, a middleweight's build, and a ready smile. His wife, smaller than him by half a head, possessed delicate features topping a pronounced overbite. Hideko, Yoshiko's brother, was three years old and perpetually in motion, alternately yammering in his native tongue or crying lustily when he'd run headlong into things.

And then there was Yoshiko … Yoshi for short.

She was a year older than me, skinny, her black hair cut in a pageboy, her eyes dark and mischievous. In just the week since her family had moved to the area, Yoshi had won the heart of every boy at Clay County Elementary School, mine included.

Some of the parents of those boys felt differently.

"The nerve of those people," my Aunt Minnie sniffed, her angular body folded awkwardly into our beaten-down old wingback chair. She and my cousin Ray were in our living room, all of us having just finished Sunday dinner. My dad was in his bedroom, sleeping one off. "It's not enough to know Auggie is still inside the *Arizona*," she went on. Auggie was my never-met second cousin, lost in the Japanese sneak attack on Pearl Harbor. "Now they have the gall to move into our town."

"They're not in town, Aunt Minnie," I pointed out from the floor, where I was working on a horseshoe puzzle. Ray lay next to me, reading a Sergeant Rock comic. "They live out in the sticks, like us."

She glanced down at me, then up at Granny. "Honestly, Cora, haven't you taught that boy better than to sass his elders?"

"I've taught him just fine, Minnie," Granny said evenly. "And he's right. They don't live in town."

"No, they don't," Minnie snapped. "They live just down a

ways from here. You could almost throw a rock and hit 'em."
Ray laughed at that. My aunt continued, "I can't believe
you're takin' it so easy about all this. After all, your brother
Nestor is still layin' where they planted him on Bataan."

"I know exactly where Nestor is," Granny replied, a
warning glint coming into her eye. "Lotsa boys were planted
durin' that time. That don't mean Mr. Suto was the one that
killed 'em."

"You don't know that he didn't."

"And I don't know that he did," Granny finished, standing abruptly. "There was killin' from both sides durin' that
awful war. Too much. But now it's over. I plan to get on with
my life, Minnie, and that includes makin' friends with Mr.
Suto and his kin. How about you?"

Minnie stood as well. "Not on my best day, Cora. You
mark my words, there's trouble brewin' with that bunch.
Come on, Ray."

As they walked through the front door onto our porch,
Ray sneered at me. "Jap-lover." Then they were gone.

Granny blew out a breath through compressed lips, then
she looked down at me. "Help me with the dishes, Joe."

A few minutes later, as we stood by the kitchen sink, her
washing, me drying, I said, "Why don't Aunt Minnie like the
Suto family?"

"Don't say 'don't,' Joe," Granny replied, taking the gravy
boat from me. "Say 'doesn't.'"

"I'm just talkin' like you."

"Well, don't talk like me. You're smarter than me. You're
smarter than any Box that ever was. So you're gonna talk

better than any Box ever did." Her tone allowed no come-back as she handed me a fresh-rinsed plate.

"Yes'm." I wiped the plate with the dishtowel for a few seconds, then said, "So why don't—doesn't—she?"

"People have funny ways sometimes," Granny answered as she took the plate from me, setting it in the cupboard on top of the others. "Your Aunt Minnie is funnier'n most."

"I don't think she's so funny," I said, rubbing my nose.

"Me neither." Granny took the towel from me and flipped it over the faucet. "That's that. Now come on back into the livin' room and let's have us some chocolate peanuts."

"Yes ma'am!"

♦ ◊ ♦

So began the Suto family's stint in perdition. Looking back, I suppose friction between them and the rest of the community was inevitable. There were too many barriers, cultural and otherwise, dividing us all, and the times just weren't right for it to work. The slights against them were trivial, but no less hurtful for their size: Mr. Suto and his wife were ignored in stores and on the street, their mailbox was vandalized twice, and in school Yoshi was shunned by the girls her own age. Even the church, and Toad Lick only had the one, seemed aloof.

Of course, not everyone gave them that treatment. Granny went out of her way to make them homemade gifts of apple butter and home-cured bacon, and I talked to Yoshi at lunchtime, helping her learn our slang terms. Others in the town tried to reach out to them as well, but it wasn't enough.

As the days passed it was becoming increasingly obvious to everyone that the Sutos simply weren't welcome here.

The events of the morning on the day the tragedy happened are seared into my memory. It was a Saturday, July the first, a scorching hot day in a series of them, portending a miserably humid Fourth of July holiday. Granny had had me bike down the road to the Sutos' house with the gift of a quart of fresh-churned buttermilk from Regina, our cow. The milk was sealed in a boiled glass bottle that had been wrapped in a wet rag to keep the milk cool, then I'd tied the bottle to my handlebars with a rope.

After I'd dropped the milk off at their house and had gotten the usual effusive, incomprehensible thanks from Mrs. Suto that our gifts always got, I made my way over to the barn. I saw Mr. Suto had pulled their Plymouth Valiant over into the shade, and he had the hood up as he worked on something inside. Hearing me approach, he stood up with a smile. "Joe. Good morning to you."

"You too, Mr. Suto. Whatcha doing?"

"Putting in new points and plugs. Maybe this old car has some life in it yet." Of the family, Mr. Suto spoke the best English; someone said he'd graduated from UCLA, but found that working for Peabody was the best he could do. I somehow doubted that. Yoshi spoke almost as well as her father, but was having trouble with our Kentucky idioms, and as I said, I was only too happy to help her learn. Her mom Reishi spoke very little English, and Hideko, the hyper three year old, less than that. Still and all, though, they were a very nice family. As I compared them point by point to the vinegar-drenched townsfolk giving them all that grief, I thought of them as better yet.

I must have been casting mooncalf looks back at their house as he worked, because Mr. Suto slammed the Valiant's hood shut with a satisfied grunt before saying, "She's around back, on the tire swing." He grinned at me, wiping his hands on a greasy rag. "Why don't you go say hello?"

I mumbled my thanks and scurried off, embarrassed.

Sure enough, as I rounded the corner of their house, there Yoshi was, perched on the swing, slowly humming and moving back and forth as she dragged her foot in the dirt. Then she saw me, and her face lit up with a grin. Her crooked teeth and dark eyes made my nine-year-old heart flutter in my chest like a caged bird.

I hid it well though, as I nonchalantly sauntered over to her. "Hey, Yoshi."

"Joe. Hello … hi." She smiled again.

"Swingin' on the old tire, huh?" I said, jamming my hands in my pockets. Master of the obvious, that was me.

"Yes. It is very nice. Hot, but … nice." Her bangs were wetly plastered against her forehead. "We did not have such heat in San Diego."

"Aw, this ain't nothin'," I drawled. "When I was a little kid it got so hot one day the fish came out of the pond to cool off."

Yoshi threw back her head, squealing laughter. "Joe! I think you are lying! But it's funny!" I joined in, pleased that I could so easily coax a laugh from that solemn face.

My chores forgotten then, we laughed and swung and drank water from their well, water so cold it made your teeth ache. So Yoshi and I passed the rest of that July the first, 1961.

The day the Suto family died.

♦ ◊ ♦

Ten o'clock that night, and I couldn't sleep. The heat and humidity always seemed worse at night, because somehow your brain was thinking if the sun was down, it should be cooler. It wasn't. I flopped listlessly in my sweat-dampened bed, trying to block out the sounds of both the crickets and peeper frogs outside and the drone of the fan coming from my dad's room down the hall. We only had the one fan, and Dad, by unspoken fiat, had hooked it. I imagined Granny was just as uncomfortable as me, and deep inside my little-boy head I'd always thought on nights like this that the first thing I'd buy when I was big and rich would be a fan of my very own.

Then off in the distance I heard another sound, a far-off, muffled crackling. And below that sound, faint screams.

I leaped off the bed, ran over to the window, and stared out. Beyond the trees, a half-mile or so, I saw orange reflected against the sullen clouds. Fire. The Dillon place.

Yoshi.

Still in my pajamas, I thundered into the hall and right into Granny. "Yoshi's house is burnin'!" I shrieked.

"I know!" she yelled back.

Right about then my dad stumbled out of his room, rubbing roughened hands through his greasy, frazzled hair. "What the Sam Hill's goin' on?" he muttered. Apropos of nothing, I noticed he was still wearing the same stained overalls he'd had on when he'd passed out earlier that evening.

"Dad!" I screeched, grabbing his wrist. "Yoshi's house is burnin'!"

He pulled his hand free. "So what am I supposed ta do about it?"

I looked up at him, giving him a look that only a nine year old can. "Nothin'. Stay drunk, I guess."

Then I was tearing down the hall and out the front door. Faintly I heard Granny yelling at me to stop, but I ignored her as I poured on the speed. That afternoon I'd laid my old fat-tired Huffy by the gate, and nearly without pausing I grabbed it and began pedaling like the wind down the road.

Two minutes later I wheeled around the bend and came upon a sight that haunts me still. The volunteer firemen had just arrived and were frantically playing water over the front of the Sutos' house. But it was no use. The fire was obviously beyond the efforts of our one puny pumper to contain.

I heard yelling, both from inside the house and out. The one yelling outside was Deacon Edwards, our unofficial fire chief. He was trying to restrain Mr. Suto.

"You can't go back in," Edwards pleaded. "It's suicide."

But Mr. Suto was past reason as he strained to pull free. "Let me go! My wife! My babies! Let me go!"

As I'd said before, he wasn't a weak man, and with that cry Mr. Suto finally broke loose and pounded the three steps up onto his smoldering porch. Then he was inside.

Mr. Edwards made as if he was going in after him, when one of his men pulled him back with a shake of his head, screaming garbled words.

Suddenly there was a loud rumble. A second later, with

a roar and crash of broken glass, one of the upstairs windows blew out. We all looked up.

Framed there, against the insane heat, was Yoshi. Her hair and nightgown were ablaze, her mouth open in a pain beyond pain. Yoshi's eyes met mine then, and she thrust her hands out of the window toward mine on the ground, seeking ... what? Relief? Deliverance? I had none.

Then her bedroom floor collapsed and she was gone.

The state sent an arson investigator out the next morning, and he and his team spent the whole day combing the smoldering ruins for clues. They yelled at me to stay out. I did, but only because the look in the investigator's eyes showed a hurt that nearly equaled mine. I overheard one of his men telling his partner something about "Frank taking it hard." The other man answered that "losing whole families is the worst." I tried to hear more, but Sheriff Dinsmore shooed me away again.

I suppose they were right in trying to keep me at arm's length, but what kept drawing me back was that final desperate look I'd seen on Yoshi's face. And in her eyes. I knew I'd carry that look with me always, as well as the knowledge of something else: the unshakable feeling of helplessness that had kept my feet glued to the grass as she burned.

Mr. Edwards showed up at noon. He gazed at me, nodded grimly, and put his arm around my shoulder. "Don't beat yourself up, Joe. There wasn't nothin' anybody could have done. God saw fit to take 'em."

I didn't answer.

"Lord have mercy," he moaned, "if I could have saved 'em, I would. You know that, don't you?"

I pulled away, still saying nothing.

"I know," he muttered with a shake of his head. He joined me in staring at the wreckage. "Worst thang I ever saw. But there just wasn't nothin' could be done."

Logically, I knew he was right.

But logic has little bearing on the heart.

23

_T_he state finally ruled the fire as 'suspicious,'" I said. "They'd found the remains of some fireworks in the basement that Mr. Suto must have gotten for the Fourth, but what set them off, they never could figure."

"So a family you'd grown close to died needlessly," Angela murmured. "And you're still having trouble getting closure on that more than four decades later."

"'Closure' is a psychobabble term, Ange," I said, more harshly than I'd meant. "Pure-grade nightmare fuel is what it is. I don't know that there's any 'closure' to that." My voice again caught in my throat. "The look in that poor little girl's eyes as the fire took her. Her screams. All of their screams ..." I swallowed again. "Do you know that I couldn't eat roast beef for three years after that? Or even be in the same house where it was cooking?" I shook my head. "That's where the fear comes from, I guess. Watching that family die, and knowing what a horror their final moments were. That fear's been with me ever since, stuck to my soul like flypaper. It's a like a voice telling me that's how I'm going to go, when it comes my time. On fire and screaming." I stared. "Now you know what I know. And what Martin knows."

Angela took my hand. Her small fingers folded inside mine as she gave me a tentative smile. "There's a scripture in the Bible I really like. It says that perfect love casts out fear. All fear. It's written to believers, and that's what you are now. You're an heir to that freedom. And there's not one place in the Word that says you have to put up with any of the devil's junk."

"Yeah?" My voice sounded hollow. "So what do I do with it?"

"Cast it over on the Lord."

"Yeah, that's just what Pastor Franklin told me." Then I said, "Okay, let's say I do that. I hand it off to God. But what if I wake up tomorrow, and there it sits on my bed, waiting?"

"Give it to the Lord again," Angela answered without hesitation. I must have given her a sour look, because she shook her head at me. "Joe, God's ability to deal with your problems isn't a zero-sum game. It's not like one day he says to you, 'Sorry, you're more than I can handle. I've only got so much strength to go around, and you've used up your share.'" She reached up, running her fingers through my hair, then cupped my face in her hand. "What you did last August was just the start of your walk with God. But he wants to walk with you every day, Joe, not just on Sunday.

And walking with him means you walk together, not running ahead or lagging behind him, but right next to his side."

I didn't answer for a moment, then I sighed. "Maybe you're right, Ange. I've carried this stinking fear in my gut for more than forty years, like some kind of a red-eyed beast. Every time I see so much as a match flare, the thing snarls up in my face and makes my bowels go loose. I'm tired of it. Beyond tired." I narrowed my eyes. "Maybe it's time to permanently dump his butt."

Angela's hand found mine again, and our fingers interlaced. "Now you're talking," she grinned.

We read some scripture then, and prayed. Then we just snuggled together, listening to the November wind howling outside as we watched the fire. And for the first time since I was a boy I was able to *really* watch the fire, enjoying it for what it was, and not worrying about what it could do.

To me or anyone else.

24

The next day, bright and early, I was at the office. Angela was right: it was past time to call Del and Marcus and Greg, and at least give them a heads-up about Martin. Whether they took action on that news, or even believed me, wasn't within my purview. I'd give them the skinny on it, and let them do with it as they would.

Before I'd left last night, Angela asked me a question, a question I was surprised she hadn't asked before. "I'm relieved you're going to call those men and tell them what's going on. But what about that other man, your lieutenant? Doesn't he need to know too?"

"Lieutenant Calhoun," I nodded. "Yeah, the Loot was the eleventh man. I think I told you he was also the only one who never took the money. But the day the rest of us got back after our all-expenses week in Saigon, we'd found that

Calhoun had already been transferred to an AirCav squadron." I shrugged. "I guess that wasn't too surprising; Bravo platoon had been essentially wiped out. His command was finished. The brass reassigned the rest of us to other units, and that was that. Then a month or so later I heard through army scuttlebutt that the Loot's slick had gone down somewhere in the highlands while on patrol. His body was never recovered. That was the last I ever heard about him."

Angela frowned. "That seems to have Baumgartner's signature all over it, doesn't it?" Once again I was amazed at how astute she was.

"Yeah," I agreed. "But if there's any justice to be had in this world, our buddy Baumgartner'll get his someday, in spades."

"And if not in this world," Angela said to me, her normally cheery voice now gone dark, "then in the next."

In college I'd taken a course on comparative religions. One of the things we'd had to read was a tough piece of eighteenth-century literature called "Sinners in the Hands of an Angry God," a happy little work written by a New England preacher named Jonathan Edwards. Edwards said in his memoirs he'd penned his words for the specific purpose of scaring the hell out of people—literally. According to historical contemporaries it had done just that. It's generally agreed to be one of the most effective sermons ever written. As a freshman, I'd scoffed at it, of course; I was too cool to buy such tales.

Now that I was a Christian and was reading the Bible for myself, I knew that Edwards, if anything, had understated his case. I suppressed a shudder. Baumgartner, and his erstwhile homicidal ward Martin, in the hands of an angry God; that was a scenario that didn't bear thinking about.

I picked up the phone and dialed information for Boise, Idaho.

The computer voice gave me Del Haggin's home number, and then it offered to connect me for "only" fifty cents. Now, if I'd been stirring pasta sauce with one hand while ripping lettuce with the other, I might have been tempted. But since I was doing neither, I politely told the thing to cram its diodes and called Del myself. You save a buck, or fifty cents, where you can.

Three rings, and the phone picked up. "Hello?" The voice was a woman's, and I remembered now that Mrs. Brake had told me her Web search had revealed Del was married.

"Mrs. Haggin?"

"Yes, who's this?"

"My name's Joe Box, ma'm. Del and I served together in the war."

There was a long pause, then she said, "Del doesn't like to talk much about that time."

I'll bet he didn't. Most of us who were there tend to try to bury our memories, until something like we were facing now forced them back up. "I just need to speak with him for a minute, Mrs. Haggin. Is he there?"

"He's at the shop," she replied after another pause, still sounding guarded; Mrs. Brake had also told me Del owned an auto parts store. "Is there something I can help you with?"

There was no percentage in alarming the woman, not yet

anyway, so I answered, "No ma'm, not really. Just some old unit business. Would you mind if I called him at work? Like I said, it'll only take a minute."

"No," she said, "I suppose not. If you're sure it's really important. Del still has nightmares about that time." She sighed. "But if you have to. He's been really busy with Thanksgiving work. It seems like everybody's on the road."

Including Martin.

I assured her it was important, really, and she gave me the shop's number.

I thanked her, depressed the button, released it again, and then punched in the number for Haggin's Auto World. The connection rang twice before the phone was snatched up.

"Haggin's."

"Hi, is Del there?"

"You got him. What can I do for you?"

"Del," I said, "it's Joe Box."

There was a pause—he and his wife fit well in that regard—then, "Joe Box! From the war?"

"Not anymore. We came home, remember? But yeah, it's me."

"Holy Mother McGonigle," he laughed. "I can't believe this. It's been, what, thirty years or more? Are you in town?"

"No, I'm calling you from my office. Cincinnati."

"Cincy, home of the Redlegs," he chuckled. "They never were the same after they let Sparky go. So what are you doing there, working for the VA?"

"I'm an investigator, Del. Private."

It took him a few seconds. His next words to me were considerably cooler. "Investigator, huh. What's this about?"

More people than you think don't like talking to a private eye, so I shrugged that off and just said the name. "Martin."

"Martin?" Del exploded. "What—"

"He's out," I broke in flatly. "And he's on the move."

For a moment I thought Del's phone had gone dead. Then he croaked out, "Doing what?"

"Killing us," I replied.

A sharp intake of air, quickly let go. "Who?"

"Eddie, Vlad, Bobby, Toby, Rafe, and Little Bit," I said. "So far."

"Brother …" Del whispered. "He's going for a clean sweep."

"All died in the last two weeks. One of us—you, me, Greg, or Marcus—is going to be number seven. If we don't act."

"Martin," Del growled, now sounding back in more control. "And Baumgartner. That stinking spook. He lied to us. He said Martin'd never get out."

"Yeah, well snafus happen, Del. At this point it's not real important to know why Martin got sprung from the nuthouse. We just have to figure who he's going to hit next. And stop him."

"What about the cops?"

"Forget that. I've already talked to an LAPD cop named Barber. Three of the guys, Eddie and Vlad and Little Bit, were killed in the LA area, but the cops there are writing it off as coincidence. I have the feeling the ones in the cities where Bobby and Toby and Rafe bought it will feel the same way. Somehow Martin's made each of their deaths look like natural events, suicide, acts of God, whatever."

"How?"

"By killing them with whatever scared them the most," I said, my voice grim. Then—"Stabbing's yours, right?"

"Stabbing? Who told you that?"

"You did. Remember that day on the trail when we were all talking about what our deepest fears were?"

"Yeah …" Del said slowly. "Now I do …" Then he said, "But how did *Martin* find out? The guy wasn't even there. And besides," he went on angrily, "this is sounding screwier by the minute. Isn't it awfully early in the day to be drunk?"

Del's response was just what I'd been dreading. "Check it yourself," I snapped. "Do a search of the names, like I did. See what killed those guys. Then you tell me if you think I'm drunk."

"Okay, okay," Del said. "But listen," he went on more calmly, as if he was talking to a child. "Think about what you're saying. Maybe Martin *has* done some killing, I don't know, but that doesn't mean he knows I'm afraid of being stabbed. You know what I mean, right?"

"Of course I know," I replied, just as calmly. Then I said, "So does the devil."

"What!"

There, I'd finally said it. And how about that, I wasn't dead of embarrassment. I was still alive and everything.

"You heard me, Del," I said. "And don't act so shocked about it. You remember Baumgartner telling us about Martin's involvement with the occult. That stuff was bad enough then to give him the ability to kill more than two dozen men without even breaking a sweat. Now he's had more than thirty years to get *really* good at it."

"But stabbing me ..." I heard Del swallow. "How could he ... How do I stop that?"

"You don't," I answered flatly. "God does."

There was no reply from him, so I said, "Listen, Del, I don't have a whole lot of time to go over the finer details of this, but I need to tell you that I became a Christian about three months ago."

His laugh at what I'd told him sounded nervous and sarcastic. "Great. Super. Just terrific. Now you're one of those hallelujah boys I laugh at on TV, out to save my soul. That'll help me a lot, I'm sure."

I sighed. "You know what? I've done what I was supposed to do. I've told you that Martin's out, he's killing our bros one by one, and you might be next. So, are you?" I snorted at him. "Look, Del, *I* don't know. But you might be. And if you are, well, that plants the ball squarely in your court. Your only hope of surviving an encounter with the freak is to put yourself in the hands of God." I leaned back in my creaky old office chair. "Now you can ignore that if you want to, that's up to you. But I'm not the one who might get a knife slipped between his ribs tomorrow." I heard Del gulp; maybe I'd been a little over the top with that last bit. "Again, up to you. But if it was me, I'd get myself to a church that has some real-world experience handling this kind of thing. I'd get them standing with me in prayer. And I'd do it like yesterday."

I heard heavy breathing, gasping really, and then the line went dead. What the … I stared at the receiver in my hand like I'd never seen one before. Then I dropped it back onto its cradle.

Well, poop.

Did he believe me? Was Del right now frantically flipping through the church listings in the Boise Yellow Pages, trying to see if one jumped out at him? Or was he laughing with the boys in the back room of his shop over the old war buddy who had slipped the rails?

In the end I figured it really wasn't my concern. Like I'd told him, my job had been to alert him to the threat. That job was now done—except for praying for him, as Angela would say.

Shaking my head with a sigh, I picked up the phone again. Where was it Mrs. Brake had said that Greg Dapp was living these days?

25

My call to Greg unfortunately followed much the same script as the one I'd made to Del. I'd called the Teaneck, New Jersey, information line, and they'd given me Greg's home number. I'd dialed it then, not really expecting to find him home. Mrs. Brake had told me Greg was a high-steel worker, and I knew those guys put in long hours. But thankfully Greg's voice on his machine told me I could either leave a message or call him on his cell phone. He gave me that number, and I punched it in.

Even if the subject matter hadn't been bad, the call itself had to rank as one of the weirder ones I've ever made. I mean, how many calls do you make to a guy who's standing on a foot-wide I-beam 312 feet in the air? (I know it was that high; when Greg told me, I turned a little green.)

Anyway, Greg's attitude pretty much mirrored Del's, up

until when I mentioned he'd said his worst fear was of dying in a plane crash.

"Joe, you're not gonna believe this," Greg said slowly, the faint traffic noise all those stories below him putting a strange counterpoint to his words, "but we're topping this building out today. Guess where I'm heading tomorrow?"

I didn't have a clue, and told him so.

"Saudi Arabia," he laughed, but there was no humor in it. "Some sheik with more money than sense wants to build a racetrack there. For horses. A racetrack in the middle of the desert, how stupid is that? Anyway, my company got the bid to hang all the steel for the hotel. My partner put me down to do the prelim site work before the rest of the crew heads over next month."

"Hotel?"

"I told you the guy's an idiot," Greg laughed again. "Yeah, the sheik's trying to make the place another Vegas. A Vegas surrounded by three hundred miles of desert in any direction you'd care to go."

I almost didn't want to ask the next. "How are you getting there?"

"Much as I'm dreading it, I'm hopping our corporate slick at mid-morning tomorrow," he answered, "taking it to New York, then from there I'm on a Delta flight to Egypt. Once I reach Cairo, they'll ferry me the rest of the way on one of Ahab the Arab's private jets."

"Greg …" I tried to put a warning tone in my voice as I felt that unpleasant jittering starting to run up and down my spine.

"Hey, don't tell me," he said. "I've been sweating bullets for a week. Last night I dreamed the thing crashed, and everybody was killed but me. But I don't have a choice. I gotta go."

"Maybe you could postpone it," I said. "At least until Martin's caught."

"Can't," Greg replied shortly. "I'm not only the senior steel pusher for the company, I'm also owner and head engineer. We're small, but we're growing. And a rivet doesn't go in until I okay the site."

I was flummoxed. "Well—"

"Oh, I'll be all right," he said, his words almost flip. "Once I'm in the air even old Martin couldn't nail me."

"Never assume."

"I'll betcha Del didn't buy any of this, did he?" Greg asked after a moment.

"I don't think so. Why do you say that?"

"He's a funny guy. He doesn't believe in anything he can't touch."

"Well, he's stupid then," I said. "We all saw what Martin was capable of."

"Del could explain away the sunrise. One day I guess he'll find out different."

"How about you?"

"Sure, I believe in the supernatural," Greg replied. "I haven't gone the route you did, becoming a Christian and all. But yeah, I believe there's something beyond us, a force, a power, whatever. And I think Martin's gone over to the dark side."

"I think he was born on the dark side. The dark side of the moon."

"The best album Pink Floyd ever did."

"Your butt. 'A Momentary Lapse of Reason' is the one." Neither one of us was wanting to think about who Martin had targeted next.

"Anyway," Greg said after another moment, "I gotta go. If I stand too long in one spot my legs cramp."

"Sure." A leg cramp, for most of us just an annoyance, in a high-steel worker's life might mean death. "Well, take care of yourself."

"You too. And don't sweat it, Joe. Martin can't run around the country too long killing people. There's laws, you know."

We both laughed at that, our hearts not in it, and I hung up. I got up then and went over and stared at my monkey.

On top of the filing cabinet in the corner of my office sits a child's toy, a sock monkey. For those unfamiliar with that term, a sock monkey is a small stuffed animal made out of a certain kind of work sock. The sock's red heel forms the monkey's muzzle. It's a poor kid's toy, or it was until it started to make a comeback a few years ago. I'd had one as a child, but this one wasn't it. No, the one I was looking at now had been found by my wife, Linda, the night she died in a car wreck, nearly thirty Christmas Eves ago.

The night she'd bought it, she'd had the shop owner make up a nametag that read Mister Monk Junior, in honor of the one I'd lost years earlier in a move. She had wrapped up the box, with the monkey now inside, in pretty paper, put it in our car trunk, and happily headed home. A mile and a half from our apartment, she hit a patch of black ice. Our car went into a spin, and now Linda would be forever twenty-two. But here's the part that still grinds my guts: in a note from her I'd found later, she'd told me the monkey wasn't for me, but for our unborn son. Surprise. The monkey remained in that box, stuck under my bed, for all those years.

But then three months ago, the day Sarge led me in the prayer that made me a Christian, I did something strange. For some reason I've yet to fathom, I removed Mister Monk Junior and put him there in my office. Why? As I said, I still don't know. Maybe my actions were fraught with symbolism; you know, taking Mister Monk from his cardboard coffin and bringing him into the light of day, just like my heart when I accepted the Lord.

Or maybe he just cheers the place up.

Some people might say it's morbid, me keeping him always in my line of sight, as if I'm mourning what might have been. And some days, I guess, maybe that's true.

But mostly when I look at him, the word I'm thinking of is "reunion."

26

I smiled gently at old Mister Monk before turning away and sitting at my desk. Why had I just done that? The answer was that I've experienced too much death in my nearly fifty years on spaceship Earth, and I needed a reminder right about then that death wasn't the end—for good or bad.

The endings I've seen are, as the saying goes, legion. They first started with the Suto family, then moved on into my dad's death, and then Vietnam and that mess. All that was followed by things I witnessed in my time as a cop when I came back from that war. That's still not counting Granny's death, as well as several dimly recalled drug and alcohol overdoses I encountered during the twelve-year blackout period that followed the passing of my wife and son.

Now things had come nearly full circle. Like Dracula springing up from the grave, an enemy from Vietnam I once thought disposed of forever was now squarely back in my life. I recalled something that Jeff Davis, the one and only president of the Confederate States of America, had said in his writings. His words concerned another war, but they still seemed entirely too apropos for what Del and Greg and Marcus and I were facing: "A question settled by force and violence remains forever unsettled and will rise again." Indeed.

I picked up the phone and called information for Waycross, Georgia.

Mrs. Brake had told me Marcus was a farmer there—no big shock at that; in 'Nam he'd told us the Crowells were farmers from as far back as anyone could recall—and she'd also said he was a widower, so I didn't hold much hope I'd find him still in the house at nine-thirty in the morning. *Unless he's laying there dead*, something whispered nastily in my head. I shook that off as I wrote the number down the computer was giving me. If Marcus's spread was big enough, maybe he'd have a hired hand around that would catch the call.

No such luck. His phone rang, and rang, and rang, without either being picked up or a machine coming on to take the message. *Marcus, Marcus. I'm trying to save your life, son, but you ain't making it easy.* Twelve rings later I gave up and sat back, scratching my head. *Now what?*

Pastor Franklin had told me something shortly after I'd become a Christian that's stuck with me. He said that in one regard the Christian walk wasn't really any different from the one you'd find in business or sports or any area of life. You needed a person, he said, one who knew the ropes, one who'd walked the same road you're walking now, but years earlier. Someone who'd fought the fight of faith valiantly and borne the scars of battle, someone who'd known both victory and defeat and the lessons each taught. More than just a mentor, the pastor had said. A spiritual father. I nodded. I knew exactly who mine was. It was past time to bring him into play.

I picked up the phone once more and dialed Sarge.

"Hello?" It was Helen, Sarge's wife of forty-five years.

"Hi, Helen, it's Joe." It only belatedly occurred to me right then that they might have known more than one Joe.

I guess not, because I could almost feel the sunshine in her voice as she said my name, and not just because she and Sarge now lived in Florida. "Joe. Heavens to Betsy, it's good to hear you."

"Heavens to Betsy"; you gotta love people who still talk like that. I know I do.

"Same here, Helen. How is that old Mick of yours? Still giving you fits?"

"As always," she laughed. "I swear, some days I'd like to see him back on the force, if only to get him out from underfoot."

I chuckled at that. Sarge had always been about as domesticated as a water buffalo. The idea of him continually being in the way in the small beachfront Naples condo he and Helen shared would have made good fodder for a sitcom. No wonder he spent as much time as he could on his small boat, the *Perpetrator*.

"Is he out striking terror in the Florida fish population again?"

"What else? He was anxious to try out this new set of salt-water lures he bought through the mail. He said his old ones were worn out, which they're not, and ever since those lures came yesterday he's been like a child at Christmas. The one he's using this morning is five inches long and looks like a lobster with two heads. What fish see in those things I'll never understand."

I laughed again and said, "Well, when he comes in, tell him to give me a call."

"I can do better than that," Helen replied. "Since we were up to see you last summer Tim and I have entered the modern age. We bought a pair of cell phones."

"You didn't. Sarge once told me he'd be boiled in oil before he'd ever stoop to using one of those 'yuppie mating calls,' as he referred to them."

"Well," she chuckled, "all I can say about that is, tell the cook to heat up the pot, because now he won't part with the thing. Let me give you his number."

She did, and I got ready to hang up. "It was good to hear your voice again, Helen."

"You too." But she didn't want to let me go just yet. "How is that sweet lady of yours?"

"Ange is terrific," I smiled. "She's always talking about you two, about how much she enjoyed meeting you both this past summer."

"We need to do that again," Helen said. "But this time we'll have you down here. You still haven't seen our place.

And of course, bring your lady. She can take the guest room."

"So where am I supposed to sleep?" I asked, faking hurt.

"Ah, there'll be no hanky-panky in the Mulrooney house, Joseph Jebstuart Box," Helen replied in a comically gruff tone. "We'll make you up a nice hammock on the porch."

Son of gun if that didn't sound pleasant. Tropical breezes, the night sounds of the ocean, gulls wheeling through the sky—I could handle a whole bunch of that right about now.

"You're on," I said. "Right now I'm in the middle of something, but when it's over, I'll be down. We both will."

"You do that," Helen said, and then the whimsy left her voice. "Joe, the Lord just told me something. He said that whatever it is you're involved in is very bad. Life and death bad. So I want you to know that Tim and I will be praying for you, just like we did last summer with that laboratory thing and the missing girl. We'll pray for you night and day. You know that, don't you?"

"Yeah, Helen," I said, my throat closing with emotion. "I know that."

"Good," she said. "Now you call my Tim, and you tell him what's on your heart."

My oh my. People like that, you cherish.

♦ ◊ ♦

"There's only two humans in this world I'll quit fishing long enough to talk to," Sarge said. "Helen's one."

"And that makes me the other," I answered.

"You guessed 'er, Chester. What's up?"

Sarge always did like to cut right to it. "I'm in trouble," I said.

"Yeah, I figured it was something like that. I could tell it from your voice." I started to reply when he cut me off. "Before you get rolling, let me get this rig laid back down in the boat before some gull snags my lure and flies halfway to Cuba with it." I heard him set the phone down, then there were various clanks and clunks as he secured his rod and reel. "Okay," he said a minute later, "that's done. Not that I'm soft on gulls, but if you've ever seen one try to lift off with a treble-hook crawler caught down its gullet, it ain't a pretty sight."

I would imagine not. "I'll try to make this short, Sarge. I hate taking you away from the fish."

"Do 'em good," he chuckled. "Give 'em a false sense of security. Kind of lull 'em into apathy before I come on like the avenging angel." I heard him sigh with contentment then, and knew he'd just sat down in his captain's chair. I could picture it exactly, because Sarge had sent me a snapshot of his boat, with him in it. The local paper had published it the day he'd brought in the largest sand shark caught in those waters in twenty years. "Okay, Joe," he said. "Lay it on me."

I did. I told him every bit of it, with the exception of what I'd done in Vietnam. That I hadn't had to go over, as we'd both shared war stories with each other the nights we'd been on patrol together. And until this week, outside of those of us who'd been in on Martin's capture, Sarge was the only one I'd ever told that tale to. I was feeling bad for bending his ear with all this, and using his air minutes, but I knew he wouldn't feel the same.

"So this mook's out," Sarge said, "and he's settling some scores."

"That's it exactly. And with only four of us left, he's just about cleared the board."

"So why are you asking me about it?" Sarge wasn't being unnecessarily gruff; it was just his way. As I said, he'd been a Marine in the Korean War, and felt that the time he'd been granted these past fifty years was a gift. He rarely squandered it.

"I guess I just need some advice."

"No you don't," he said flatly. "You need some guts."

"What?"

"You heard me. When did you say your friend Little Bit called you? What was it, Wednesday night? So here it is Saturday morning. If what you told me is right, about all you've done since then is sit on your butt and whine."

I was glad I wasn't expecting sympathy from Sarge, because I knew I'd never get it. "That's a bit harsh, isn't it?"

"Is it? I'm not the one this guy is gunning for."

"No, your only enemies are the fish."

"Not enemies. Adversaries. College boy like you ought to know the difference."

I knew what he was doing now. He was trying to make me mad so I'd distance myself from the horror bearing down on me. Distance clears the mind, Sarge had often told me during my rookie time on the force, and sharpens the eye.

"Okay, adversaries," I said. "But I've got an enemy roaring down the turnpike toward me, and I was just thinking you might be able to give me some ideas about that."

"You've told your pastor, and Angela, and turned it all over to the Lord, isn't that what you said?"

"Yeah."

"Well, let me give this some thought here." There were quite a few seconds of silence, while Sarge ran the information through his uneducated-but-still-analytically sharp brain. "Okay," he said then, "how about this. You say this fool's dad is a United States senator?"

"Was. He retired a few years back. But I checked with my sources in Columbus, and it turns out he still lives right outside the city on some sort of gentleman's farm."

"Hold on a minute," Sarge said. "Columbus? It's all coming back to me now. Yeah, Henrik ten Eyck. He was some kind of big old muckety-muck when you and I were still on the force."

I laughed at that. "Your ignorance of politics is as bad now as it was then. Didn't you *ever* follow it?"

"Nope." He snorted his derision. "Why should I? I haven't voted since Eisenhower. Most politicians are as a big a bunch of crooks as you or I ever saw on the street. They just have better haircuts, and their fingernails are polished. Underneath those glad-handing smiles of theirs they're all a bunch of double-shuffle, three-card-monte con men."

"Well, this particular con man was head of the Senate Appropriations Committee."

"Yeah, I remember. Big old fat greasy cuss. Teeth as white as a toilet tank lid and every gray hair on his head looking like it was nailed in. Always on the eleven o'clock news, telling the homefolks how he was making sure the boys doing the fighting had the best of everything." Sarge snorted again. "Not quite true, was it?"

"I'm the wrong guy to ask," I said. "As long as they kept me in bullets and Spam, I was happy."

"Maybe. But when it comes settling-up time in glory, old Henrik is gonna have to face a Judge he never expected."

"Could be you're right. Anyway, back to Martin," I prompted.

"Don't rush me," Sarge snapped. "I'm old, so I go off on tangents sometimes." A moment later he said, "Okay, see how this hits you. What if Martin's doing all this as a rehearsal?"

"Rehearsal?" I must have sounded baffled. "You lost me on that one. A rehearsal for what?"

Sarge's answer was simple. "Killing his father."

"Killing …" The light clicked on. "Of course. I think I'm getting it. But tell me your read on it first. See if we're on the same page."

"Okay. You say Martin's story is he was neglected as a boy. The only thing close to a real father he ever had was this Baumgartner guy, with some various bodyguards thrown in the mix. Let's say that's true. Doesn't excuse him, but it helps to understand him. God knows how tough it is for a boy to make it in this world without guidance from someone stronger than himself."

I gave a silent amen to that, and once again thanked God that in his mercy he'd given me a man like this one to be my own surrogate dad.

"So," Sarge continued, "Martin rebelled. He did whatever

he could to wake his dad up to the fact he was losing a son. Including shooting his bodyguard. But even that wasn't enough. He needed something more outrageous. So, he became a traitor."

"Makes we wonder if he hadn't planned it all from the start," I mused. "Even from the day he enlisted."

"Could be," Sarge allowed. "We'll never know, and it's probably not important. I imagine he would've revealed himself to the world sooner or later so he could really rub salt in the wound. The thing is, he tried to cause as much harm to his father, and his father's reputation, as he could. Getting captured screwed that up, but now he's out, and he's ready to finish the job."

"So killing all of us is just exercise."

"Yep. I'll bet he's been croaking people since the day he got sprung. Guy like Martin fits the classic serial killer profile. He can't quit it any more than you or I could stop breathing. And I think that him sharpening his rusty skills on you guys, as well as on the general populace, is like a pitcher warming up in the bull pen before facing a heavy hitter."

"His father," I nodded. "It fits. It stinks, but it fits."

"It's the only thing that does, at least to me."

"So the question I'm left with is—"

"What to do," Sarge finished. "Here's what I'd tackle next, if you want to hear it."

"That's why I called."

"Okay, first I'd make sure to call this guy Marcus tonight, when you're reasonably sure he's gonna be home."

"Well, sure," I replied. "I was figuring on that."

"What time do you think that might be anyway? You're the guy who used to live on a farm."

"It's hard to say. This time of the year the crops are long since in, but a farmer's work never really stops; take that from someone who knows. I'd say no later than ten, at the latest."

"Okay," Sarge said, "but before that call, you need to make another one first. To ten Eyck."

"To warn him," I nodded again. Then I said, "That's not going to be easy to pull off. I may end up having to go there in person. On the phone he'd probably just consider me another Vietnam burnout trying to cause him grief."

"That's not your problem. Your deal is to let him know."

"Okay," I said. "While I'm at it, I think I'm also going to find out which hospital had Martin."

"And why they pronounced him cured. Which he obviously ain't."

I sighed at the enormity of the problem. "Baumgartner told something to the Loot back when we caught Martin," I said then. "Something to the effect that it would have been better all around if the boy had been strangled in his crib."

"That's pretty strong," Sarge said, "but I can't fault the feeling. Too late now though. This is the hand you've been dealt."

"Yeah," I said. "Lucky me."

"I guess it goes without saying that Helen and me are gonna keep you on the front burner of our prayer time."

"Thanks," I answered simply. Heartier thanks would follow later, when Martin was either in jail, or under the sod.

"Just watch yourself, Joe." Sarge's tone had grown dark. "And those around you. A demon-possessed fool like Martin ain't too particular who he murders, as long as he gets to do it. If he can't kill you, he'll settle for somebody close."

With those words, my blood ran cold.

Angela.

27

here is no more boring drive on God's green earth than the one from Cincinnati to Columbus. Yes, I've heard about western Kansas, I've heard about the Australian Outback, I've heard about the trackless depths of the Gobi Desert. Put them all together, and they still wouldn't equal one mile of tedium that the I-71 corridor produces in such boundless measure. Disregarding the November weather outside, I had the Goddess's heat off, the window down, and the radio cranked full tilt to the paint-peeling sounds of a Stones' oldie. Anything to keep me from nodding off and slamming into a bridge abutment.

I made it though, and it was going on 1:00 PM when I circled Columbus and started on the last leg, toward New Albany. In another ten minutes I was off the loop and into farm country. But this area I was cruising past was about as close to the farm country I'd known as a child as rap music is to … well, music. Whatever tillers of the earth had once toiled here were long gone. In their place were "estates," a nice word for farms that had been carved up and sold to the idle rich so they could erect large brick monstrosities on half-acre lots. But it was the names these developments had been given that were the real hoot: The Ponds. The Pines. Willowwood. Any ponds, pines, or willows still extant were only in the fevered minds of the builders who'd filled them in, torn them down, or bulldozed them under. The day I'm elected emperor, there'll be some changes made.

I checked the name of the "estate" I'd written down that my source at the cop house had given me for Henrik ten Eyck: Grand Possibilities. Cute. The only grand possibility Henrik needed to concern himself with was waking up with his throat slit, courtesy of his boy. I had a bad feeling about this whole trip as I pulled up to a massive iron filigreed gate set firmly into the high brick wall on either side of it. There wasn't a guard shack like I'd suspected, but only a speaker box set into the brick next to the gate. As I pressed the button on it, I reflected that a human guard probably wasn't needed; I'd bet I was under surveillance from no less than three hidden cameras as I waited for someone to acknowledge my existence.

I didn't have to wait long.

The male voice razzing at me from the speaker's grill carried not a modicum of warmth. "Yes, who is it?"

"Hello the house. Joe Box, coming to call."

"This is private property, Mr. Box," the metallic voice intoned. "Please turn your vehicle around and leave."

Metallic or not, I picked up the tiniest sneer as it said the word "vehicle." I knew I was on-camera now, and I highly resented the insult to my car. My thoughts grew dark. *If I wouldn't take that attitude toward the Goddess from Sarge's son Jack, I sure won't take it from you, Robot Bob.*

"Sorry, I can't leave," I said.

"Can't or won't?" The voice carried a veiled hint of a threat. "We're equipped here to handle either scenario."

"Whichever you'd like. But I need to see Mr. ten Eyck."

"A ten-second countdown has begun, Mr. Box. Don't let it reach zero."

"Tell Henrik I have one word for him," I said. "A word that'll pop this gate."

The voice now sounded contemptuously amused. "And what word would that be?"

My tone was flat as I said it. "Martin."

Ali Baba had nothing on me. Fifteen seconds later there was a buzz and click, and darned if that gate didn't swing wide.

I drove on through and began the long pull up the jet-black driveway as I headed toward ten Eyck's house. I glanced out the driver's side window as I went. The landscaping was as nicely done as a veterans' cemetery ... which, considering the rumors that had plagued ten Eyck during the late sixties and early seventies about huge sums of soft-money contributions coming into his coffers from munitions makers and aerospace tycoons, wasn't too far off the mark. Lots of trees and ornamental bushes were planted here, maybe in memory of boys whose guns had jammed or whose planes had exploded at inopportune times. I finally passed between two gigantic sycamores, and there before me was the ten Eyck "estate."

At first glance the place reminded me of the David O. Selznik mansion you'd see on the screen before one of his movies would start: wide, and three stories high, filled with white pillars, white dormers, white gables, and enough French doors to satisfy Charles de Gaulle. The blacktop ended in a stretch that came up under a sheltered entrance before looping back on itself and rejoining the main drive. In the center of that loop squatted a huge marble fountain, replete with idiot-faced Cupids spitting water at each other. I knew the outside temperature had to be below freezing, so that meant that fountain was heated. To what end? I guess just because Henrik ten Eyck could. What a wastrel, I thought. Maybe Sarge was right about politicians. I was tempted to pull right on around and start heading home, leaving the man to deal with his mad son any way he chose, when God gave me a nudge. *Oh, all right,* I said silently as I parked. *Just let this be over quick; I've got better things to do with my time.*

So did I, the Lord answered right back, *but I spent that time dying for you anyway.*

Whoops.

I got out of my car, pocketed the keys, then walked up three steps of dark-red brick and onto a flagstone porch big enough for a family of four to set up housekeeping. Before me loomed a set of massive oak doors that would have given William the Conqueror pause. I stepped closer. Those doors might have been imported from a castle at that. Both were five feet across, nine feet high, and each had a circular iron ring as big as a dinner plate set in the center. Knock, knock, would you like a *Watchtower*? I was tempted to try to heft one of those rings and let it drop back down—I've always wanted to do that—but before I could do so the right-hand door swung wide. I half-expected to see Lurch standing there, but the greeter I got was gruesome enough: John Baumgartner.

For a second we regarded each other. I don't know what he thought of my looks, but to me Baumgartner was one of those men who simply do not age. Sure, his reddish hair had a few wisps of silver, and maybe there was the slightest dip to the jawline, but by and large the man appeared much as he did the day he paid us our blood money. I understand it's hard to judge a snake's age too.

His smile was as warm and effusive and real as a prostitute's. "Mr. Box. Please, come inside, won't you?"

I didn't drive all the way up here to stare at your shrubs, I thought. But I kept that to myself as I smiled and followed him in.

Once inside the main foyer, Baumgartner reached his right arm out to the side and snapped his fingers, his eyes never leaving mine. Instantly a sixtyish, grim-faced woman in a maid's outfit appeared.

Still smiling at me, Baumgartner spoke. "Willeena, take Mr. Box's coat, please."

She did, saying, "Shall I place it in the cloakroom, sir?"

His grin at me grew sunny. "No need. The gentleman won't be staying that long. Just drape it over that chair." He brightened even more. "That's all right with you, isn't it, Joe?"

So now it was Joe, was it? Weren't we friendly. "Oh golly, John, sure," I waved, "anywhere is fine. I'm easy." I grinned back at him. We really did hate each other.

Baumgartner's smile slipped a bit. I don't think he liked getting sassed. "Wonderful. Follow me on back to the sunroom. The senator's having a bit of late lunch, but he can spare you a few minutes."

"Nice of him," I said, as we began moving down the wide hall. Not surprisingly, it was full of art objects. Was any of it any good? Don't ask me, I'm a Norman Rockwell man. I passed a painting whose canvas looked like it'd been pelted with tomatoes and toothpaste. I suppose to the rich, if it looks like it was done by a chimp with distemper, it's art.

I pointed at it as we walked. "Is that an expensive piece?"

"Quite," Baumgartner said. "It's a von Schumpter. The valuation on that one is, oh, maybe two hundred thousand."

"Dollars?"

"Dollars."

Wow. Maybe I needed to buy me some tomatoes. And a chimp.

After a journey only ten yards less than the Bataan Death March, we were finally there. Baumgartner pushed aside the white French doors—see?—and motioned me on through. I entered a domain with enough tropical plants and humidity to rival the Florida Keys. I had the feeling a blizzard could have been raging outside its glass walls and it wouldn't have bothered the bald, corpulent, pajama-wearing old man seated before me in the huge wicker chair. He looked up from his plate of meat and veggies long enough to nod at me as I walked up to him.

"That's fine, John, you may leave now," the old man said.

Baumgartner didn't budge. "I'd be happy to stay if you need me to, sir," he replied. "I can sit right here." What a loyal fellow. There was a good deal of the lapdog in John Baumgartner.

The old man—ten Eyck—waved his fork at him. "No, no, go on. I'll ring you when we're finished."

Baumgartner dipped his head. "As you wish, sir." He turned to me. "Don't be long, Joe. The senator tires easily."

"Not to worry, John," I said. "Check on my coat, will you? It's a London Fog."

Seething, but still smiling, Baumgartner exited the room.

I turned to the old man. "That looks tasty. Pork?"

"Chicken. My poor heart can't take too much even of that." Ten Eyck wiped his floppy lips with a linen napkin and leaned back, regarding me with red-rimmed eyes. "You said the magic word to get in here."

"I know. If I had a son like yours, I'd want to know what sort of mischief he was involved in too."

Still staring, ten Eyck stabbed another bit of grayish meat and transported it to his mouth, where he began chewing it lazily. "So what do you wish to tell me about him?"

"With your connections, senator, I imagine you already know. Martin's been busy. I'd like him stopped before he gets any busier."

"And you think I'm able to do that?"

"Sir, no offense, but you've heard the phrase, 'money talks'?" I smiled as I motioned around. "You're rich enough to make it scream. I'd just like for you to do the voodoo that you do so well." I leaned down. "Find your freaking son, senator. Lock him away. Make him leave me and my friends alone." I straightened. "That's all. Nothing too difficult for a man with your resources."

"You ask a hard thing, Mr. Box. I'm not so sure that I can accomplish it." He looked at me differently now. "Or want to."

I narrowed my eyes, understanding dawning. "I'll be—So that's it. You'll have to forgive me, senator, sometimes I'm a little slow." I nodded at him. "I get it now. You're more than willing to let Martin take the rest of us out, because when that's done, the last of the men who could tell the world of the deal you cut is history." I puffed out a small, humorless laugh. "Pretty raw, Henrik."

"I have no idea of what you're talking about, Mr. Box," ten Eyck said, returning to his plate.

My fingers flexed in and out for a few seconds, balling themselves into fists and releasing, before I answered him. "Pity. And that's only the first reason I came up here today."

He looked up at me, squinting one eye as he chewed. "Oh?"

"The other was to warn you."

"Warn me? Of what?" His eyes grew large. "Of you?" He wheezed a wet chuckle. "Remove that idea from your mind, sir. It's been tried before, by worthier men." Picking up a pea pod, he examined it critically before popping it whole into his mouth.

I could feel my composure slipping by degrees. "No, the same subject as before. Martin."

Now ten Eyck brayed a laugh at me, spraying food particles in all directions. "Good grief. Martin? Coming here? To do me harm? That's insane." His laugh grew even more raucous. I'd bet he was the kind of guest invited dead last to cocktail parties.

"Sure, why not?" I replied. "You're not immune. Matter of fact, a friend of mine thinks this is all leading up to you."

Ten Eyck took a sip of something—wine, it looked like—before answering, the humor gone now. "Mr. Box, I'm seventy-seven years old. I'm not near ready to die yet, at anyone's hands, your friend notwithstanding." He motioned around him with his glass. "I'm as rich as Croesus, and have the security here to prove it. I've spent over two million dollars on home defense, including hiring sixteen full-time armed security guards, as well as installing heat sensors, motion detectors, silent alarms, video cameras, and other things I don't feel like telling you about."

"Impressive. But as the little girl said in *Aliens*, it won't make any difference."

"And why is that?" ten Eyck folded his filthy napkin into a neat square before placing it on his tray. "Go on, Mr. Box, tell all. I get little enough to laugh at, and you're an amusing man."

"Are you saying you're not aware of your son's involvement in the occult? Or even care? You're not that stupid."

"Are you saying you believe any of it's real?"

I gave him a disbelieving look. "Come on, ten Eyck. Your houseboy Baumgartner could tell you more of that than me. According to him he practically raised your son. He knows what Martin is capable of. He saw it."

Ten Eyck stood, not an easy task for a man of his advancing years. And bulk. His words at me now were measured. "John Baumgartner saw what he chose to. He's loyal, but dull. Given his limitations, however, John is a dedicated man. Much like you, I'd wager."

If John Baumgartner was like me I'd jump off the Carew Tower. I just stared at ten Eyck as he shook his head and continued.

"When Martin's mother died giving him birth I turned my son over to John for rearing. By and large he's done a fine job, a job I had absolutely no desire to do. I was none too pleased that Martha had turned up pregnant in the first place; my career was just beginning in earnest then, and that baggage wasn't needed. With her death, any interest I may have had in my son dropped to zero. Had abortion the approval from the populace then as it enjoys today ..." ten Eyck spread his hands. "Who knows?"

Then reaching over, he pulled a palm frond close for examination. It obviously didn't pass muster, because he drew what looked like a small pair of scissors out of his pocket and snipped it off. As it fell to the floor, he looked up at me with a smile. "Insect-ridden. Useless things disturb me. Every item should carry its own value."

It occurred to me right about then that Henrik ten Eyck wasn't entirely sane. Which led me to ask: "What about the hospital that kept Martin for all those years?"

"What about it?"

"I'd like to know the name of it, and the name of the head dog there who let him out."

Ten Eyck's eyebrows climbed. "To what possible end?"

"You may not be interested in keeping your skin intact, senator," I said, "but keeping mine ranks way up there. Any intel on your son would be good."

He gave me a look of irritation. "Oh, all right. Anything to get you on your way. Not that it'll do you any good. The hospital is called Longwood. It's quite an exclusive facility, located not far from here, in Worthington. The chief administrator's name is Dr. Claude Winter." His smile was bitter. "Will that do?"

"It'll have to." I decided to go for it all. "Will you give him a call for me?"

Now ten Eyck's slobbery lips twisted in a sardonic grin. "Why would I do that?"

"Call it leveling the playing field," I answered. "Giving me a fighting chance."

He was still grinning. "You know, maybe I should at that. Your visit here has brightened my day. A lot. This whole thing is becoming more entertaining than I would have imagined." His nod at me was mocking. "All right, Mr. Box. After you've gone, consider it done."

"Thanks." Then I said, "Not to spoil your upcoming fun, senator, but let me ask you once more, appeal to whatever conscience you may still have left. If Martin contacts you, will you call him off?"

"No," he answered simply. "You said it before, sir. For the first time in his useless life, Martin is providing a service I can actually take advantage of. He's handling my problem for me."

"And the fact that when he's done with us, he's coming after you doesn't even enter in."

"No. Because I simply do not believe he will."

"So you're not going to do anything at all," I said.

"On the contrary," ten Eyck replied. "I'm going to do this"—he slipped the scissors back in his pocket—"and this"—he picked up his wine glass and polished it off in one gulp—"and this"—he reached down and pressed a button next to his chair—"and wish you a profitable day, Mr. Box." His smile at me now was that of dismissal.

"I haven't penetrated your thinking one iota, have I?"

"Even less than that." He looked past me as the door behind me opened. "There you are, John. When you've escorted Mr. Box out, please join me in my office." Turning back to his plants, I saw him reach in his pocket for the scissors again.

I walked the two steps over to ten Eyck, Baumgartner right on my heels. I ignored him as I said, "Even though I want to, senator, the Lord won't let me leave yet without one more appeal."

"The Lord?" ten Eyck laughed. "Good God."

"Yes, he is. Martin won't stop when he's finished with me. I know that, but how can I make you understand?"

"You can't," the old man said as he began tugging and yanking on the fronds again. "Good day, sir."

I'd just taken another step closer when I felt Baumgartner's hand clench the back of my left arm, right above my elbow. If you want to bring out the English in me, as Granny used to say, that'll sure enough do it. I whipped around, ripping his fingers free, and stuck my nose a quarter inch from his. "Don't. Not unless you want to see if I can tear your freckles off barehanded."

My threat must have worked. He backed up a few paces.

I turned back to ten Eyck, my voice flat. "You're bound and determined to die, senator, and I can't stop it. I suppose I was a fool to try." I shook my head. "What a wasted trip."

"High comedy is never a waste, Mr. Box," ten Eyck smirked, looking back over his shoulder at me. "You have a rare gift."

Setting my jaw, I pivoted around and began heading for the door that led back into the main house, Baumgartner right behind. Reaching it, I turned. "Ten Eyck. One last thing."

"Yes," he sighed as he fiddled with the fronds, peering closely at them.

My words were even. "What are you the most afraid of?"

He turned again, pursing his lips in disapproval. "What an odd question. I wouldn't feel so led as to share that with you."

"No need to share," I said. "Whatever it is, it's only enough for one. That's for true, as another one of Martin's victims, my dead buddy Little Bit, used to say. So watch your back, Henrik. You'll never hear him coming."

Ten Eyck smiled and stared at me like I was another not-quite-up-to-snuff palm frond. I again shook my head in absolute consternation, and with that Baumgartner and I left the sunroom.

He only stopped long enough to make sure the door was securely closed, then caught up with me, matching my stride. "I wish I could say I told you so," he smiled. "But you already know that. The senator's security measures are far beyond anything you or your friends are capable of, so of course he's confident. Should Martin attempt the unthinkable here, which I doubt, he'll find he's more than met his match. The senator has things well in hand."

Coming into the foyer, I picked my coat off the chair. I still hadn't answered him. As I pulled the door open to leave, Baumgartner placed a hand—lightly—on my shoulder. "Don't feel too badly about your efforts here today, Joe," he simpered. "You can die confident in the assurance that you did nobly in warning the senator. Real Medal-of-Honor stuff. Not that it was needed."

Shrugging him off, I smiled. "Martin specializes in wet work, John. We both know that. And with him being completely hooked into hell now, when the time comes that he decides to take the senator out, he'll do that very thing, 'measures' or not. And *you* can die confident in knowing he took you off the board as a bonus." I cranked my head around at the house and its grounds. "What that boy's going to do here will be something special."

With that I walked down the steps, got in my car, and left. In the rearview mirror, I saw Baumgartner watching me as I drove off. His expression was too distant to make out.

28

Hello, my name's Joe Box. I'm here to see Dr. Winter."
I hoped so anyway. I was banking on the fact that ten Eyck
had done as he'd promised and called here after I'd left him.
If he hadn't, I knew I wouldn't get ten feet inside. I was standing in the middle of the richly appointed—what else?—lobby of
the Longwood Memorial Hospital. I didn't know who
Longwood was, nor was I interested in why this place was
named for him, but I cared greatly whether Dr. Claude Winter
would be willing to tell me more about Martin's stay here.

The severely dressed matronly receptionist gave me the
look I expected. "And you are—?"

"Joe Box. As I said."

"Does Dr. Winter know you?"

"No, but he will," I told her, adding mentally, *he will if
you'll lift the stinking phone and call him.*

She didn't seem inclined to do that. "Dr. Winter is a very busy man, Mr. Box."

"As are we all, Mrs. DeHaven," I smiled. I'd checked her nameplate as I strolled up.

She gave my blue serge suit the up and down once-over. It was the only suit I owned, but I'd had it professionally dry-cleaned after my last case, and it sure didn't deserve the fish-eye this old bat was giving it. "Perhaps if you made an appointment …"

"I believe that's been done ma'am," I told her. "By Senator Henrik ten Eyck."

"Well …"

"Mrs. DeHaven," I said, what little good humor I had melting like a Popsicle in July, "just buzz the man, will you?"

Maybe she wasn't used to being talked to in such a manner, but she did as I asked and picked up the phone. After punching in the digits for Winter's extension, she told him that "some man named Box" was here to see him. She couldn't have packed more sneer into my name if I'd been here to serve him papers in a paternity suit. Whatever he said though must have worked, because Mrs. DeHaven put the phone back in its cradle, giving me a look of sour disbelief as she did. "The doctor's expecting you, Mr. Box." She pointed to her left. "That first door is his office. Please. Go on in." She then dropped her hand in her lap and gazed at me the same way Troy's soldiers must have done as the Greeks stormed their way through the city's open gates.

But I was gracious to the vanquished foe. "Thank you, Mrs. DeHaven." I left her and made my way the twenty feet or so over to Winter's door. When I reached it, I knocked twice and waited.

"Come in," a basso profundo voice intoned. I did.

Once inside I gave the room a quick glance. It was very nicely furnished in blonde oak and nappy cream carpet, with an expensive-looking leather sofa off to my right and plenty of von Schumpter-style chimp art on the walls. That alone told me the man had money.

"Mr. Box?" that same deep voice boomed, and I turned, seeing now who'd spoken. I hope I hid my incredulity. A more unprepossessing-looking fellow you'd be hard pressed to find. The man was small, slim, balding, in his late sixties, and the upper part of him that I could see above the huge desk was nattily dressed. This was Dr. Winter?

He motioned to a visitor's chair directly in front of his desk. "I'm Dr. Claude Winter." Well, that answered that. "I can only spare you a few minutes, so please, be seated."

I did. "Thank you, doctor." I still was finding it hard to believe that huge sound was coming from that small throat. I thought back to a *Star Trek* episode I'd seen in the sixties, one where the crew of the *Enterprise* had been captured by an alien with a tremendous voice. It was only at the end they discovered their captor was basically a child with a beard. That had to be one of the sillier ones the network ever did.

But the effect from Dr. Winter was just as strange.

He folded his hands on the desk. He still hadn't cracked a smile. "The senator told me you'd be stopping by, and he asked me to help you, if possible. What he did not tell me is why."

"My visit concerns his son, Martin."

Winter leaned back. It seemed as if the room's temperature had just dropped ten degrees. "Martin." His tone was contemplative. "Dear, mad Martin. I might have known."

I smiled. "I thought the heads of mental hospitals didn't use words like 'mad.'"

"In Martin's case, the term hardly does him justice."

"Really. I'd like for you to tell me about that, sir."

"*You'd* like?" Winter said flatly. "I've acquiesced to the senator's wishes in allowing you entrance here, Mr. Box. But as I've said, you have yet to tell me why I should go any further."

That was true, I hadn't. "All right," I nodded, and I then proceeded to give him the quick version of both what had happened more than thirty years ago, and what was still going on today.

Winter frowned at me. "We are aware of Martin's traitorous service time, of course. But you believe he's responsible for these murders?"

"Not just believe it, doctor," I said. "I'm convinced."

"It hardly seems possible," he muttered.

Now I leaned forward. "Tell me why that is."

"I'm not sure that I can," Winter said. "Patient confidentiality—"

"Is hereby waived," I broke in. Then I said, "Doctor

Winter, the senator asked you to extend me every courtesy. Didn't he?"

"He did," Winter admitted. "He also mentioned something about 'giving you a chance.'" He shook his head. "It was quite unusual. Now, I don't know if he meant giving you a chance to speak with me about Martin, or—"

"I know exactly what he meant. It's kind of a private joke."

"Joke?"

It was my turn to shake my head. "It's not important. But I'd like for you to tell me whatever you can about Martin's time here."

Winter sighed. "Very well. For the sake of my relationship with the senator, I shall. And since Martin *has* been officially removed as one of our patients, I suppose technically I'm not violating his confidentiality." His tone sharpened. "But I must ask you, Mr. Box, to keep what I'm about to tell you under the strictest confidence. Do I have your agreement?"

He did, and then Dr. Claude Winter proceeded to tell some of the things Longwood Memorial Hospital had done to dear, mad Martin.

◆ ◊ ◆

Martin ten Eyck, twenty-one years old, was admitted to Longwood on 18 January, 1971. At the time Dr. Winter was on staff, but only in an advisory capacity. Martin's attending physician, Dr. Taylor Hanford, Yale, class of 1947, was also the hospital's chief.

"Dr. Hanford was a brilliant man," Winter told me,

"years ahead of anyone in his treatment of the mentally ill. Longwood was considerably fortunate in securing him."

"Longwood the hospital or Longwood the man?" I interjected.

"Longwood the hospital. Longwood the man has been dead for a hundred years." Winter frowned at me. "Please stay on track, Mr. Box."

"Sorry." How was I supposed to know Longwood was dead? I hadn't even heard of the boy until today. "Go on, sir."

Winter settled himself deeper in his chair. "The day Martin arrived here, we knew he was a special case. A challenge awaited us. And not just because of what he'd done, or who his father was; the senator had been quite generous with his funds to assure our silence concerning his son."

I knew all about that.

"One of Senator ten Eyck's family friends, a John Baumgartner, brought Martin in that day," Winter said. "Baumgartner was accompanied by a ... the name escapes me at the moment ..."

"Mr. Carlton," I prompted.

Winter frowned again. "How did you know that?"

"I saw him once," was all I said.

The doctor cleared his throat. "We'd known they were on their way, of course, but Martin's arrival still came as a bit of a shock. The senator had made us aware of his son's activities in Vietnam, so all of us here expected Martin to arrive in an ambulance, locked in a straightjacket. You can imagine our surprise when he climbed out of one of the senator's staff cars, clad not in restraints, but in normal, everyday street clothes."

"That was unusual?"

"It was unheard of." Winter leaned forward. "Mr. Box, you must understand the purpose of Longwood. We get the cases that, save for the wealth of those involved, most mental hospitals wouldn't touch. And as I've said, the senator had made us fully aware of Martin's activities overseas."

Activities. Winter made it sound like Martin had been caught spray-painting highway overpasses. I banked down my anger as I said, "So why is it so hard for you to accept what he's doing now?"

The doctor held up a warning finger. "Allegedly doing."

"Whatever."

"The answer is, because of the treatment he received here."

Now we were getting to it. "Treatment?"

"Yes. As I told you, Dr. Hanford pioneered techniques that, at the time, were considered revolutionary. Today they are quite common. But in 1971, with the arrival of Martin, it was a classic case of the perfect doctor meeting the perfect patient. And Senator ten Eyck assured us we would have availability of whatever funds necessary, plus full use of his considerable connections, to do whatever was needful to effect a cure."

Caramba. If Martin hadn't been screwed up enough before he came here, being securely in the hands of Dr. Frankenstein would have fixed him up good. It was hard to say who was the bigger monster, Martin or his father.

"Could you tell me some of what was done?"

"I suppose so; as I said, what was unthinkable then is now accepted in the mainstream of mental health treatment. Included in Martin's treatment were not only the usual electroshock therapy and hypnosis, but crystallography, handwriting analysis, Rolfing, primal scream, past lives regression, drugs—"

"Drugs?" I broke in. "What kind?"

Winter waved a hand. "The names would be meaningless to you. Psychotropic medications."

"You mean LSD?"

"Yes, LSD was one of them," he grudgingly admitted. "That and its derivatives."

Lord have mercy. Nothing like giving acid to a madman. "And all of that worked?"

"Better than we'd hoped," he smiled. "Of course, the time element involved in such treatment was considerable."

"More than thirty years' worth, if I'm not mistaken."

"Yes. As I said, Martin was quite the challenge."

I cautiously broached the next. "Was anything ever done concerning his involvement in the occult?"

"Of course," Winter said. "We made great use of that as well."

That stopped me. "Come again?"

He smiled. "It's not bandied about much in the media, Mr. Box, but many in the medical community are well aware of the reality of the occult. And of its efficacy in the treatment of both the physically and the mentally ill."

I stared. So while in public the intellectual elite glee-fully bashed the power of Christian prayer, in private they embraced with both arms the nostrums from hell. Incredible. I'd bet Luke Franklin would have a comment or two about that.

"You encouraged it, huh?"

"With the greatest enthusiasm, Mr. Box. As I've said, Martin's father gave us full reign. And money was no object. As of his twenty-first year Martin was heir to his own large trust fund."

"You also allowed him books on the occult, tapes, that sort of thing?"

"Yes. Plus the time alone for him to practice what he was learning."

Good grief. With guys like Winter running them, I made a mental note never to get locked up in a nuthouse.

"Let me see if I can sum this up, doctor," I said then. "Martin was given full access to anything he wished con-cerning any part of the occult, and that indulgence was supplemented by you giving him New Age therapy, drugs, and whatever else that struck your fancy."

"Dr. Hanford was a brilliant man, and Martin a most willing subject," Winter smiled again. "I've told you that."

"And this went on for more than three decades."

"Yes. About that. After Dr. Hanford's death ten years ago, I not only assumed headship of the hospital, but that of Martin's treatment as well. His episodes had nearly ceased by then."

That perked my ears. "Episodes?"

Winter waved it away. "The usual ravings of the unbalanced. Threats against certain unnamed men, ravings against his father … We know now it was attributable to a new drug regimen we were trying on him at the time. We record all the sessions with our patients on tape, and when these were later played back to Martin, he was horrified, and quite chagrined."

Yeah, I'll bet he was. "How did you know the threats weren't to be taken seriously?" I asked.

"Because we are professionals here, Mr. Box. It was all pure fantasy, a wish. One month ago, we had our final staff meeting concerning Martin, and the consensus of all present was that his cure was complete. He was joyful. We released him with a clean bill of health, his records expunged."

It was my turn to frown. "You can do that? Clear his record of his time here?"

Winter chuckled. "Money talks, Mr. Box. As you may have heard."

"Yeah," I said. "I know."

"That's why I find it so difficult to believe Martin could be doing the things you say he is," the doctor said.

"Because that would mean your 'cure' of his madness had failed," I smiled. "And that simply is unacceptable in your paradigm."

"Unthinkable," Winter agreed. "Martin had more than thirty years of the finest help money could buy, Mr. Box. If we say he's cured"—he nodded—"he's cured."

I put my hands on my knees and stood. "Thank you for

your time, doctor. No need to show me out. I know the way."

"You're satisfied then?"

"Satisfied?" I shook my head. "No. But you've helped me to understand him better." I started walking toward the door. I was nearly there when I turned. "How did Dr. Hanford die?"

Winter furrowed his brow. "Now that was an odd thing. An aneurysm, a huge one. The man was as healthy as a horse, but the subsequent autopsy showed Hanford's brain had practically exploded." He shook his head in wonder. "One never knows, does one?"

"This one does," I said as I left.

29

It was now going on late afternoon as I pulled the Goddess in the Agnes' pothole-strewn lot. I entered my apartment, and Noodles greeted me in his usual way, head-bumping my shins and threading his way between my feet as I walked. My cat must either have very good radar or the ability to count the rhythm of my strides, because I hardly ever step on him. The times I do, he stores those in his favor bank for when he wants extra treats. Who says people own cats? I think it's the other way around.

He was giving me the full treatment, purring for all he was worth as I checked my mail. Not much today. Two bills, electric and phone, plus an offer from the cable company to hook me up with high-speed Internet access. Ha, and ha again. The Internet thing I roundfiled , then I put the bills on the counter. Noodles was still in full cry.

"Oh, all right," I told him as I pulled a can of cat food out of the cupboard. He only gets treats at night, after he's had his regular meal. "You act like you haven't eaten for a week." As the can whirled on the electric opener, he was nearly beside himself. It was only after I'd poured the contents into his bowl that he looked up at me in confusion.

"Sorry," I said. "The store was out of Kitten Kuddle. This'll have to do."

He sniffed it, then turned and stalked off, mortified that I'd insulted him so. "Don't let it get too dry before you eat it," I told him as he went. "I imagine it's worse that way." He switched his ruined tail at me as he disappeared behind the sofa. "Up to you." I picked up the phone to call Angela.

She answered, and I tried to make my voice low. "Hello, madam, I'm taking a survey. Are you as beautiful as people say you are?"

"Oh, even more so," she breathed. "But my taste in men is awful." Then she laughed loud and long.

Nuts. I've yet to fool Angela with one of my telephone gags. Either my jokes aren't that good, or there's more to this intercessor stuff than I know.

"All right, all right, so you knew it was me," I groused. "You've bruised my ego irreparably. I've half a mind not to ask you out to dinner."

"Where's the other half gone?" she laughed again. Before I could answer, she went on, "Oh, Joe, I wish I could, but I start that new class tomorrow, and I'm swamped going over this curriculum."

"Class? Oh, yeah, I remember now." Angela had agreed

to Pastor Franklin's request—I called it being shanghaied—to teach the Sunday school class for the five year olds. "How much bookwork can there be for kids that little?"

"You'd be surprised," she sighed. "Count on me to leave this until the last minute."

"But Ange, the plans I had in mind," I told her. "A steak dinner at La Normandie—that is, steak for me and fish for you—followed by a leisurely drive, watching the lights of the city flow by, followed by—"

"Enough," she groaned. "Don't make it worse than it is."

I laughed. "Sorry."

After a moment Angela said, her tone crafty, "You could help me, you know."

"What? Go over lesson plans for five year olds?" I laughed again. "What I know about that stuff begins and ends with Curious George."

"Okay, then how about helping me out in class tomorrow?"

"Good grief, Ange, that's even worse." I brightened. "Hey, I could show them my gun. That's always a crowd-pleaser."

"Joe Box!" she gasped. "You bring a weapon into my class-room, and I'll call the police myself!"

My laugh this time was heartier, Angela joining in.

"I'm sorry," I told her, "but I'm going to take a pass. A man should play to his strengths, and being locked in a room-ful of sugared-up tots isn't my best."

"Oh, all right," she sighed again in fake petulance. "So where should I meet you before the main service starts? I'd still like to sit with you, even if you are being rotten."

"How about right next to the bookstore? I'll buy you a

couple of chocolate mints before we go in. I know you're hooked on them."

"Joe, you're too good to me."

Before she could hang up, I said, "Listen, Ange, I know you have to get back to your stuff, but before you do, I need to ask you something."

"Sure."

"There's something that's been niggling at me since last night. Somehow Martin understands what our deepest fears are. But you never told me how. *How* does he know?"

"Only God has the answer to that," she replied. "But you need to stop worrying about what you don't know, and go with what you do. Because this is all tied up with his walking in darkness."

"I don't understand."

"The spirit world is real, Joe. That includes both sides. The Bible tells us that one of every three unseen spirits is a fallen angel."

"Now *there's* a scary thought."

"Yes. And hard as it is to consider it, there is the possibility that something besides Martin was listening in on every conversation you and your friends had in Vietnam."

"Here I was wondering if maybe it'd been because the guy'd been trained as a LURP, and knew about camouflage and ghilly suits and such. That all the time maybe he'd been just a few yards away from us that day, biding his time and gathering intel. Now you're saying it might have been something else, kind of like spies."

"Could be. We don't know for sure. But if that's true, they

were only too happy to pass along to Martin every scrap of information he needed to carry out his plans against you all."

"Caramba. Either way we handed him the knife to cut our throats." I shook my head. "I wish I would have known that. I would have watched what I'd said more closely."

"Joe," Angela said, "you've touched on a key part of spiritual warfare. Two items are absolutely critical: number one, keep God's Word foremost in your heart and mouth, and number two, remember the name of the Lord is our strong tower. The righteous run to it and are safe."

"It's simple when you put it that way."

I could almost hear her rueful smile coming over the line. "It is simple. But that's not to say it's easy. Following God's Word should be the lifelong pursuit of every believer. When it's not, we always pay a heavy price."

◆ ◊ ◆

Turning off the TV, I checked the time. Ten o'clock. As I picked up the phone to call Marcus, my stomach rumbled again. Not that I was hungry, far from it. Earlier tonight my supper had consisted of two nuked burritos, covered in cheddar cheese, with nachos on the side and root beer to drink. It wasn't the steak dinner I'd envisioned, but still a satisfying blend of brown things and yellow things. But now my stomach was reminding me that I wasn't a kid, and I couldn't eat like one. What was left? Drinking prune juice and watching *Matlock* reruns?

Noodles hadn't fared any better. He'd still not touched his food, and he was also still sulking under the couch. That cat held a grudge the way Ted Williams carried a bat.

I punched in the digits for Marcus's phone I'd written down earlier. The thing rang in that distinctive, muffled, tinny way country lines always do, before it was picked up.

"Hello," Marcus answered in the snuffly manner I recalled so well. He sounded exactly the same as he always had.

"Hey, Marcus. You'll never guess who this is."

"Uh, Reverend Miller?"

Reverend Miller? Who was he? "No, man, it's Joe Box. You remember. From the war."

There was a pause, and then—"Joe. Well, good night nurse. I ain't heered from you in a coon's age!"

My, it was fine to hear Southern dialect again. I like living in Cincinnati, but sometimes a man just has to go back to his roots.

"Same here. How've you been?"

"Aw, fair to middlin'. Waycross didn't get near the rain as usual, so my spuds and beans fared poorly, but the corn came up right smart, so I guess it all worked out. You know what I mean." I surely did. "So what in the world are you doin' with yourself these days?"

"I'm a private investigator, working out of Cincinnati."

"Naw. Is that right? I figured you woulda been some kinda professor or somethin' by now."

"Not hardly. I tried a few things before settling on this."

"Well, I bet you're a whiz at the thing. I always said you was the smartest man I ever knew."

That touched me. "Well, thank you kindly, Marcus."

"Don't mention it. So what can I help you with, Joe?"

There was no easy way to say it. "I've got some bad news."

"Tell me, Joe."

"You're not going to like it, but here it is. Some of our bros—quite a few of them—are dead."

"Aw naw! What? Lemme settle back here. Okay, tell me."

I did, relating each man's name and how he'd died, and after that there was a long pause. I then heard Marcus blow his nose. Was he crying? "Merciful God ..." he said thickly. "All them men ... It don't hardly figure."

"It does when I tell you who's doing it."

"I already know. Martin."

That stopped me. "Now how did you know that?"

"It's the only thing that makes sense," Marcus said, sounding better now. "When you told me how each man had died, I just put two and two together. They all died of what they was skeered of most, right? I remember us talkin' about it. I figured that Martin somehow got wind of that, and now he's croakin' us all just as fast as he can, makin' it look like somethin' besides him."

I whistled. "It's taken me days to get that. You make me sing pretty small."

"So now what?" he said.

"I'm giving the three of you left, including Del and Greg, the heads-up on it. What you all do with it from here on out is up to you."

"Did they buy any a' this?"

"Greg? Yeah, I think so. He's leaving for overseas tomorrow morning, and I guess he thinks that makes him safe." I shook my head. "Del, I don't know. He hung up on me."

"Well, I believe you," Marcus said simply. "And I got the

means to stop him. I got me an old Purdey over-and-under my grandpap bought in England a long time ago. She shoots double-ought buck in the tightest pattern you ever saw. If Martin comes on my land, I'll blow that boy clean in half."

"That'd normally be the way to do it, but my girlfriend says there's more to Martin than we know."

"Girlfriend?" Marcus laughed. "What's your wife have to say about that?"

"Not much," I told him. "I've been a widower for nearly thirty years."

"Oh Lordie, Joe, I'm sorry." Marcus genuinely sounded upset. "I didn't mean—"

"It's all right," I said.

"I know how that is, losin' a wife, I mean," he replied. "I lost my Becky a dozen years ago. The pain's still there, some."

"Yes it is," I said.

"So what did you mean," Marcus asked then, "about your girlfriend sayin' there was more to Martin than we know?"

I told him the rest of it then, about my conversion experience and how that tied into my limited understanding of what was empowering Martin. When I was finished, I somehow knew I'd get a better reaction from Marcus than I'd gotten from Del. I wasn't wrong.

"So you're a Christian now," he said. "Ain't that somethin'? Me too!"

My face lit up in a smile. "Really? When?"

"Right after my Becky died. She was strong in her faith, even when the cancer was takin' her by inches. The last thing she asked me to do was to meet her in heaven someday. At her funeral, Becky's pastor, Reverend Miller, told everybody where she was now, and that she was free of all that pain at long, long last, and asked would anybody like to know how they could see her again someday." So that's who Reverend Miller was: Marcus's wife's pastor. And his too, now, I guessed. "I was the first one to hold up his hand. How about you?"

"Mine doesn't go near that far back, only since last August. It happened right at a really bad time in my life."

"Funny how that works, ain't it?"

"That's a fact."

"Well, now that you got us all warned and all, what's next?"

"I just don't know. From here on out, I'm stumped."

"I know what I'd do, if'n I was you ..." He sounded pensive.

"I'm all ears."

"Get inside the boy's head," Marcus said. "Be him. Think two steps ahead."

I nodded. "Go from hunted to hunter, you mean." It made sense.

"That's the way. What kinda game you ever gone after?"

"Rabbits on up."

"Same here. You know the sayin', that the bigger a critter gets, the craftier the thing is?"

"Yep."

"Well, there you go," he finished. "Give you a for instance. Me 'n a coupla boys from church went on a moose hunt up in Canada two years ago. I nailed me a moose inside of thirty hours, while them other boys stomped around purt near a week and never even got to smell one. Bet you know why."

"Because you thought like your prey. You got inside its head." I narrowed my eyes. "I can't say I care much for the idea of thinking like Martin though."

"I bet not. But you ain't got much of a choice, seems to me."

"You know, this would sure be easier with help," I told him. "And since Greg's going to be gone, and Del doesn't believe it, that leaves just us two." I grinned, warming to the idea. "So what do you say, you old stump-jumper? Couple of Daniel Boones like us ought to make short work of Martin. You could fly up here, or me down there, and we could coordinate how we're going to it."

There was a pause, then Marcus cleared his throat. "I don't know how to say this, and I hate to, but you done struck out with me too."

"Huh?"

There was a longer pause, then—"I ain't got no legs, Joe."

Now it was my turn to be speechless. "But … But how—?"

"It happened a year ago," Marcus said. "One day last fall I dragged the chipper into the barn, so's I could grind up some old rotten barrel staves for mulch. I was in the loft, pitchin' 'em in, when I slipped and fell in myself. The thing ground my legs off right above my knees, quicker'n I could spit."

That his account of the accident was stated so starkly, and with not one ounce of embellishment, made the horror that much more real. "Oh, Marcus," I croaked. "That's—"

"I know," he replied. "I durn near bled to death, and prob'ly would have, if the mailman hadn't found me. And if it hadn't been for some of the men from my church helpin' me along, as well as some neighbors—and they most usually was one and the same—I woulda lost this farm, sure as breakfast."

I still couldn't speak. He went on, "So there's the reason I can't be much help on this hunt. If Martin comes to me, I'll drop him where he stands. Otherwise ..."

Marcus didn't have to finish that for me. I knew what "otherwise" meant. "Otherwise" meant I was completely on my own. Well, except for God, of course. But the idea of a crippled, legless man waiting helplessly as the stalker drew near wouldn't fly either.

"Listen," I said. "Let me come down there. I can stay at your place. It'll be like old times. Between the two of us we can—"

"I can't let you do that, Joe," Marcus broke in. "You got friends up there, maybe kin. A girlfriend anyway. Martin's liable to try for any of 'em. Down here, it's just me."

My voice grew raspier still. "What are you saying? Do you think I'm going to leave you down there helpless while a maniac draws down on you?"

"Helpless?" Marcus shot back with some heat. "I've might have lost my legs, but my eyes is as good as they ever was. Let Martin try anything here, and I got a deer slug that'll settle his hash right smart."

I still didn't like it, but didn't know what else I could do. He was right. To be able to go after Martin I needed mobility, and, as much as I hated it, that let Marcus out. My voice thickened. "Well, okay. But—"

"I'll be fine," he said, cutting me off. This was getting too maudlin for both of us. Then he said, "You know, one of us shoulda parked a round in that boy's chest more'n thirty years ago. We didn't, and now we're payin' the freight. So you handle him from your end, Joe." Marcus's voice was grim. "And if you miss, I won't."

30

I'd gone to bed then, the first part of what I was supposed to do done. All three men had been warned, and now as I lay there I was running different scenarios through my head of how I could anticipate Martin's next move. Thankfully my stomach problems had eased, although Noodles was still giving me the treatment as he skulked under the sofa. By tomorrow his food would be crusted over the top, and he'd really be put out. It's not like I hadn't told him though. Without even noticing when it happened, I was asleep.

And then I was awake.

The room was pitch black as I propped myself up in bed on my elbows, every sense tingling. What had awakened me? Sometimes that happened when Noodles knocked something over, but that wasn't the feel this time. No, something was most definitely wrong, something beyond my cat tipping over a vase. I got up, slipping into my deck shoes as I did. If something was broken in the kitchen, I didn't want my bare feet to be the first to find out.

My bedroom connected directly into the living room, and as I came in I flipped the light on, peering around. I couldn't see anything out of place, but the feeling of *wrongness* was stronger here. What was going on?

Then without warning two words blasted into my mind, words I instinctively knew were from on high.

Get out.

What the—? The warning came again, more urgent still.

Get out. Now.

There was no time to argue. Deep inside, a switch had been thrown. I didn't know how many seconds were left, but I knew they were few.

Thankful that I slept in cutoff shorts and didn't need to change, I rocketed out my door, pounding down the hall and up a flight of ill-lit stairs.

My neighbor just above was an old German expatriate by the name of Mr. Platz. I sincerely hoped he was still awake, as his hearing was starting to go.

I banged my fist on the side of his door, just as hard and as fast as I could as I screamed his name. "Mr. Platz! Wake up! Wake up, Mr. Platz, it's Joe! Mr.—"

His door flew open. "Vhat on *earth*?" As he clutched a magazine—idiot that I am for detail, I noticed it was *Der Speigel*—the old man's eyes were as big as a lemur's. "Vhat are you doink, Joe? Haff you gone mad?"

I grabbed him by his arm, not much caring whether he liked that or not, and began pulling him from his apartment. "Something's wrong, Mr. Platz! We need to get out!"

He was still befuddled. "Iss it a bomb? I do not understand …"

"No time." I was now tugging him down the hall toward the staircase. "Who else is in the building?" Mr. Platz normally made it his business to know the comings and goings of the Agnes's few tenants. As a rule I didn't much care for that part of the old man's habits, but tonight it was critical.

"Who else?" he muttered as I yanked him along. "Most people are gone, left for ze holidays …"

We reached the stairs, and I spun the old man around so he was facing me. "Mr. Platz. *Who?*"

His eyes still weren't focused on me. "Mrs. Dobrowski, I think, in 3-C. And zat artist fellow, zat new man, in 1-A. Vhat iss his name …?"

"I'll get them," I said, giving him a slight shove. "Just go!"

For a second I didn't know if he was going to do that, and that I might have to carry him. Then he started moving down the stairs, only a lot slower than I liked. As he made his way down, I ran back down the hall. The building only had three floors, and Mrs. Dobrowski's unit was next to Mr. Platz's. As I reached her door, she wrenched it open. Mrs. Dobrowski was a formidable woman in her late seventies, a widowed schoolteacher, so I'd heard. The stories must have been true as she gave me a glare that would have turned a sixth-grader into goo. "Joe. Is that you making all that racket? What in the world is going on?"

I grabbed her hand. "No time to explain. You need to leave."

She slapped my hand free. "Don't touch me. Have you been drinking again? I thought you abandoned that when you got religion."

This was definitely neither the time nor the place for a theological discussion. I needed to get the old crank moving, and something Mr. Platz had said fit the bill. "Bomb!" I said. "There's a bomb in the building!"

"A *bomb!*" Mrs. Dobrowski nearly turned me into road pizza in her haste to rush past me on her way to the stairs. She made good time down them, moving faster than a woman her age had any right to, me hard on her heels. As she flew out the main door, I kept going around, down one more flight into the basement.

The four apartments down here made the ones on my floor look like magazine ads. Dank, dark, and spidery, it was no wonder the landlord only had one of them rented, to the "artist" Mr. Platz had spoken of. Artist was a relative term. I, too, couldn't place the name of the young guy who called the joint home, but I'd helped him the day he moved in, back last spring. As I'd carried in the stretched canvas with his finished works on them, I'd gotten a gander of what he termed art: bright, messy, impressionistic claptrap. Maybe the man's name was von Schumpter. Whatever he was called, I could tell he was feeling no pain as he answered my pounding.

"Hey, man." Rail thin and disheveled, his eyes were dull, glazed, and moving in two separate directions. "Who started the war?"

I pulled him out of his place by one of his paint-splattered hands. "Nobody! Just run!"

He easily slid his hand free, and now I saw my own was covered in an oily rainbow. "You need to chill, dude," he slurred. "Life's too short." His pupils were pinpricks, and whatever he'd been doing in there, he'd been doing for a while.

I grabbed him by the belt holding his nasty jeans up. "Partner, you said a mouthful!" And with that I practically dragged him bodily up the stairs. A few seconds later all four of us were standing by the fountain.

"Is everybody here?" I panted.

Mr. Platz continued to look befuddled, the young guy more so, and Mrs. Dobrowski was going for the patent on that glare. "Well, Joe? What—?"

The Agnes exploded.

The sound was unbelievable, a throat-ripping roar that squeezed the body as it violated the mind. I'd never heard anything like it, and that included my time in combat. All four us were way too close, and we tumbled every which way like marionettes with our strings cut as the intense heat washed over us like surf. All of us were screaming, because all of us thought we were dead.

I ended up flat on my back on the far side of the fountain, so I had a world-class view of the hideous fireball rolling out of the Agnes's roof. Then doing a pretty fair imitation of a sand crab, I moved as fast as I could, still on my back, away from the heat. Clambering to my feet, I ran to check on the others. The fire department trucks must not have been too far away, maybe on their way back from another call, because in the distance I could faintly hear approaching sirens. I say faintly, because it seemed my hearing was 90 percent gone.

The first person I came to was the "artist." He was sitting on his butt, clapping his hands and grinning as he stared rapturously into the inferno. "Bravo, man! Rock and roll! I gotta paint this." He looked around. "Hey, where's all my stuff?" Forget this guy. I looked over to my left. There, a few feet away, lay Mrs. Dobrowski, clutching her head.

Kneeling beside her, I gently pulled her hand away. Swiftly flowing bright-red blood coursed down the side of her face. I gulped. I'd seen this before. I swallowed again as I tried to put the picture out of my head of how my wife's face had looked the night she died in that wreck. Talk about a flashback. Blinking back tears, I smiled at the old lady. "Lay back and rest, Mrs. Dobrowski. Help is on the way." I reached down and ripped the lower part of her nightgown off, wadding it up and using it to staunch the blood.

"What's going on?" she was moaning, over and over. "What's going on?"

"Press that tight," I said, my voice sounding distant in my own ears. "I'll be right back." As I stood up to look for Mr. Platz, another crash came from the Agnes. I turned to see. One of her flaming walls had now fallen outward, flattening and burning the vehicles parked on that side. The Goddess was one of them. I shook my head, then I thought I heard a cry. I whipped around toward it. Mr. Platz.

I ran over to him, finding his clothes scorched, his eyebrows gone, and his *Der Speigel* smoldering. I slapped it out of his hand. The sirens were getting closer. "Mr. Platz! Are you all right?" I quickly spun him around, finding nothing else on him burning.

He was gazing at me in horror. "Joe. Vhat happent? Vhat happent?"

I lowered him to the grass as the first of the engine companies pulled in. "Rest easy, Mr. Platz. Everything is going to be all right." Kneeling beside him, I turned back to the Agnes. She was fully involved now, and even as the firefighters frantically began unrolling hoses, I knew it was hopeless. Nothing in that building was going to be saved tonight.

Then I felt Mr. Platz squeeze my hand, and I looked down. "Joe?" His eyes searched mine. "Joe, vere iss Noodles?"

31

*J*ack Mulrooney mashed his cigarette into the beaten metal ashtray lying in the center of the equally beaten old metal desk. As he grinned down at me, smoke trickled out of his nostrils like a low-rent dragon. He'd told me he'd specifically asked to be the one to interrogate me, even though he's vice; I guess fun's where you find it, and old Jack was obviously enjoying himself tonight. How I'd ended up here, I was still trying to figure out. The firemen were finally getting the blaze under control when the police arrived on scene, and they immediately began taking statements from all of us who'd called the Agnes home. The "artist" and I were invited to give a more complete accounting downtown, no big surprise there, while Mr. Platz and Mrs. Drobrowski were taken on to Mercy Franciscan Hospital in Mount Airy for observation. Something must not have jibed in what I told the first batch of cops, because the artist was released right about the same time I was escorted down here.

Jack and I were now both deep in the bowels of police headquarters, down in one of the interrogation rooms. Back when I was on the force we called the place the Dungeon. The name still fit. The walls around me were a nasty institutional puke-green, the harsh light above hidden behind non-breakable mesh, and the trashy furniture was old back when Kaiser Bill was still launching U-boats.

Jack bent down over me, his breath rank from smoke and whatever he'd had for dinner. His grin hadn't left. "Comfy enough, Joe?"

Solicitous cuss, wasn't he? Comfy? Not even close. Battered though it was, the metal chair I was parked on felt as hard as titanium, and my left wrist was throbbing, because it was manacled to a chain. The other end of the chain was fastened to a D-ring bolted into the floor. I was far from comfy. But I wasn't about to tell him that.

"Oh yeah," I said. "I've never sat on a better chair. Who's your decorator?"

"That doesn't matter," he grinned. "Not to you, at any rate. You got burned out tonight, remember?"

"Yeah, Jack, I do," I nodded. "Thanks for reminding me."

"Don't mention it." He pulled out yet another cigarette and lit it, his fifth since two uniformed cops had brought me in earlier. If you smoke—filthy habit—that'll give you an idea how long I'd been held. He blew a plume of carcinogenic gas up toward the lights. "So. Care to make a statement yet?"

I shook my head. My hearing was slowly returning, but

every sound still had the background noise of a dentist's drill. "Say that again?"

His grin slipped a bit. "A statement. Would you care to make one?"

"Yes, Jack. I'd like to state that it's a miracle you keep your teeth so white, smoking as much as you do. What's your secret? Gargling bleach?"

His eyes narrowed. "I'm glad to see you haven't lost your sense of humor, but I don't think you appreciate yet the delicacy of your situation."

I smiled, even though my skull was still ringing. "Enlighten me."

"Sure, glad to," he said. "The charges that could be made against you include arson, incitement to panic, terrorism—"

My smile dropped. *"Terrorism?"*

Jack spread his hands. "It's the times, Joe, what can I say? These days people are looking for terrorists under every bush."

I slumped back in my chair. I wanted out of there. Now. "How about cracking a window?" I said. "This place stinks."

He chuckled. "No can do, pal, house rules. Something you would've remembered if you hadn't quit the force."

"Look, not that again," I sighed. "Look, Jack, we've danced around long enough. Either charge me or spring me. My fanny hurts, my ears are ringing, and the longer I smell your breath, the better a forty-day fast sounds."

"Gosh, I hate to hear all that," he said. "But I imagine the charges will be coming soon enough. The DA's working on them even as we speak. When he's done, don't worry, we'll find a nice cell for you." Jack lowered his voice. "And just between you and me, he's not any happier at being dragged down here in the middle of the night than I am." He grinned again. "But I'm taking it better. I've dreamed of this night. I really have."

I sighed again. "So you think I'm an arsonist." I shook my head. "That's insane. What kind of arsonist burns the building he lives in?"

"The worst kind. The kind who plants a firebomb, then shows how much he's a hero by pulling everybody out right before it goes off." Jack's smile was wry. "But I do have to say, Joe, you've got guts. Your neighbors tell us you cut it pretty close, all things considered." He drew another lungful of smoke, letting it puff out of his lips as he went on, "You might consider copping to insanity. I would, it's easy time. I'd think the police shrinks would love to take a stab at seeing what makes you run."

"Funny. I was thinking the same thing about you."

He again leaned down over me, just like I'd done to Henrik ten Eyck—when was it, earlier today? could that be?—only Jack put his hands on the arms of my chair. "We've got you, Joe, face it. That old woman, Mrs. Dobrowksi, already told us how it went down tonight. You were running all over the building yelling 'bomb,' and then sure enough"—his eyes bulged—"Boom!"

So that's what had put me in the Dungeon. "It won't wash, Jack. Where could I get enough explosives to take out an entire building?"

"You're a combat vet," he replied. "I'd bet there's lots of

things you know about. Including where to get the makings for a bomb."

"But what would be the *point*?" I rasped, on the verge of losing it. In one fell swoop tonight I'd lost my dwelling, my belongings, my car, and my cat.

Noodles' dying was the worst. I almost wanted to scream at the unfairness of it all. I'd rescued his little self from being burned alive, and he'd ended up being burned alive anyway. And now, instead of being able to grieve in peace, I was having to spend what energy I had left staying out of lockup.

To top it off, Martin had blown his chance to kill me tonight, and I didn't know how he was going to deal with that failure. All this pressure; I couldn't stand it. Right at that moment, as I sat homeless in that dank, grim hole, staring up at Jack's smirking puss, God seemed to be on Neptune.

"I want a lawyer," I croaked.

"First smart thing you've said all night." Jack reached into his inside suit pocket, pulling out a small cell phone. "Here. Use mine. I insist." And he grinned again.

I was in the process of using it to call an attorney I'd done some work for in the past when somebody knocked once and opened the door.

Jack turned, irritated. "I thought I said I didn't want to be disturbed."

"Sorry, Lieutenant," the young uniformed cop said. "Inspector Ravine from arson is here and wants to speak with you right away."

Jack shook his head. "Tell the inspector to wait. I'm not finished yet."

"Oh, yes you are," I heard an authoritative voice—a woman's—say. With that a weary-looking African-American lady in her late forties pushed the door wide and the young cop aside. She was dressed in business casual, and wouldn't have looked out of place behind the desk in a bank, except her outfit was smudged and soiled, and her pants' cuffs were wet. As she came in, the smell of smoke on her overpowered what was coming off Jack.

The uniformed cop shrugged as he left, and Jack frowned at the woman. "Olivia, can't this wait? I'm interrogating a suspect."

"You may be interrogating him," she said, "but he's not a suspect."

"What?"

"I finally got inside the place. Still a few hot spots, but I saw what I needed to." She waved a manila folder at him. "It's all in here, and you're going to hate it. Prelim findings show no evidence of a bomb. No evidence, no suspect. Sorry."

"But—"

She pulled a chair close and sat down heavily in it. "Read it yourself. I'm beat." Jack still looked lost, because the woman said, "Okay, to give you the skinny, what we found in the basement has all the earmarks of a faulty gas line."

"*Gas line?*" Jack's eyebrows climbed in disbelief. "I saw the coverage on the news tonight. The fire chief said he'd never seen one burn so hot. You're saying a gas line explosion did that?" He pointed a finger at me. "And if Box isn't guilty, how did he know what was going to happen beforehand?"

"I'm not saying anything, Jack, not yet. What I am telling you is we did a gas chromatograph scan of the building's interior and found no traces of TNT, flammable liquids, C-4, or anything else. What we found instead was a natural gas furnace older than Methuselah attached to cracked feeder lines coming in from the wall. Maintenance was not a high priority at the Agnes Apartments."

"That's true," I spoke up. I'd hung up Jack's phone before the attorney had answered. "We either roasted or froze every winter. That furnace hadn't been checked since Wendell Wilkie ran for president." They both looked at me as if they were amazed I could talk. "Well, it hadn't," I said.

The inspector shook her head at me and then said to Jack, "This is going to hurt, but I'm recommending we cut him loose."

He gritted his teeth. "Not on your life, Olivia. No way."

The inspector stood. "Jack. The whole department knows you've had issues with this guy for some time. But think. Is he worth a civil suit for false arrest? Or departmental hearings? I understand internal affairs has been given a quota to root out the 'bad actors,' as the new chief puts it. Don't let one of them be you."

"IA plays their games, and I play mine," Jack said, his words clipped.

The inspector lightly touched his arm. "Listen, Lieutenant," she muttered, obviously trying to stroke his ego. "It could be this guy is dirty on a lot of things"—she shot me a look—"no offense."

"None taken," I smiled.

She turned her attention back to him. "But not on this. I'm sure of it."

They looked at each other a moment longer, then Jack slumped like he'd sprung a leak. "Oh, all right," he sighed. He rubbed his face, then yelled out, "Carnetti!"

The young cop who had spoken earlier stuck his head back inside. "Yeah, Lieutenant?"

The words squeezed out of Jack like they'd cost him a month's pay each. "Carnetti, take this guy out of here. Give him back his wallet and keys and throw him out the door. Tell booking to cancel his cell."

Cracking his gum, the young cop furrowed his brow. "You sure about that, Lieutenant?"

"Do it!" Jack barked.

Carnetti nodded, "Yes sir," then he glared at me, giving me his tough-guy look. "Come on you, let's roll."

I held up my chained hand. "Can't."

Sighing again, and muttering obscenities, Jack bent down and undid the metal clasp holding my wrist, letting it fall clanking to the floor. The blood rushed back in, making my fingers tingle. I wiggled them as I stood. "Thanks, Jack. Here's your phone." I held it out to him, and he snatched it from me. I went to push past, but he stopped me with a heavy hand on my shoulder.

"Next time, pal." His voice was soft and full of menace. "Next time you're mine."

"Next time, *pal*, you'll screw up and catch the right guy." Before Jack could reply, I looked at Carnetti. "Let's get my effects, kid. I need some air."

32

I checked my wristwatch. The crystal face was badly scratched from my gymnastics performance last night by the Agnes's fountain, but I could still read the time: 6:05 AM I'd been a free man for the last three minutes. I was standing in front of police headquarters, with everything I owned in the world, except for what was back at my office, held in two pockets of the cutoff jeans I was wearing. I pulled everything out, doing a quick inventory: in front were my car and apartment keys (no longer needed), office key, and a little more than fifty cents. My back pocket held my wallet, containing my driver's license, PI ticket, concealed-carry permit, Social Security ID, eleven dollars, and a maxed-out Visa card. I didn't even have on a shirt.

I checked my sockless feet. My old deck shoes had seen better days. Maybe Jack should have booked me at that; at least I'd be wearing an orange jumpsuit, and my cell would have been reasonably warm. My teeth picked that time to start chattering. I was dressed okay for a day in Key West, but right now the temperature in Cincinnati had to have been no more than forty degrees, and the leaden sky looked like snow. Wouldn't that be dandy.

Even though the population on the street at that hour had to have seen their share of odd sights, the looks I was getting from the few folks up and around at that early hour were ones of wonderment. One particular old wino stopped and stared, and he wasn't such a prize himself. Replete with matted gray hair and scraggly beard, dressed in dumpster chic, and smelling like he'd been dead a month, the codger appeared to be the aboriginal grit, yet he was looking at me like I was the one deserving pity.

"It's okay," I grinned, my heart not in it. "I'm a nature lover."

Muttering and shaking his head at me, the old man shuffled on.

The shivering was getting worse. I needed help, right away. I looked up and down the street for a pay phone, finally spying one a block and half down. Praying it was still in working order, I began double-timing it down toward the thing. Mentally I knew that if it was broken, I could still go back and entreat the desk sergeant for use of one of the department's phones. But I knew that act of desperation would get back to Jack, and I simply didn't want to give the boy the satisfaction. So here I was sprinting like a half-naked, rapidly-freezing 220 runner toward a possibly dead phone, instead of turning around and asking for aid from the cops who'd held me. Isn't pride dumb?

I reached the phone and lifted the receiver, trying to ignore the fact the handset was gummy with something I didn't want to think about. Putting it to my ear, I was grateful to hear the soothing sounds of a dial tone. Now if only Angela hadn't left yet. Muttering a quick prayer under my breath, I dropped in the money, punched in her number, and waited. Four rings, and her machine kicked on. Great. Not only wasn't she there, I'd wasted my change. But I began to leave a message anyway.

"Ange, it's Joe. Listen—"

There was the sound of her phone being snatched up. "Joe? Are you all right?" She sounded out of breath.

"I need help," I said simply.

"Where are you? What's happened?"

"I'm outside of District One headquarters, on Ezzard Charles. The Agnes burned last night, and the cops just now released me."

"What? The Agnes—"

"I'll tell you all about it later, but I need you to come and pick me up. Bring clothes, Ange. Anything. I only got out with my cutoffs and shoes."

"So that's what had me up all night praying," she said. "Did you—"

"Could you hurry it up?" I broke in. "I'm so cold right now I'm doing the Charleston, and I don't even dance."

"I'm on my way."

"Meet me outside of the lobby of the cop house," I said. "And bring coffee too. Lots."

Without waiting for an answer, I hung up. Then, shaking like a malaria victim, I ran flat-out back up to District One. I only slowed down when I reached the doors, sauntering in like I was enjoying a fine summer day.

The old sergeant behind the desk put down what he was working on and frowned. "Forget something?"

"Nope." I was trying to keep my teeth from clacking. "Got somebody coming for me. I just thought I'd wait here."

"Lieutenant Mulrooney has a bet going," the old cop told me, resting his chin on his fist. "He was saying you'd be back, freezing and begging a ride."

"Not a bit of it," I replied with a smile of dismissal. "I'm fine." The fact that my skin had bigger bumps on it than next week's Butterball turkey made that an obvious lie.

The old cop shook his head and went back to his work.

Fifteen minutes later Angela pulled up in her 1997 white Pontiac Grand Am. Those never were my favorite cars, but right now pickiness wasn't an option. She swung the passenger door wide, and I trudged across the sidewalk and climbed inside. The events of the last eight hours were beginning to crash in on me. I slammed the door shut with a grunt.

Pulling away from the curb, she handed me a Styrofoam cup. I leaned my neck back into the headrest. "Thanks," was all I said.

"There's some of my brother's things in that paper bag by your feet," she said. "He's still in Guatemala, so I don't think he'll mind me snagging some of his clothes. The shoes may be a tight fit, but everything else should work."

"Thanks," I said again. I took a long pull of the hot coffee, then began to slowly root through the bag. Inside were a blue sweat suit, gray socks, and a pair of off-white running shoes. "This is great, Ange," I said, trying for enthusiasm—and failing— as I pulled everything on. Between the coffee and the clothes, I was already getting warmer. Now fully dressed, I fell silent once again as I resumed staring out the passenger window.

We rode on that way for a bit. I had no idea where we were going. Worse, I didn't care.

She must have been reading my mind. "I just thought we'd drive for a while. Okay?"

"Whatever." I was still staring out the window at nothing in particular. Then I said,

"Today's Sunday. What about church? And your class?"

"I'll miss it this morning," was all she said. We rode that way for another fifteen minutes, then I sensed her eyes on me.

I turned to her, spreading my left thumb and forefinger an inch apart. "I came this close last night. This close." My throat felt raw, and I dropped my hand back into my lap, staring out the windshield. "Everything's gone."

Her voice was soft. "Tell me."

I did. In a monotone, I related all the events from the time we hung up last night to my phone call to her this morning. "Where did you say we're going?" I asked then.

"Nowhere. We'll see."

My brain felt like an old record slowing down. "I lost it all," I said.

"I know."

"Noodles is dead, Ange." My eyes were tearing. "He

burned up." I again put my head back, closing my eyes. "I could sleep for years."

"Let him sleep, dear Lord," she whispered.

Blackness floated down on me like a benediction.

◆ ◊ ◆

I came awake with a start. Where was I? I whipped my head around. Angela and I were still in her car, still moving. Soft instrumental music was flowing out of the CD player. I had no idea who the guitar player was, but he was very good.

Angela glanced over at me with a smile. "Welcome back."

Rapidly I drywashed my face. "Where are we? How long was I out?"

"A couple of hours. We're going to the pastor's house. I called him from here. I've just been driving around until you woke up."

I tried looking at my watch, but my eyes wouldn't focus. "Couple of hours? What time is it, around eight? Who's that playing?"

"Nearer eight-thirty. Donna said she'd have breakfast waiting. That's Doyle Dykes."

"Breakfast ..." My brain still felt fuzzy. "Wait a minute. Doesn't Luke have to preach this morning?"

"Pastor Tony has it covered," Angela said. "Pastor Franklin wants to talk to you, see how you're doing."

The memories came flooding back. "Well, for this being my first time as a homeless person, I'm top-notch."

There was a pause, then Angela said, "There's a thermos on the back seat with more hot coffee. Take some if you want."

I realized that last crack of mine had sounded bad. "I'm sorry, babe." I'd said that word again. "I didn't mean—"

She reached over and patted my leg, the love liquid in her eyes. "I can't imagine what you've been through, Joe. But Pastor Franklin said to tell you the Pike is ready to help in any way they can. Just ask."

My throat tightened, and I didn't trust myself to answer. I just put my hand on top of hers and squeezed. We rode the rest of the way to the Franklin's house in silence.

In another twenty minutes we were there. Luke and Donna, along with their sixteen-year-old daughter, Sally, lived in a huge old refurbished farmhouse right next to the new church property. If you stood on their porch facing the highway, the sanctuary and its acreage were on the left, and on the right was a pasture and barn where Luke kept two ancient swaybacked nags he'd had since he was a young man. To the jaundiced eye, those horses were good for nothing, years past their prime. But to someone who loved them, that argument was meaningless. Some animals you keep just because. My eyes began stinging again. I knew how that was.

Angela and I pulled through the gate and made our way on up to the house, parking on the side. As we got out, Luke and Donna came out on their porch and then down to the car. Donna took Angela's hand as Luke embraced me.

"How you doing, man?" he whispered.

"Hurting," was all I said.

He released me. "I'll bet that's true." He looked over at Angela. "Y'all want to come on in the house? I think we're ready to eat."

Donna smiled, "It's not much. Bacon and eggs and grits. Toast if you're a mind to. Joe, Angela said you like pineapple juice, so we picked some up."

With all I had left, I loved all these people. "That would be fine," I managed to say. As the four of us climbed the porch steps, I said to Luke, "Where's Sally?"

"She's already gone on to service this morning," he replied. "I told her I thought it'd be a good idea for the four of us to have some time alone."

"Sounds good," I nodded. "I need it."

After all of us were seated at the kitchen table, we held hands around it and bowed our heads. "Lord," Luke said, "I'm gonna make this short. Bless this food, and bless our time. In Jesus' name, amen." As we let go of one another's hands, he picked up a steaming bowl of eggs, handing it to me. "Scrambled. I hope that's okay, because Donna made a bunch."

I ladled a huge mound of them on my plate. For some reason, my appetite had come roaring back. "Good. I think I could eat a bunch."

The four of us dug in for the next twenty minutes, eating and smiling and drinking pineapple juice and coffee, making small talk all the while. Healing comes in many ways.

Finally Luke wiped his mouth with his napkin and stood. "Let's take our coffee on into the living room. We can talk better there." He looked over at his wife. "Darlin', it's okay if we leave the dishes until later, isn't it?"

"Fine with me," Donna smiled. "It's your turn to do them anyway." We all grabbed our cups and followed Luke on into the adjoining room.

Once inside, he pointed. "Park yourself anywhere you want." He lowered himself down into an old imitation-leather easy chair. "This one's mine," he said, "as long as I get here before the dog." Angela and Donna took opposite ends of the couch, while I took the easy chair's mate next to Luke.

"Man, this feels nice," I said, settling in.

"I know," Luke answered. "The dog likes that one too. It's hard to fool a hound." He set his cup on a small table next to the chair, then turned to me. "Now then. Angela told me on the phone pretty much of what happened last night, so we can go into it more later, if you're up to it. What I'd like to know now is what we can do to help."

His request threw me, because it covered so much ground. "Well—" I started, but Donna cut me off.

"Let's start with the basics," she said. "You'll need a place to stay for a while. You know Dempsey Miller, one of the maintenance men at church, don't you?"

"I think so," I said.

"Sure, you'd remember him if you saw him," Luke jumped in. "He's a big old guy, around seventy, six-foot-five, ruddy face and gray hair. Burps a lot."

"Oh yeah," I said then. "I've seen him around."

"Anyway," Donna said, shooting her husband a look, "Dempsey owns an apartment building in downtown Hamilton, and he said you could take one of his units for free until you find something permanent."

My eyebrows rose. "Are you sure he wants to do that? That seems awfully generous."

"Dempsey got burned out once," Luke replied. "He knows how it is."

"Well … Tell him thanks. I accept."

"Next is food," Donna said. "Angela can tell you about that."

She smiled at me. "You know I'm on the benevolence committee, don't you?"

I shook my head. "I didn't even know there was one."

"Sure," Luke said again. "We set it up for emergencies."

"It's a money fund and food bank," Angela told me. "The storeroom where we keep the nonperishable items was restocked only last week, and the freezer and walk-in fridge are kept full, so we'll head over there in a bit. Feel free to take whatever you need." She looked over at Luke. "Is it okay if we have Irma cut Joe a check for a hundred dollars or so for incidentals?"

"Absolutely," the pastor said.

"Don't forget the car," Donna said to him.

"Car?" My thoughts were swimming. Nice as it was, this was all coming too fast for me to assimilate.

"You ever heard of Tom Gage?" Luke asked me.

"No."

"Tom owns a couple of car lots," he said. "He's also a member here. Not as regular with his attendance as I'd like, but Tom blames that on his business. Anyway, I called him earlier this morning, and he said he could fix you up with something. Now, it's probably not going to be as snazzy as that old Cougar you drove, but it'll be reliable, and Tom'll be more than fair on the price. Unless you've got your eye on something else."

I shook my head. "No," I said again. "Up until last night I hadn't planned on buying another car anytime soon. I guess I can take the guy up on his offer for right now, and use the insurance money from my car for something else later if I need to."

"Speaking of insurance," Donna said, "did you have coverage on the contents of your apartment?"

"Yeah, I did. And I also heard the arson inspector, Ravine I think her name is, tell Jack Mulrooney it looks like the fire's going to be ruled accidental. That should speed up the processing of all our claims."

"All that's left then, I guess, is some clothes," Angela said. "We can raid my brother's things again, but it's pretty picked over. Almost everything else he took with him on his mission trip."

"There's some stuff in the thrift room at church," Luke offered, "but not much in the way of business duds."

"I've never had a whole lot of use for those anyway," I said. "I only had the one suit, and it's history."

"Well, let me do some checking around today," he said. "With four thousand members, we ought to find some clothes that'll work."

For some reason, that last bit made me uncomfortable. "Listen—"

He cut me off. "I know. You feel like a charity case with all this. You're probably harking back to when you were a kid, and your church or relatives helped out strangers. Right?"

I remembered the Suto family. "Yeah."

Luke leaned forward. "Remember what 'charity' means in

its original form. We'd translate the word today as 'love.'" His look was intense. "You're one of us now. A member not only of a local body of believers, but a worldwide one as well. The biblical model tells us that when one laughs, we all laugh. And when one hurts, we all hurt. Sometimes we lose sight of that, but it's still true."

Donna smiled at me. "Let us help you, Joe. We want to. And then, when it comes time, you pass it along to somebody else."

Angela nodded. "Walking with Jesus is just as simple—and as profound—as that."

I put my hands on my knees, staring at the floor, and blew out a breath. "Thanks." The tears came then, unchecked. And I didn't even care.

33

After we'd talked some more, I started feeling tired again. This whole business had taken more out of me than I'd thought. We finished our coffee, and Luke told me to take their guestroom so I could nap. He said they'd all be back directly. A nap sounded good, and so I didn't argue. What woke me up three hours later was Luke slamming something down on the bed.

"Rise and shine, Joe," he laughed. "Take a glance at what we found." I sat up, rubbing my eyes and staring at two big cardboard boxes perched next to me. "Clothes," he said. "Winter ones. I had Pastor Tony make an announcement from the pulpit this morning about what all you needed, and your basic size, and several of the folks went home and brought back these." He opened one of the boxes, pawing through its contents. "Let's see, you've got jeans in here, casual shirts, sweatshirts, a couple of flannels—I'd like those myself—tennis shoes, deck shoes, slippers ... hey, dress shoes too. Black Bostonians. Nice." He flipped open the second box. "Well look here. Collette Weik clerks at Wal-Mart. She must have bought you some underwear and socks. She's an older single lady, you know. Bless her heart."

I still didn't know what to say.

"Oh yeah, here." Luke dug in his pocket, pulling out a key. "I already talked to Dempsey, and this is to your apartment: 2611 Hampshire, number 6. I know the building. It's old, but nice. Dempsey keeps on top of things there. He told me it's yours until you get something permanent. Angela's already taken a couple of the ladies from the benevolence committee over there with some food. She said she knew pretty much what you liked. Brown things and yellow things." He laughed again. "Guy food, right?"

"Right," I grinned. I was overwhelmed, but wasn't minding the feeling.

"All that's left now is the car," Luke said. "Angela asked me to have you call her as soon as you were up. I guess she's still at your new place. Tom said he'd meet you both at his lot on Route 4 whenever you're ready."

"I'm ready now," I said, getting out of the bed. "Uh, is there someplace I could get washed up first? My BO could be classified as a new life form."

"Sure," Luke laughed. He pointed through the bedroom door down the hall. "The main bathroom, the one with the shower and tub, is there. Towels are on the shelf over the john; soap, shampoo, and razors under the sink. Take your time. The water heater we have here's big enough for a missile cruiser."

"Good," I said as I started down the hall. "As my Granny used to say, I'm not fit for decent company."

Twenty minutes later—and a good deal cleaner—I was out of the shower and into some of my donated clothes: new Jockeys, black jeans, gray sweatshirt, sneakers. I'd come back into the bedroom to give Angela a call before I bathed, figuring to shave some time off. I wasn't wrong.

I was just combing my hair when Luke knocked on the bedroom door. "Joe, you decent? Angela's here."

"On my way," I said.

As I came into the living room, Angela and Donna were seated there, and Angela smiled. "Wow. You clean up pretty good."

"I know. You can't tell it by looking that only last night I was one step away from the dude with the sickle." I held the two boxes. In one I'd combined all the clothes I'd been given, and in the other were my dirty things, mine and Angela's brother's. "We need to find a Laundromat," I told her.

"There's a washer and dryer at your building," Luke said. "Dempsey said to tell you it's in the basement."

"That'll work," I smiled. Then my smile fell away. "This isn't over yet. All of you do know that, right?"

Luke nodded. "We know."

"Martin missed nailing me last night by a whisker," I said. "He's out there now, somewhere. Maybe he's planning on trying again right away, or maybe he's going to go after Del or Marcus or Greg, and save me for last, right before he makes a try for his dad. I just don't know."

"I talked to John Bohe earlier today," Angela said. "He and I have called a special meeting of the intercessory prayer group for tonight, after the evening service. You're not alone in this, Joe. You never have been."

I nodded grimly. "I'll need every prayer you've got, and then some." I put down the boxes and held out my hand to Luke. "Well, I guess I need to go grab some wheels. Thanks, pastor. For everything." We shook, then embraced.

"Go with God," he said roughly. "And remember, keep his Word first place. It's your sword and shield."

From there Angela and I left to meet the car dealer at his lot. It took about fifteen minutes to find his place on Route 4, and as we pulled in, he came out of his little trailer office.

"Well, I'll leave you to it," Angela smiled as I got out. "This is guy stuff. Call me later, okay?"

"You've got it." As she pulled away, the man walked up.

"Hi, I'm Tom Gage," he smiled, extending his hand. "And you must be Joe." Gage was in his early thirties and pleasant looking, with the blackest hair I'd ever seen.

"I must be," I said as we shook. "Pastor Franklin said you might have a car for me."

"Yeah, I think so. It's over here." As we walked I got a view of the inventory. Gage's dealership was one of those "pay-on-the-lot" places. You've seen them: usually they're the fourth—and last—incarnation of whatever business had tried the location before. Mostly the stock consists of used cars of roughly ten-year-old vintage. A lot of folks give them a wide berth, but fifteen years ago I'd found the Goddess on just such a lot down in Richmond.

"Here we are," Gage said as we rounded the corner on the last row. "Not pretty, but she'll get you from here to there. And the price is right."

I stopped, staring. Then I looked at him. "You're kidding. Right?"

"Not at all," he answered. "I always thought the Yugo had gotten a bad rap. This one here only has thirty-five thousand miles on it."

"And every one of them a stone-cold embarrassment." I walked around the car. Being a Yugo, that didn't take long. To me a Yugo always looked like the box a nicer car would come in. This one was no exception. It was a squatty mustard-yellow, with the left taillight plastered with red repair tape and the back bumper held on with rope. I bent down by the driver's door. Right in the center was a bullet hole. Nine millimeter, if I wasn't mistaken. "Thirty-five thousand miles, you said?"

"Yep."

"I thought they used kilometers in Beirut."

"Beirut? No, this one was involved in a drug bust in Withamsville."

"A *drug* bust?" I stood, shaking my head. "What self-respecting drug dealer would drive this vehicle?"

"A dumb one," Gage laughed. "The driver caught one in the belly."

"So you'd like to sell me a drug-dealer's death car. Tom, I'm touched."

"Who said sell?" he asked. "I guess the pastor didn't make it clear. I'm giving this to you."

That stopped me. "What? Giving?"

"The pastor told me what happened last night," Gage said. "That Cougar of yours sounds like it was one sweet ride. Now I don't have anything on either of my lots close to that, and I'm not likely to either, but I've seen my share of hard times. This is how I'd like to help. It'll hold you until you get something better."

My voice felt rough. "Man. When you said the price was right, I—"

"Aw, I picked this thing up at a police auction a month ago," Gage said, waving off my emotion. "I figured if I couldn't sell it, I'd donate it as a tax write-off. So yeah, the price is right." He laughed again. "What's better than free?"

"Not much," I smiled.

"Come on back into the office for the title and keys," he said. "In five minutes you'll be the proud owner of the world's most under-appreciated car."

And so I was. The owner, that is. Not necessarily proud. As I pulled away from his lot, Gage waved like a father watching his son leaving the nest. I slouched down as I drove. I'd told him I was really thankful for his gift, but mercy. I hoped I wouldn't see anybody I knew.

Route 4 intersects with the I-275 exchange, and on impulse I turned west on it. For lack of anything better to do, I thought I'd take a look at the site where the Agnes once stood. Morbid? Possibly. But it had been my home for a dozen years. Noodles' too.

Unbidden, the picture of the last time I'd seen him—only last night?—entered my mind. I swallowed and clenched the wheel tighter. Get a grip, Box. He was just a cat. But a different part of me answered, no. He was my friend.

Then another picture floated into my brain, that of the bridge of Martin ten Eyck's nose centered square in my crosshairs.

I smiled.

Soon, Martin. Soon.

34

Five minutes on the highway led me to the Mount Healthy exit, and then I turned left on Hamilton Avenue. It wasn't far now. A mile and a half down, I turned left onto Riley, my street. Former street.

Approaching the site I slowed down, then stopped. I extricated myself from the little car, then just stood and stared. There was almost nothing left of the Agnes. Ignoring the police tape that had been strung clear out to the curb, I stepped over it and onto the property.

The Agnes was a shell. Three walls were all that were left of her, the fourth having collapsed outward onto the parking lot. The rubble was still there, and I knew that several cars and trucks were entombed under the brick, the Goddess among them. Sorry, hon. The scraggly grass out front was trampled and torn from the feet of the firefighters who'd done their best to save the building. It had been hopeless. I remembered Jack saying to the arson investigator that the fire chief had "never seen one burn so hot." I didn't doubt that, considering the Agnes's demise had been fueled from hell's fire.

The stench of smoke was overpowering. As I picked my way around toward the back, a woman from one of the adjoining buildings came out on her stoop. Thankfully the places on either side of the Agnes had been spared the apartment's fate.

"Hey," the woman called. "The cops won't like you hanging around here."

I looked over at her. She was dowdy, in her late forties, hair in curlers and sixty pounds past her prime. A cigarette dangled dangerously from her lips as she gathered her ratty housecoat closer. "It's all right," I said. "I used to live here."

"Says you," the woman shot back. "How do I know you're not a thief?"

"You're right," I nodded. "I'm a thief. I steal scorched brick from burned-out buildings. Call the cops. I'll go quietly."

Scowling and muttering curses, the woman turned and went back inside.

I shook my head and made my way back around to the front of the building. After climbing the steps to the stoop, I peered past what was left of the doorway into the foyer. The stairs leading down were still somewhat intact, but I wouldn't have tried them on a bet. Remembering that Inspector Ravine had traversed these very stairs last night, even before the fire was completely out, made my admiration of her, and those like her, crank up several points. I looked up to where my floor should have been and saw only gray sky. The fire-ball I'd seen had cored this building as neatly as a pineapple. Noodles never had a chance.

Jamming my hands into my pockets, I trotted the three steps back down to ground level, walked down the sidewalk, climbed into the Yugo, and drove away.

As I took a final glance at her in the rearview mirror, the wreck of the Agnes jutted up like the remnants of a broken heart.

♦ ◊ ♦

After that happy jaunt, I cruised on down Hamilton, another mile or so, to my office. This being late on Sunday afternoon, I didn't figure there would be anyone in any of the other businesses the building hosted: the Allenby Insurance Agency, Whizzer Jokes and Novelty, or Pronto Printing, Mr. Yee/Lee's place. I wasn't wrong. This time of year the sun set early, and even though it was only going on five-thirty, it was nearly dark as I pulled the Yugo up in front of the old refurbished apartment house that held our places of employment.

I climbed the stairs up to the second floor and unlocked my door. As I stepped in, I flipped on the lights, then I just stood there, looking around. What was I after here? Blamed if I knew; maybe just the assurance that this part of my life, at least, was still intact. Then I spied Mister Monk Junior next to the picture of Linda on top of the filing cabinet, and once again I thanked God I'd had the foresight to bring them here last summer. It was bad enough losing Noodles in the fire; if I'd lost those last links to my wife and my son, I don't know if I could have stood it.

I went over and checked my machine for messages. Nothing. After standing there stupidly for another minute or so, I turned and left, locking the door behind me. Time to head home—wherever that was. Where the heck *was* Hampshire Drive anyway? I didn't have a clue; what I knew about the city of Hamilton you could fold up in a flea's navel and still have room for lint. Sighing, and feeling dumb, I went back into the office and retrieved an area map from my desk.

As I sat jammed in the Yugo, I turned the map to the Hamilton streets. I flipped on the car's radio as I began my search, wanting some background noise to drown out the pain of my losses. I was just narrowing the grid down when the song ended, and the news came on. National and international stuff at first; vitally important, I knew, but not to me, not now.

Then I dropped the map as my attention was riveted by the third news story.

"… crashed outside of New York City. To repeat, a Bell helicopter carrying six people on their way from Teaneck, New Jersey, has crashed into a maintenance hanger at New York's Kennedy International Airport. All six people aboard the craft, which had been leased to Gregory Dapp Construction of Teaneck, were killed. Among those was Dapp, the company's president. Included in the dead were his pilot and crew, along with four aircraft service personnel on the ground. The cause of the accident remains unknown, but tower workers who witnessed the tragedy stated the helicopter was on its final approach when it began flying erratically. Moments later, and still several hundred feet from touchdown, it reportedly lost power and crashed into a hanger, killing four. Six workers were injured in the mishap, which caused massive damage both to the hanger and the three Boeing 767s it housed. The ensuing fire is currently being battled by four engine companies from New York, as well as by emergency airport ground crews. The FAA has dispatched investigators to the scene. Because Dapp had been on his way to Saudi Arabia to do initial work on a desert racetrack being funded by billionaire oil magnate Sheikh Abu Ibn-Assad, elements from both the Homeland Security Agency and the FBI have been alerted, although at this time officials are cautious about the possibility of this incident being terrorist related. More later. Sylvia Wagner, CBS News."

I flipped the radio off, staring. Martin again. "The dark side of the moon ..." I whispered. "Sorry, Greg." Silently I said a prayer for him, hoping it would make a difference. Then I fired up the Yugo and headed up the road.

♦ ◊ ♦

"You the new guy?" The words were said to me in a menacing tone as I was in the process of swinging my new apartment door wide. I turned to see who it was, which wasn't easy, since I had both boxes of clothes balanced in one hand while I held the door key in the other. The young man who'd spoken stepped up closer to me. He didn't offer to help.

"That's right."

The guy cocked his head. "What's your name?"

I almost said "Puddentame," but didn't. Call me judgmental, but I didn't care much for this kid's looks. He was maybe twenty years old, beefy, with a shaved head, chin beard, and enough tattoos to cover the Seventh Fleet. Everything about him screamed "tough guy." His eyes were red, and he squinted them at me, waiting me out. "Joe Box," I said at last.

"Well, Joe, here's how it is. I knew the guy who lived here before you. Tilly Natchilo. We called him Nacho." The kid put one fist on top of the other. "We were like that, man. Tight. Partied all night."

"I'm thrilled for you. Now, if you'll—"

"They call me Honcho," the kid said. "After a John Wayne movie."

Dimwit. The movie was *Hondo*, but I didn't bother to correct him. "Do they now?"

"Yep. See, the thing is, I run this floor."

"Is that a fact?"

"Yep," he said again. "Truth is, I run this whole building. It's my job to keep people from bothering you. Insurance, like."

"Really. It's good to have employment. Who hired you?"

The kid frowned. "Nobody, man. Nacho and me, we thought it up ourselves." Then he grinned, "Gotta lot of old people around here. Scared, with brittle bones. It's sad, but things happen, you know?"

"I do indeed. And it's your job to stop it."

The kid's grin grew bigger. From his rotten teeth, you could tell he was a stoner. "Now you got it, Joe. I knew you would. See, I'm a peacekeeper. I'm offering you my services."

"For a price, right?"

"Sure, man. It's more than fair. Ask anybody. Ten percent

of whatever your monthly rent is, payable in advance. It's worth every penny."

"Quite a bargain. And if I don't pay …?"

The kid shrugged. "Then you get bothered."

I set my boxes down, turning to him. "Honcho and Nacho. You know, I like it. It's better than Heckel and Jeckel."

He frowned again. "Who?"

I used my foot to scoot my boxes on into my apartment. "What does Dempsey Miller have to say about all this?"

"Him," the kid laughed. "Not much. Maybe when he was younger he coulda done something about it, but he's an old guy."

"That's true," I said. "But I'm not."

The kid laughed again. "Oh, man. What are you telling me here, Joe?"

"I'm telling you to go back to sniffing airplane glue, and to leave me alone."

"Oh, man," he said once more, his eyes shining. "You're not going to pay? You're the first. That makes you … what's the word? … *unique*."

"I'm every bit of that," I smiled. "My girlfriend would agree."

The kid licked his lips, his eyes half-closing now. "Girlfriend, huh? Hey, maybe I'll see her around sometime. I kinda dig older women."

"Honcho," I said, my smile vanishing, "I've had a rotten twenty-four hours. And you know what?" I set my feet, balancing my weight. "I'm one inch away from taking every one of them out on you."

The kid balled his fists. "Oh, man." His laugh now was crazed. "I'm gonna like this. I'm gonna like this a whole, big bunch." He rolled his shoulders. "Anytime you're ready, Joe."

"Wait a minute," I said, relaxing. "How old are you, Honcho?"

"Twenty. Why?"

"Old enough," I nodded. And with that I fired my left leg straight up and out, putting all of my weight into the task of planting the arch of my foot on either side of Honcho's nose. You pick up the oddest things in wartime.

The kid never even squawked. He smashed back into the wall, his head slamming it hard, then he fell face first onto the floor, flattening his flat nose even more. But he never felt that. He was out before he hit the deck.

"Honcho?" I said, looking down at him. "I'm ready."

35

There was a knock at the door, and I flipped off the TV and got up. When I'd come in earlier I'd been pleasantly surprised to find the apartment had come furnished. Not the newest or the best, of course, but right on par with the kind of stuff I'd had back at the Agnes. The only difference was that the TV here was a thirteen-inch black and white job. Still it beat watching the walls.

I opened the door, and Angela walked in. She gave me a quick peck on the cheek. "You were supposed to call me."

I motioned around with my hand. "I would have, but no phone yet."

The door was still open, and she pointed back out in the hall.

Honcho lay where he'd fallen. He'd been there an hour. One old guy from across the hall had timidly rapped on my door fifteen minutes earlier, asking if I knew what had happened to Honcho. I told him he was rethinking a career move. The old man grinned toothlessly and left.

Still pointing, Angela raised her eyebrows at me. "Some of your work?"

"Just a local punk. I'll haul him out of here directly."

"I imagine God will have something to say to you about that when you do," she said. "Joe, you always seem to spread sunshine wherever you go."

I ducked my head modestly. "Brighten the corner where you are. That's my creed."

Shaking her head, but smiling, Angela came on in, and I shut the door behind her. She looked around in approval. "Dempsey's done a nice thing here. As far as I know, this is the only one he has that's furnished."

"I'll be sure to thank him tomorrow," I said. "This is beyond 'nice.' Everything that's been done for me is."

"What kind of car did Tom have for you?"

I was evasive. "Oh, an interesting one."

"Really? Not another Cougar."

"Be still my heart," I said. "I wish. No, it was a ..." I mumbled the rest.

"A what?"

"A Yugo," I said. Then I frowned. "What's so funny?"

"You," Angela laughed. "A guy your size, cramming yourself into a Yugo. What a picture." She laughed harder. "Oh, Mister Ringling! I have a new act for you!" She bent over, holding her sides.

My gaze was stern. "I'll have you know, Miss Swain, the Yugo is a fine automobile."

"Oh, no doubt," she wheezed, then she started singing "A-yoot-doot-doodle-doodle-doot-doot-doot" like a circus calliope.

"Are you quite done?" I asked a moment later.

She wiped her eyes. "Yes, quite. But please. Let me get you climbing out of it on video one time before you get rid of it."

"Oh, all right," I said, smiling at last. "I guess it does look kind of funny at that." I pointed at the couch. "Let's sit down. I know that thing looks like it came up the Natchez Trace, but it's really comfortable." I plonked myself down, Angela joining me.

"Wow, this is all right," she said, wiggling her rump.

"Horsehair," I replied. "Granny had one like it when I was a kid. You never forget the smell."

Angela wrinkled her nose. "I don't smell anything."

"You're not country. But it sure takes me back." We sat that way for a few minutes, then I said simply, "Greg's dead."

Angela stared at me. "What?"

"I heard it on the radio earlier. The helicopter he was on crashed in New York today. He's dead."

She squeezed my hand. "Oh, Joe."

"I tried to warn him. He blew it off. He said Martin couldn't kill him once he was airborne. Looks like he managed it though. The next call will be from Del."

Angela frowned at me. "Don't say that."

"I feel it, Ange." I tapped myself on the chest. "Right in here."

She blew out a breath, staring ahead. "That's discernment. So I guess it's true." Then she looked hard at me. "You told me earlier that your friend Marcus is the only one besides you who's a Christian, right?"

"As far as I know, yeah."

"That's his only hope," she said. Her eyes now were probing mine. "What are you going to do?"

"Marcus said something about getting inside Martin's head. So I'll have to figure out how to do that."

"The mind can be a dangerous playground," Angela warned. "And from what you've told me, Martin's had a lifetime to develop his weapons there." Her gaze now was level. "No offense, Joe, but if you meet him on that field, he'll take you."

I frowned. "So what do you suggest I do? Wait for him like a staked goat?"

"That's exactly what I'm telling you." She gripped my hand again. "The Bible says the weapons of our warfare aren't carnal. But that's where Martin has developed his strategies. You can't win there. In order for you to fight him, and defeat him, you've got to take the battle to a higher plane."

"You're talking about spiritual warfare again," I sighed. "I thought I was through with all that last August with the GeneSys case."

Her smile was tender. "That's just it. We're never going to be finished with it, not as long as we're walking the earth."

"Never?" I tried to keep the anger out of my voice. "Even earthly armies get leave, Ange. When's it our turn?"

"There are respites," she said. "God in his mercy grants us those. But leave? Not until we cross over, then our leave is eternal."

36

Monday morning. Three more days until Thanksgiving. I hoped I'd have something to be thankful about when it arrived, because I knew this game with Martin was winding up. On some unseen spiritual plain, swords had been drawn. Like Greg's death, and Del's imminent demise, I felt that knowledge inside too. I rubbed my face. I also felt like forty miles of bad road. Very little sleep, and most of that lousy. Angela had stayed late, but it's not what you're thinking. We'd prayed, and prayed hard. That is, she did most of the praying. I'm still too new at this spiritual warfare business to be much good at it. She'd told me how the intercessors' meeting had gone. Once again, as with that case last August, the prayer machine at the Pike was cranking up. As Angela left, she said she was going to tell them to amp those prayers up even further. Sounded good to me. I knew I'd need every one they had, and then some.

I got up from my desk, walked over to my office window, and stared out. It wasn't the first time that I was glad I wasn't paying for a spectacular view, because I sure didn't have one. My office has two windows. One faces the street; the other, the blank brick face of the building next door.

Mr. Yee/Lee had stopped by earlier, offering his condolences on my losses. He's a nice old guy. Not too long after that, the other tenants in the building had done the same. But now it was just me, and I was simply waiting. For Martin. Being a staked goat isn't as much fun as it sounds.

I checked my watch again. Ten o'clock, straight up. I'd been here since five. If my cell phone hadn't been in the Goddess when she was crushed, I might not have been here at all, electing instead to stay in my new apartment and checking my messages by remote whenever I felt the need. But that was speculation. My cell phone was as flat as my car, so here I was in my office alone, waiting it out.

I was just pouring my third cup of coffee of the morning when the phone on my desk rang. I looked at it. It rang three times. Four. Then I sighed, walking over like I was a thousand years old. Before I even picked it up, I knew.

"Box Investigations."

There was a long pause. During it I heard faint gasping, the sound someone makes when they've been crying for hours. I waited. Then a woman's voice said tentatively, "Is this Mr. Box?"

"Yes."

There was a sharp intake of shuddering air, then the woman said, "This is Marjorie Haggin. Del's wife."

"I know." She must have gotten my number off of Del's caller ID at work.

"It's Del, Mr. Box," she said. "He's been hurt …"

"Can you tell me what happened?"

"I … I'll try. It happened … late last night. Del had stayed at the store, doing inventory. He called me then, and said he was on his way home. He asked me if we needed anything at the grocery. But he never came …" She gulped hard before saying, "The police found him by his car …" There were some incomprehensible sounds. I waited; then she came back on. "They took him straight to the hospital, but … but he …" She stopped again, unable to go on.

"What happened to him, Mrs. Haggin?" I asked her softly. Even though I knew already.

"He'd been *stabbed!*" She almost screamed the word. "The doctor said he'd never seen such a horrible wound. Del's heart was … was nearly … They've called in some specialists but he's …" I heard her pull in a breath. "Mr. Box," she sobbed. "Del's *dying!*"

I almost dropped the phone right there. Dear God in heaven. Sweet, sweet heavenly Father. "Getting stabbed was your fear," I'd glibly told Del. "Is that what scared you the most, Delbert boy? Is it?" Colors swam behind my eyes. Sometimes it's a sin to be right.

"How can I help?" I asked thickly.

"You can't." The woman's voice was hollow with

defeat. "They said Del's got ... maybe an hour. Maybe a little more. There's blood ... pouring ..." She swallowed. "But then right before ... right before he ... couldn't talk anymore, he asked me to tell you something. Two things, really." She gulped again. "He said to tell you that you were right. And then he said ... he said for you to get him." Her voice was raspy. "Get who, Mr. Box? Do you know who did this?"

"I don't have a clue," I lied. "Find a preacher, Mrs. Haggin. Now."

And I hung up the phone.

For the thousandth time that day I checked my watch. Ten ten. Forget the staked goat, I had to get out of here. I grabbed my coat off the brass rack and headed out. I let my feet take me where they willed, and found myself walking north on Hamilton, up toward the deli I'd given a ton of business to over the years. As I came in the door, the bell over it jingled—a childhood sound of Toad Lick's general store that still took me back—and the owner, old Mr. Sapperstein, looked up from his task of cutting tongue for sandwiches.

"Mr. Box," he smiled. "Welcome, welcome. How are you this fine November morning?"

"I'm fine," I lied again. I hoped that wasn't going to turn into a habit. My Granny had always drilled into me that the two worst things in the world were a liar and a cheat.

Mr. Sapperstein laid his knife down on the gouged old wooden chopping block with a frown. "I don't think so. You've looked better, I think."

I smiled and didn't answer as I bent low, perusing the wonders in his refrigerated case.

He held up the remnants of the tongue. "I have the item you need right here, Mr. Box. My dear departed *babushka*, Grandmother Marina, may she rest in peace, always said a nice tongue sandwich and a bowl of chicken soup can solve almost anything."

Not this, I thought to myself. *Not hardly. Plus I always make a point of never eating anything that can lick me back.* "The soup sounds good, Mr. Sapperstein, but I'll pass on the tongue."

He clucked his disapproval as he ladled a generous helping of hearty chicken soup from its large steel kettle into a thick cardboard take-out bowl. I knew this soup. It could take Campbell's to the mat and hold it down for a three-count without breaking a sweat. Putting a plastic lid on it, the old man said, "No trouble with your young lady, I trust." He smiled again. "Ah, Angela. Such a nice girl. And so pretty." Mashing the lid down with his thumbs, he said, "Forgive the meddling of an old Jew, Mr. Box, but you could do worse, I think. You should settle down with her. Grow old. Raise a houseful of children."

"They're like arrows in the quiver of a righteous man," I said. I'd just read that somewhere recently in the Bible.

Mr. Sapperstein's eyes lit up in delight. "Ah, and so they are, Mr. Box!" He touched the side of his nose with his finger, and then wagged it at me—his finger, not his nose. "Solomon. *There* was a man. He knew." He handed me my soup container. "So, I didn't know you were religious."

Taking it, I smiled again at him. "Just recently, Mr. Sapperstein."

He nodded. "In this crazy world, when everything falls, God stands."

Those words nearly rocked me back. *God stands.* Old Mr. Sapperstein had nailed it down as neatly as anyone could: the deli owner as theologian. Why not? God had done it with a shepherd. And he was right. I needed to brand those words into my mind, and into my heart. In the middle of all this mess, God stands.

"Give me a tongue sandwich with that soup, Mr. Sapperstein," I said.

He grinned. "A wise choice. Solomon would be proud." Turning to make the sandwich, he said, "Speaking of crazy, that was some news from Columbus this morning, eh? Go figure."

I wasn't really paying attention. I was trying to imagine how tongue would taste. "Plenty of mustard on that," I said. "What news?"

Mr. Sapperstein held up two plastic squeeze bottles. "Brown or yellow?"

"Brown."

"Good choice," he nodded. "On tongue, brown is best." As he slathered the bread with it, he said, "The news about that senator. That ten Eyck man."

I felt the room tilt. "Ten Eyck man?"

Mr. Sapperstein was still bent over his work. "Sure, you remember him, Mr. Box. Henrik ten Eyck. He was many years retired, but it was said he was still the man with the influence. And money? *Nu*, the man had money."

I set my soup up on top of the case before I dropped it. "What about him, Mr. Sapperstein?"

He put my sandwich on wax paper, folding the corners flat. "He's dead."

I swallowed. "What?"

The old deli owner glanced up at his clock. "It's almost ten-thirty. I'll flip on the news. Maybe there will be more." Wiping his hands on his apron, he walked over to the small color portable up on the counter and turned it on. The updates at the bottom of the hour were just starting.

The Ken-doll clone stared into the camera. "And in further national news, retired senator Henrik ten Eyck, five-time legislator from Ohio and often embattled former head of the Senate Appropriations Committee, is dead. The bodies of both Senator ten Eyck and his chief-of-staff, John Baumgartner, were discovered at eight-thirty this morning, Eastern Standard Time, in the solarium of Grand Possibilities, the senator's palatial home outside of Columbus, Ohio. We go there now for a live report."

The camera cut to another reporter who could have been the anchor's twin, standing outside the gate I'd been at on Saturday. He pressed his earpiece in tighter, looking appropriately grim. "As was reported, both former senator Henrik ten Eyck and his longtime aide, John Baumgartner, were found dead this morning in the senator's home from what Columbus coroner Dr. Clarence Milliard has termed 'massively poisonous' insect bites. Fifteen minutes ago a press conference with Dr. Milliard was held. Here's some of what was said."

The scene switched to an office where a harried-looking jowly man was trying to talk into the half-dozen microphones jammed in his face like anteater snouts. The caption at the bottom of the screen listed him as Dr. Clarence Milliard.

Over the din of the reporter's voices a woman sang out, "Sir, are you saying the official cause of death for the senator and his aide will be listed as insect venom?"

"Ms. Swenson ..." All the reporters quieted down so the doctor could be heard. "Ms. Swenson," he said again, "we are only in the beginning stages of the investigation. All I can say is that the initial signs point us in the direction of some variant of arachnid-type poison, hitherto unknown. That scenario would fit in with this last shipment of plants from the Pacific Rim the senator received as a gift from an unnamed benefactor sometime on Friday. I understand the identity of that person is still in question."

The babble rose again, then a man's voice called out, "Arachnid? Are you saying it was a spider, doctor?"

Milliard nodded. "That's correct. Early toxin reports list the poison as a type of spider venom."

That got the bunch of them cranking again, then the same man's voice asked, "What kind of spider?" A woman shouted, "How many bites did each body receive?"

"Several poisonous spiders are indigenous to that area," Milliard replied, "including the New Zealand Redback. The lab reports are still somewhat sketchy. But since the plants delivered yesterday came from there, that appears to be where our search is directed. As to the number of bites, they were extensive, leading us to believe several of the creatures were involved."

"Are the spiders still in the solarium?" another reporter yelled.

"That remains unknown at this juncture," Milliard said patiently. "But I can tell you that after the bodies of Senator ten Eyck and Mr. Baumgartner were removed, the room was sealed and gassed. Sometime later this afternoon a full entomological sweep is planned."

The gaggle started chattering again, and Milliard held up a tired hand. "That's all I have. Now our work of toxin identification begins in earnest. Thank you."

He was turning to go when another reporter hollered, "Sir, were their deaths painful?"

The other newshounds muttered their disapproval at such a question, but Dr. Milliard stopped and wearily looked back at the reporter. "Judging by their final expressions, young man, I don't have adequate words to convey that."

Mr. Sapperstein flipped off the TV with a shake of his head. "Such sadness," he said. "There's too much sadness in the world, I think." He handed me my sandwich and bowl of soup. "There you are, Mr. Box. Enjoy."

With almost a physical effort I tried to shake off what I'd just heard. Easier said than done though. Although I held zero affection for ten Eyck or Baumgartner, those men had still died hard. "Thanks. How much do I owe you?"

"For the soup? The soup is good, I think a dollar for the soup is fair." The old deli man shrugged with the whole upper half of his body. "But the tongue? Maybe you won't like the tongue, and if I charged you, it wouldn't be right." He grinned then, again wagging a finger at me. "But maybe, maybe you'll say, 'This tongue? This tongue is good. What was I thinking?' And the next time you come in, you'll pay me a little extra for what you get, eh?"

I handed him my dollar with a smile of my own. Just being around people like Mr. Sapperstein makes folks feel better. "Sounds like a plan," I nodded.

I left the deli then and walked back up the street to my office, this time against the wind. The temperature was dropping, and I glanced up at the sky. The clouds looked like they were only ten feet up, as solid and gray as a battleship. We'd have snow this week, sure as anything. I pulled my raincoat tighter against me as a particularly savage gust nearly pulled my food out of my hands. I wished the coat had come with a liner, but you know about beggars not being choosers. I also hoped the soup would be warm enough to drink when I got there; Mr. Sapperstein's chicken concoction has been known to awaken the comatose. I wanted to savor every drop. But if it got cold, too bad. I'd drink it anyway. I'd been meaning for a while now to buy one of those little microwaves for the office. One of those would be custom made for a day like this. I could warm up this soup if I needed to. Maybe whip up some hot chocolate, and plenty of it, made the old-fashioned way, the way Granny used to, with Hershey's powder and a dash of vanilla. Graham crackers would be good too.

As I trudged along, part of my brain knew exactly what the other part was doing: immersing itself in minutiae against the horror I was facing. But it's hard to compart-mentalize death.

Only Marcus and I were left now, I mused, out of the whole star-crossed bunch. I bent into the wind. Acey-deucy. This one or that. One potato-two.

Which one of us would Martin try for next?

37

Ten minutes later that question was answered. I'd come back to my office, hung up my coat, and spread a paper towel to lay my sandwich on. I'd just peeled back the lid on the soup bowl, letting the aroma waft up in my face, when the phone rang again. The knowing sank into my heart. Oh no.

I shakily picked it up, hoping I was wrong about the subject of the call. I wasn't. "Box Investigations."

"Yeah, is this Joe Box?" The voice was an older man's, rough and clotted and Southern, a smoker's voice. I know, because he sounded exactly like my dad, a three-pack-a-day Viceroy man, had.

"Yes." I cleared my throat. "Yes, it is."

"This is Clovis Chastain," the man said. "I'm a neighbor of a fella I think you know. Marcus Crowell?"

Oh my God. Here it comes. "I know Marcus."

"Well," Chastain said, "there's been an accident."

The word hung. "Accident?"

"Yeah, a pretty bad one. On his farm."

"Not another shredder foul-up," I moaned without thinking.

"Naw, it weren't the shredder," Chastain rasped at me. "Tractor wreck at his grain elevator."

"A *tractor* wreck?" I'd never heard of such a thing, and I'd spent a good deal of my life on a farm. Turnovers, yes, engine fires, or even a slow-moving one being rammed by a car. Maybe that's what Chastain meant. I had to ask the next. "Is he dead?"

"Purt near," the man allowed. "The doctor at the hospital said maybe I should call Marcus's next of kin. Now Marcus don't have no next of kin, just a few neighbors and friends from his church. Though I 'spect he told you that. Before Marcus passed out for good in the emergency room, he grabbed my shirt and croaked out, 'Call Joe Box. Cincinnati.' I called information, and the gal there gave me two numbers, your home and your office. This was the first one I tried."

"So what happened to him, Mr. Chastain?"

"Well, it's like this. I help Marcus out with his taxes and such, 'cause he ain't got much of a head for figures … you might know that too." I didn't, but kept silent. "Anyway," the man went on, "I was over ta Marcus's house this mornin', and he couldn't find the ledger book for 2001 for nothin'. We're doin' a refile, see. Marcus then told me he keeps old stuff like that in the barn, so's it wouldn't be lost if his house burned. Stupid, but there you go."

Was this man going to get to it? He had more wind than a life insurance agent.

"Marcus wheeled himself out the door—you do know Marcus ain't got his legs no more, right? Sure you do, you mentioned the shredder. Right?"

I gritted my teeth. "Right."

"So anyway Marcus wheeled himself outside, to his tractor. He hadn't used it for the past coupla days. He has this pulley thing he rigged up after his accident to help get him up on the seat. Works too. I declare, he drives that tractor around his land like it was a car."

As I held the phone up to my ear, I looked down and realized I was unconsciously making a circling motion with my hand. Come *on*, Chastain, tell me already.

"So he starts off across his back lot at a good clip," the man said, "headin' toward his barn, when the craziest thing happened. That there tractor started speedin' up!"

Speeding up? I shook my head. "I don't understand."

"You would if you ever saw his rig," Chastain said. "Marcus may be a slouch at figures, but he's a stone genius when it comes to mechanics. After his accident last year he fixed that tractor up personally, movin' all the controls and makin' the whole thing driveable by hand. It can really get after it too. You never saw such a clever piece a' work."

"So what did—"

"It started goin' faster an' faster," Chastain rushed on, "bouncin' over that hard ground like a rabbit, with ol' Marcus hangin' on an' yellin' like crazy. Stuck throttle, I guess. Which is weird, because when he converted it over, he put in a brand-new one. The way he was screamin', it was almost like somebody was holdin' the thing down."

So Martin had somehow in the last few days gotten onto Marcus's land and fooled with his tractor, fixing the thing so it would accelerate dangerously the next time it was fired up. The boy surely was getting around with his mayhem. But seeing as how there's no place in the continental U.S. any more than seven hours by air from anyplace else, that wasn't so hard to do.

Chastain's voice pulled me back. "Anyway," he said, "that's when it happened."

I was about out of patience with this guy. "*What?*"

"Marcus an' his tractor missed his barn completely," Chastain said, "an' ran full tilt into his grain elevator, which was loaded to the top with feed corn."

Good grief. That'd do it, all right. I knew that for a fact. Right before my family and I had moved from Toad Lick to Cincinnati, a neighbor down the road from us had died when the corn in his grain elevator had fallen and crushed him. One kernel of corn is negligible; nine million of them dropping on you from a height of thirty-five feet will make your wife your widow.

"Yeah, that tractor tore through the elevator wall like it weren't even there," Chastain said wonderingly. "The only reason Marcus didn't die straight off was the cage over the cab. It took some of the weight, but not all. By the time I got him dug out, he weren't breathin'. I used the phone in his barn to call the county ambulance, then I dug all the corn I could out of his gullet and started givin' him mouth-to-mouth.

I learned how to do that in the Navy, and I did it till the squad showed up. They took him on to the hospital, an' I followed, an' that's where I'm callin' from."

"What are they saying there, Mr. Chastain?" I asked.

"Nothin' good," the man replied, his tone flat. "All kindsa internal stuff, lungs collapsed and such. He might have brain damage too, but seein's how he's in a coma, they ain't sure of that. They got him hooked up to pumps and wires. I over-heard one of the older nurses callin' it a death watch. I just reckon he wanted you to know."

Death watch. You're not dead yet, Marcus. Hang on. Pastor Franklin always says it's not over until God says it is. "What can I do to help?"

"You might want to say a prayer for him," Chastain said. "I ain't a prayin' man myself, but I reckon it couldn't hurt."

"Is Marcus's pastor there? He's not all alone in that room, is he?"

Chastain wheezed a laugh. "Not hardly. Yeah, his pas-tor's there, and the pastor's wife, and about half his little church. Carryin' on like a buncha nuts. Prayin' and shoutin' and jabberin'." Chastain lowered his voice. "Penny-costals, y'know."

I knew. It sounded like Marcus was in good hands. "Well, thanks for the call, Mr. Chastain."

"I'll let you know when he passes," he said shortly, and hung up.

What a cheery old dude. With friends like Clovis Chastain …

Shaking my head, I picked up a new Eberhard Faber and

started walking around, gnawing as I went. An uneasy feeling had started. Something wasn't making sense here, I mean beyond the obvious item of being stalked by a madman. I kept walking and chewing as the feeling grew. I dithered and pondered and chewed half the pencil before it finally came to me: Martin had gotten off schedule.

I pulled over a pad of paper, using the pencil to rough out a timeline. Okay, on Saturday night he'd tried to kill me by rigging my furnace to explode. He'd failed. He knew that, of course, but for his own reasons had let it slide. Then somehow he'd stabbed Del that same night, and today Greg's slick had gone down in New York, after Martin had probably sneaked onto the airfield earlier and scuttled the linkage. Greg and Del, both now dead. Then Martin succeeded in killing both his father and John Baumgartner—with tropical spiders, for Pete's sake—*before* he knew for sure his stunt with Marcus's tractor had worked. And he still hadn't made a second try for me. I began gnawing again. What the heck was going on with the boy?

A moment later I had my answer. Martin was rattled. Rattled enough that he'd killed Henrik ten Eyck and John Baumgartner out of turn, his moment of crowning glory spoiled. But why? He'd felt himself to be in total control—up until he'd failed with me. That blew his schedule. And then today he'd failed again with Marcus, but I don't think he knew it yet. I believe he thought Marcus was dead, or as good as. Which meant he'd be back to try to finish me off. But why were Marcus and I still alive, even after Martin had taken a cut at us?

And then I knew. The common thread was staring me right in the face.

Our Christianity.

Martin hadn't been stopped from making another try for me because of his own reasons. He'd been stopped by the hand of God. If I ever needed proof our God was stronger than his, there it was.

I sat back down at my desk. Okay, summary time. Out of the ten members of Charlie company, Bravo platoon, third squad, eight were dead, one was comatose, and the last one was seen walking around his office eating pencils.

But not any longer.

Angela had told me the weapons of our warfare weren't carnal. True enough, but I'd also read somewhere in the Bible, I think it was in Luke, that Jesus had told one of his men that if he didn't have a sword, he should buy one. Sounded like a plan to me. I looked down at my food, and sadly pushed it aside.

Time for a trip to the gun shop.

38

I f you're ever looking for a place to take your tree-hugging, latte-drinking, pacifist liberal friends for a really good scare, I highly recommend Dave Harrow's Gun Shop.

The first thing they'll encounter upon entering the store is Dave himself. That alone would be worth the price of admission. Dave Harrow is probably sixty years old, but don't let his gray ponytail fool you. He's a former Army Ranger and firearms instructor, with three tours in Vietnam under his belt and a boxful of medals he only shows to friends. He has a sixty-five-inch chest, Popeye forearms, and a raspy voice, courtesy of a shrapnel wound suffered on his last tour. That was the one where he rescued three Belgian nuns and five screaming kids in the middle of a firefight involving two PRU death squads and a platoon-strength NVA troop. He got a medal for that one too. He also has a glass eye, his left, but it's well made and hard to tell from a real one. Sometimes he pops it out and pretends to swallow it. I've seen him clear bars with that trick.

"Joe," he smiled as I came in his store. "Where the heck have you been keeping yourself, bubba? You look pretty rough."

"Thanks. I've had a bad week."

"I heard that," Dave said. "My business always slows down right before Thanksgiving."

"How come? I thought this time of year people remembered the pilgrims, how they hunted their own food. You know, back to the land."

Dave shook his head. "People today are too soft. The real hunters have already gotten their gear together back in the early fall. If most folks had to kill their own Thanksgiving turkeys," he laughed, "they'd starve. Oh well, it just means I might get to head home early today. So what can I do you for? You ready to throw away that popgun you pack and get a man's gun?"

Dave had been after me for a while to ditch the .38 Smith and Wesson Police Special I carry for something with a little more authority. I'd been resisting, but it hadn't stopped him from pitching me each time I came in. "I'll stick with what I know." That's what I always said.

"A six-shooter with a four-inch barrel," Dave said, his tone despairing. "The things I could do for you here. Take a look at this." He pulled a handgun out of the case, laying it down on top. "I just got some of these in. If you like it you can sign the forms, and I'll date it from last week."

I leaned down. "Hey, that's kind of nice." It was too, but

I'd only come in to buy a box of shells for the Smith. Thankfully, I'd left it in my shoulder holster back at my office the night the Agnes burned. I'd been meaning to clean it. The week before, I'd run out of bullets doing my range proficiencies. Plus, what Dave was offering was a federal offense. He could go to jail.

"Browning Hi-Power 9mm Pathfinder," he said proudly. "Right along the same lines as the .45 the officers carried in 'Nam. Here, pick it up."

I did. "Heavier than the Smith."

He raised his eyebrows. "Well, duh. How do you figure that?"

"You don't do sarcasm well, Dave." I sighted down it. "Feels good in the hand though."

He could sense I was weakening. "It's perfect for concealed-carry. Ten in the clip, and one up the pipe. Five shots more than you have now."

My resolve melted further. "How much?"

Dave grinned, looking more than ever like Ernest Borgnine on a bad day. "These babies retail new for six ninety-nine. But I'll give you my today-only, I'm-desperate-for-a-sale price of five ninety-nine."

I pondered on it for a moment. Me, give up the Smith for this? Somehow that sounded like cheating. The Smith and I had been through a lot. And as much as I didn't like recalling it, I'd taken my first life since Vietnam with it this past August. We had some history together. Plus, buying the Browning would pretty much wipe out what I had left in my checking account. "Well, I don't know …"

"I'll even throw in the first box of shells," he said. "On the house."

Dave was giving me a puppy-dog look. A rabid puppy dog. But I knew his heart was right, and I also knew that in this day of Geraldo Rivera and the PC police, little one-man gun stores like his were hurting. I felt the nudge to help. And he was old enough to know what he was risking.

"Oh, why not," I grinned. "I guess I really should have a backup piece." Who knew, maybe I'd need them both for Martin. "And since I didn't buy myself a birthday present last year, I might as well spend my money here."

"My wife will kiss you for this," Dave said, putting the shells next to it.

"You don't have a wife," I reminded him. "You're divorced."

"True," he said, "but I'm behind on alimony. She'll kiss you."

"Wrap that up for me," I laughed. Then I stopped. Oh boy. Ohh, momma. That weird niggling on my spine was starting up. "Wait a minute. Is your range downstairs still open? I ought to run a few shells through this."

"Yeah, it's open," he said. "I just had it inspected and paid the annual fee for it last week. But what's the rush? Bring the Browning back tomorrow, and I'll have the candy machine down there filled for us." Dave was a fool for Snickers.

I shook my head. The fluttering was growing worse. "Tomorrow won't work. I need to check it now."

"Why, you planning on shooting somebody?" he laughed.

I didn't answer, and Dave's smile left. "Wait a minute here, Joe. What's happening? What's going on?"

"A mess," I said simply. I hadn't even wanted to say that much. The problem is, Dave would dearly love to be a private eye like me, but due to some indiscretions when he got back to the world in 1969, he has a record. Misdemeanors, true, but barring a miracle, his dream will remain just that, a dream. He still dogs me about my cases though. And as I said, he's a former Ranger; breaking heads is what he does best (he'd also dearly love to be able to fight and get paid for it). So why isn't he a bouncer? He says it's not exciting enough. "Nothing you'd be interested in," I told him.

His one good eye was drilling me. "Try me."

"Dave—"

"I'm serious, man," he said. And he was. Dave lived on the ragged edge. "I need to get back in the mix. Bring me in. Just tell me—"

"I can't," I said. "It's a private beef. Just me and an old enemy from the past. I gotta travel light on this."

The look on his face was hurt. "You think I can't cut it because of my eye."

"Now that's a lie. Up at Target World I've seen you put five shots into a silhouette from thirty feet out you could cover with a quarter. Your marksmanship isn't in question here."

"Then what is?"

I looked at him. "Your spirituality."

"My *what?*"

"You heard me."

"Oh, man, does this have something to do with that religious kick you're on?"

"It's not a 'religious kick,'" I said. "It's my life now."

Dave scowled. "Yeah? So where does that leave your old friends?"

"With a seat on the bus next to me," I said. "If they want it. I've told you all this before."

"And I still don't buy it."

"Your choice, bro. The door's open though, and the bus is still idling." I thought back to Greg and Del and Little Bit and all the rest. "Just don't wait too long."

"Okay," he sighed then. "But what does what you're into now have to do with whoever it is you're after?"

Good thing I'd known Dave long enough to understand his circumlocution. "The man's a killer," I told him. "Stone cold. A LURP gone bad."

"I can handle a LURP," Dave said. "I've done it before."

"Not one like this. He's gone over to the dark side. Way over. Occult powers, mind control, you name it."

Dave cocked his head at me. I could tell he wasn't buying the idea.

"This guy's killed over thirty men that I know of," I told him, "probably more. A lot of them he wasted with weapons you can't even imagine." Dave still had his arms folded, glaring at me. "Partner," I frowned back, "you're big, and you're tough. But you know something? This guy could kill you cold dead without half trying. And we go back too far for me to allow that to happen." I picked up the gun, putting the box of shells into my coat pocket, along with a box for the .38. "What's the freight on this?"

"Pay me tomorrow," Dave growled, his frown so deep it looked like somebody had cleaved in his skull with an ax. "If you're still here."

39

I'd left him then and come back to my office. I knew he was still mad at me, but he'd get over it. Better mad than dead. Bringing Dave into the case at this point would be like letting a Saint Bernard run out onto thin ice. He'd caper around out there just long enough, ignorant of the danger, until he fell through and was lost. No, God was my partner in this. And that was enough.

I picked up the Browning and checked it. Clean as a whistle. Knowing Dave, that wasn't surprising. There's not a gun in his store, used or new, that he doesn't personally disassemble, clean, and reassemble before it goes in his case. That's just the way he is. Old habits die hard.

Humming tunelessly, I ejected the magazine, loading ten fresh shells in it before putting it back in. Pulling back the slide I chambered a round, then safed the weapon and ejected the magazine once more. I put one more bullet in it before reinserting it a final time. As Dave said, ten in the clip and one up the pipe. Surely that would be enough, provided this was the gun I took when I met Martin. Because deep inside I knew we'd meet, face to face, before this day was done. That's what my feeling back at Dave's store was telling me. Today it ends.

For one of us.

The task with the Browning done, I set it aside and placed the Smith on the desk. Loading a wheel-gun is far simpler. I swung it open, put in six .38 bullets, then closed it and slowly spun the cylinder. The soft ratcheting sound it makes always put me in mind of pearls rolling against each other in butter. That finished, I put my hands down on either side of the guns, considering them. Which one do I take to meet a madman? The tried-and-true, or the new? Gary Cooper never had this problem in *High Noon*. Practicality finally won out over sentimentality as I slid the Smith over and put it in the desk drawer. Eleven shots beat out six. Sorry, old girl. Not this trip.

I looked at my watch and sighed. Three twenty-five. Nothing left to do now but wait for Martin to make his move. But then I thought, no. That's not right. There *is* something to do. And I reached one more time into my desk drawer, pulling out my Bible.

I rubbed my hands over its leather cover before opening it. On my last case back in August, the day I became a Christian, Sarge had given me the New Testament he'd carried during his time in Korea. I'd argued with him, but he'd insisted. I still had that, now in a special place on my small office bookshelf in the corner. Then the day I'd joined the Pike they'd given me a nice red paperback Bible, which I'd read, excuse the term, religiously, but Saturday night it had burned in the Agnes. Fine Bibles both, but not like this one.

No, the one I was lovingly caressing now was a *King James*, decades old, the leather fading and cracked from too many years of neglect. Linda had given it to me the day we were married. I opened it, reading the inscription to me inside. That was the year she'd been trying calligraphy, and she wasn't very good at it. The lettering height and spacing were uneven, too scrunched in some places while being too far apart in others. But like the words in the Bible itself, it was the message that counted.

My dearest Joe, it read, *this is our road map, yours and mine. Our destination is long, and the way unsure, but with his Word as our guide, our arrival is certain. I love you, now and forever. Linda*

I no longer tear up when I read that inscription, and that faintly disturbs me. Is it because of my new relationship with Angela? I'd ask her about it, but I'm still feeling my way along. When this is over, I decided. Then we'll see.

I opened the Bible to the book of Psalms and started reading. I was still at it an hour later when the phone rang. The receiver was in my hand before I realized there wasn't any feeling of dread. "Box Investigations."

"Hi Joe, it's Angela."

"Hey," I grinned.

"Hey yourself. You sound better."

"Yeah, I've just been reading some psalms. It turns out

David had some of the same problems as me, getting chased all over the place by that crazy king."

"It's funny how that works, isn't it? The Bible is thousands of years old, but it's still as fresh as if it was written today."

"I'm finding that out. So what have you been up to?"

"Putting out fires," she sighed. "Joe, that building has caused more headaches than any three I've ever designed."

I guess I'd better explain. Angela may have been one of Harvard Pike's intercessors, but what paid her bills was that she was one of the state's—scratch that, the country's—most sought-after architects. One critic called her work a "sweeping revival of Neo-Classical romanticism combined with Frank Lloyd Wright audacity." Well, maybe, but her buildings sure were pretty.

What was giving her fits now was a fifteen-story apartment complex going up near the Serpentine Wall on the riverfront. Some serious scratch had gone into the design, as these units were going to house some of Cincinnati's toniest residents. The construction, sadly, was a different matter. Now what I know about putting up high-rises is right on par with what I know about Etruscan pottery, which is to say, zilch. Angela had tried to tell me what the ongoing problems with the place were, but every time she did, inside of two minutes my eyes would glaze over. I didn't even bother asking what it was this time.

But she told me anyway. "Two walls, right in the lobby, that the owner wants moved a foot farther out. Just so he can put in a bigger koi pond."

"A foot doesn't sound like so much," I said. "What's koi?" It sounded like that stuff Hawaiians eat, but I knew that couldn't be right.

"A foot means a lot when you're talking about a load-bearing wall for a fifteen-story building," Angela said. "Koi are goldfish."

"Goldfish? Why doesn't the guy just get a big aquarium and sidestep the whole problem? Maybe put in a few castles and snails."

"Now you're thinking like an architect," she laughed. "Then to top it off, this morning our project manager came down with the creeping crud, and some other temp guy is taking his place."

"A temp guy? I didn't know temp agencies handled people like that. Pretty ritzy."

"Not temp from an agency," Angela said. "I meant there's another project manager filling in for our guy temporarily. I was with him all afternoon. I couldn't seem to get him down out of the penthouse. He seemed fascinated by it."

"You do good work, Ange," I said. "I'm fascinated, and I haven't even seen it."

"I've seen it, and I'm tired of it. We're way over budget on this whole project, and all I've done today is show the new guy around and argue with the owner. I'm worn out, hungry, and in need of a back scratch. How about if I bring us some dinner?"

"Sounds good. Chinese?"

"What, again?"

"What can I say? I'm hooked on MSG."

She laughed and said she'd be over at five. We said our good-byes, and I hung up the phone. Oddly, she hadn't mentioned Martin during the call, and neither had I. We both knew in our bones the curtain was rising on the final act.

40

My egg roll flew out of my chopsticks, skittering wildly across the desk. I managed to snag it with my fingers just before it slid over the edge. "I hate these things."

"Egg rolls?" Angela sipped her green tea, giving me innocent eyes over the rim.

"Not egg rolls," I scowled. "These." I held up the chopsticks. "There's a trick to them I just can't seem to master."

"It's simple, Joe. Watch." Deftly Angela used hers to pluck a piece of sweet-and-sour chicken out of its cardboard box. In one smooth motion she transported it to her mouth and began chewing. "Yummy."

I gave her a sour look of my own.

She smiled at me. "I can't believe you served a tour in Vietnam and never learned how."

"Oh, I learned," I said. "This is what I learned." Using one chopstick, I thrust it down in the box, impaling an egg roll. I pulled it out, holding it up in triumph. "Egg roll fishing, the South Sea islands way."

We were both laughing when my phone rang again.

"I wonder who that could be," Angela said, licking her fingers.

"Maybe news on Marcus." I picked it up. "Box Investigations."

The voice on the other end was a young woman's. "Hi, is Angela Swain there?"

"Yes she is," I said, puzzled. "Who's calling, please?"

"Tell her it's Margie."

"Just a second." I put my hand over the mouthpiece. "For you. Some gal named Margie."

"My assistant," Angela said. "I told her I was coming over here when I got off work. But she knows my cell phone is broken. She shouldn't be calling here unless it's an emergency."

Angela took the phone from me. "Hi Margie, what's up?" She listened for a moment, then said, "Oh, that's crazy. What's he thinking? Can't he read prints? Everything is up to spec. He should know that." Another pause. "No, I'm not going to bother Mr. Delvecchio with this." Delvecchio's name I knew. He was the money man behind the project. Angela now sounded exasperated. "Oh, for heaven's sake. I'm on my way down. No, no, that's all right, you go on home. I'll take care of it. You too, Margie. Good night."

"On my way down"? That didn't sound good. "I have the feeling our dinner is over," I said.

"Yes, and it shouldn't be." Angela rarely got angry, but I

could tell she was steamed as she got up and stalked over to the rack, pulling off her leather coat. "Joe, I hate to do this, but that new project manager is turning out to be a pain. Now he's saying the sprinkler heads in the penthouse aren't up to code. If I don't get down there now to meet with him and check it out, he'll call Mr. Delvecchio with it, sure as anything."

I stood as well. "You're leaving? Ange, it's going on six-thirty. You've already put in a long day. What is this guy, an eager beaver?"

"Ambitious is the word. We see it a lot in construction." She buttoned her coat and picked up her purse. "This shouldn't take too long. I hope. Where are you going to be later? Here or at your new place?"

"Right here." I walked over to her. "Look at that. Your collar's flipped under again." I fixed it, and then turned her toward me. "Tonight's it, Ange. We've been dancing around the issue the whole night, but we both know it. I'm staying here until I get the call."

"Call?"

"From Martin. He's going to call here. Tonight."

She gripped my arm, her voice even. "Then I'm not leaving."

I gently disengaged her fingers. "You have to, babe. It's down to just him and me. I can't have you in the middle."

"But—"

I pointed back to the Bible still lying open on my desk. "That thing is either real, or it isn't. God's words inside it are either true, or they're not. I pick true." I softly held Angela by her shoulders. "I'm taking God at his word. It's time for me to start believing him. Really believing. When I see you again, this'll all be over. I guarantee it." Her eyes filled with tears, and I leaned down and kissed her. "Now take off."

She started to say something else, then stopped and placed her delicate hand against my rough cheek. "Go with God, you sweet man." Then she was gone.

I stood in my doorway, listening to her footsteps as she took the stairs down. I heard the front door open, pause, and then softly close.

Sighing, I sat back down at my desk, curling a lip at the food scattered around. Not surprisingly, my appetite had vanished. I didn't even bother checking my watch for the time, because I knew it was only ten minutes later than the last time I looked. Martin, if we're gonna dance, let's take it out on the floor and boogie.

Then I saw something on the corner of my desk, and I frowned. Angela had left a folder there, one of those manila accordion jobs. I reached over, spinning it around so I could read it. The Avery stick-on label read RiverTower Notes. That was the name of the complex she was working on.

Did she need this? Part of me almost wanted to chase her down and give it to her, maybe snag a kiss, but brains won out. That would only make what I was doing harder. Being the nosy sort, I pulled the folder over and opened it, making a mental note to put everything back as I found it. No sense courting trouble.

The contents lived up to their name. Graphs and drawings and charts, all laced with plenty of architectural-type terms that meant less than nothing to a layman. Behind all those were pictures of the building in various stages of progress, all of them dated, most of them taken by someone obviously other than Angela. The first one showed the obligatory shot of the mayor digging up the first spadeful of dirt. He was surrounded by dignitaries and press and folks from the construction firm, all wearing yellow hardhats with their suits and dresses. Angela was the only one of the group not looking self-important. Instead she was grinning good-naturedly at the camera, seeming to say, I know this thing clashes with my clothes, but it wasn't my idea. I smiled as I leafed through the rest. There were Polaroids of rooms under construction mixed in with shots of Angela either staring at blueprints or pointing as she talked with the crew. That was my Angela. Doggedly determined to be in on every phase. Some of the crew I recognized, but not all of them. Then I came across another picture, one of her talking with the project manager, the man who had gotten sick today. I remember she'd told me his name was Vic. Vic was ruggedly handsome, with excellent teeth and thick, bushy hair, and a clear, *look-forward-to-the-future, graduates* expression on his tanned face. He and Angela were laughing. She was touching his arm. I hoped Vic had diarrhea.

I got to the last picture, taken just this morning, hidden halfway under the others, and I pulled it out. Angela, blueprints rolled loosely in one hand, was talking with some man. She'd obviously forgotten his name, because she'd written in ink above the guy, *new project manager*, then circled it with an arrow pointing to him. Whatever had been said between them, she was frowning, while the man laughed, his hand lightly placed on hers.

And then my breathing grew ragged as the room spun. I blinked.

It was Martin.

No! I violently shook my head. No, it couldn't be. I stared harder at the picture, willing the image to change. As I did, ice formed around the walls of my heart. It was Martin, no question. In the past thirty years he'd hardly aged at all. But *how* in the—

The phone rang. Willing my hand to be steady, I picked it up. "Yes."

The whispery voice was a man's. It too hadn't changed. I'd heard that voice before, a world away, in the ash of a scorched jungle where no living thing moved.

"How will it be," Martin said softly, "losing both the women you've loved on your watch?"

And softly, softly, he disconnected the line.

41

My mind was racing faster than the engine of the battered Yugo as I whipped through traffic. Angela had less than a ten-minute lead. If it meant tearing the guts out of this little rust bucket, I had to catch her before she reached the job site. If only my cell phone hadn't gotten flattened, and hers hadn't been on the fritz.

I'd underestimated Martin. All the time I'd been waiting for him to show up at my office, he'd been with Angela. I clenched the wheel in anguish. He'd *touched* her. Had she known, even then? Is that why the expression on her face in the picture, the one where Martin had stroked her hand, was so awful? I shook my head in self-incrimination. Oh, he was a clever boy. It must have seemed simplicity itself to put something in Vic's coffee, giving him the "creeping crud," as Angela had termed it. Then, *voilà*, here's the "new guy," Martin. But how had he passed himself off as a project manager? I'd probably never know, and in the end it was meaningless.

The rush-hour traffic on Hamilton Avenue slowed once again, and this time I nearly snapped the wheel in half in frustration. Come on, come *on* … But I didn't have a choice. I knew Angela had taken I-75 downtown; I would have, it's the most direct route. But I also knew it would be crowded as well, and I had a plan to beat her there. If only I could get down Hamilton. In two more lights the traffic miraculously thinned, and I punched it. If a cop saw me, fine, bring 'em on. I knew the Yugo didn't have a chance of outrunning one of those big old Crown Victoria squads, but maybe I could convince him to give me a ride.

Blowing every light, I shot down through Northside, to the accompanying sounds of screeching brakes and angry horns, then blasted past the lesbian bookstore and rocketed across the viaduct to where Ludlow changed to Central Parkway. Merging with it, I bounced over an uneven piece of roadway, and the little car went airborne. Coming down, sparks flying, I nearly clipped a U-Haul van, and at the same time said good-bye to my muffler. The eyes of the older lady driving the van nearly hung out on stalks. I gave her a savage grin. Just like on TV, huh? As I cleared her, I risked taking a look down at the car seat next to me. Good. The Browning was still there. I hadn't bothered to rip my shoulder holster off the coat rack as I'd flown out of my office; seconds counted. I'd figure out some way to conceal the piece when I got there. I checked the road ahead. Still fairly clear, and I pressed the gas pedal down further. By now there were some uncomfortable sounds coming from under the hood. I ignored them. Surely I wasn't treating this car any worse than the drug dealer had.

And as I drove, I prayed. I'd been praying ever since I thrust the keys into the Yugo's ignition. What was I praying? I don't know. Prayers of mercy for Angela? Certainly. Prayers that I'd make it on time? Without a doubt. And a prayer that when I found Martin, my aim would be true. It went against Christian charity, but to my thinking, that boy had lived way yonder too long. It was past time for him to blow hell wide open.

As I approached downtown, I started slowing the car down, shaking my head in amazement. I'd broken enough traffic laws in my flight down here to have my license lifted for ten years, and I still hadn't seen a cop. Was that the hand of God intervening, or just the inattention of the CPD?

Now I was close, and at every intersection the clanking and wheezing coming from the engine was growing worse. But instead of cursing the car, I began speaking nonsense words of soothing to it. "Come on, little Yugo, we're almost there, almost there ... not far now, you sweet little baby ... not far, then you can rest." It must have worked, because there I was on Pete Rose Way, and straight ahead loomed the darkened silhouette of the RiverTower building.

I pulled the dying Yugo right in front and shut it off, getting out and glancing around. I didn't see Angela's car, but that didn't mean anything. As one of the executives, she had parking privileges at the underground garage. She'd told me just last week they'd gotten the security system down there installed, so the only way in and out of the building now was with a key card. She said she felt safer with it being operative. I suppressed a bleak laugh. *Right.*

Again I looked around me. At the intersection a block ahead of me, cars were crossing, but no foot traffic. That wasn't surprising. It was now fully dark, freezing, and windy. Overhead the streetlights were on, but to me their cold blue glare only made the surrounding shadows seem darker. I reached back in and pulled the Browning off the seat. Taking one last side-to-side glance, I shoved it into the waistband of my jeans, and tugged my sweatshirt down to cover it. Now that's an extraordinarily dumb thing to do, and I'm sure both Sarge and Dave Harrow would have reamed me good for doing it, but it was only going to stay there until I got inside the place. Then it would be back in my hand where it belonged.

I came up to the six-foot-high security fence, but it was "security" in name only. I could tell in a moment it had come from one of those rent-it-all places, and had seen better days. Scaling it wouldn't have posed a problem, but I saw there was no need. The padlock and hasp holding the gate shut looked to be even older than the gate itself, and there was enough play where the two halves came together for me to get down on the ground and shinny through. So that's what I did.

Once on the other side, I stood. No alarms were hooting, so far. I wondered at the thinking that would surround a twenty-million-dollar apartment and office complex with a fence that wouldn't cause a nine year old a problem. Angela had said there were construction screwups here; to me, that fence was Exhibit A.

And then another thought occurred to me: if I'd had no problem getting this far, neither had Martin.

I trotted up to the entrance, where the big double glass doors would go in another two months. Right now the doors were thick plywood, and the lock holding them shut was several steps beyond the one at the gate. Without bolt cutters, I wasn't getting in that way. But somehow Martin had. I craned my neck higher. One floor up was the mezzanine level, and I saw that the opening for one of the huge windows had been left unsealed, ostensibly for supply delivery. But how could …?

Then off to the left I saw the crane.

It was one of those huge kind that somehow grows as the building goes up. Angela tried to tell me once how that was done, but I never did get it. At any rate, that crane was my way in—if I had the guts. Because with my fear of heights, that meant me climbing the leg of that monster up to the window opening, then jumping the four feet across the gap to get inside. *So what, it's only the second floor,* I told myself. *Grow some guts, man.* But Angela had told me she'd designed this building to be one of those "showcase" jobs, with the lobby eventually holding sculpture and rocks and big tropical plants. Not to mention that stupid goldfish pond. The net result was that the first floor of this baby was nearly thirty feet high. Thanks, babe.

Remember when you were a kid, and you went to the circus, and you watched the trapeze guy scale that center tent pole with the ease of a Barbary ape? That wasn't me. Cotton mouthed, my palms sweaty, I started up.

It wasn't pretty: gasping, sweating, moaning, even whimpering once or twice ... that climb wasn't one of my finer moments. And as I went, it occurred to me how Martin had gotten Angela inside: keys. Even as a temp project manager he would have had keys, and as chief architect Angela would have had an entire set. My breathing was getting worse. Finally I was at the window opening. Now came phase two: jumping across that four-foot gap. *It's only four feet, Box. That's less wide than you are tall,* I tried to assure myself. Yes, but it was thirty feet *down,* and construction guys call falling from a building "going in the hole" for a reason.

But I didn't have a choice. Three decades ago, I hadn't been able to keep Linda from dying senselessly. Regardless of Martin's taunt, I wasn't going to let it happen to another woman I loved. And with that thought, I tightened the grip on the crane's leg with my left hand, stretched as far as I could with my right, tensed my legs ... and jumped.

It wasn't so bad. I hardly screamed at all. A second later I found myself prone on the plywood floor of the mezzanine. Shakily I got to my feet, touching a hand to my waistband to see if my gun was still there. It was. Quickly I felt myself all over. Yep, still alive. Okay, let's not do *that* again for a while. I almost reached around back to check my pants, but didn't; I think I was okay there too. I pulled out the Browning, remembering I'd chambered a round in it earlier. Flipping off the safety, I began to walk.

For the first time I noticed how *dark* it was in here. I knew enough about construction to know there were almost always lights left burning all night when buildings were going up, for security if nothing else. But, except for the dim illumination flowing out from the stairwell I was approaching, this place was blacker than Charlie Manson's heart.

Cautiously I eased the stairwell door open, putting the Browning in first. Nothing. I followed the Browning in with my whole body, every sense I possessed quivering like it'd been sandpapered. Still nothing. I released my breath. I hadn't realized I'd been holding it. I looked up the stairs, listening. Not even the wind from outside could be heard.

I swallowed and started up.

As stairways went, these were pretty typical. A half-flight to a small landing containing a twenty-five-watt bulb in a cage, then a turn and on up to the second half. When I reached the floor above the mezzanine, I saw that the door off the landing carried the label, First Floor. In my mind it was the third, but why quibble? So was she here, or on another floor? It would take me until tomorrow to search each floor. And Angela didn't have that long. Tonight at dinner she'd told me the "new guy" had been fascinated by the penthouse, that she'd had a hard time getting him to leave it. Even then, Martin was dropping me a clue. So to reach her, I'd have to climb twelve more flights. Truth is, I'd have climbed a thousand. Setting my jaw, I started.

It was on the fifth floor that I heard a distant noise. I

stopped breathing, listening hard. The sound was that of a slow creaking, back and forth like a metronome. And below that creaking, a dripping. I sniffed. There was also a faint smell here, like hot copper. I knew that smell. Thrusting the Browning ahead of me, I slowly started up the dark stairs once more. By the seventh level the sound had gotten louder. It was all I could do to keep from calling Angela's name. Wiping my mouth with my left hand, I came up onto the landing. As I did, my feet slipped in something slick. The copper smell now was overpowering.

That's where I found the body.

It was hanging by the neck from a rope in the almost nonexistent light, and when I saw it I almost did two things at once: gag, and sink to the floor in relief. It wasn't Angela, thank God. But it was *somebody's* corpse, and I forced myself to look at it again. A guard. The guy was young, not yet thirty, maybe a family man moonlighting for some extra Christmas money. Instead of that, now they'd get his insurance. Happy holidays, Mrs. Jones. Even though it was pointless, I reached up with my left hand to check for a pulse in his neck.

My hand sank into blood.

I jerked my hand back, but it was too late: it was covered in the stuff. But why was I so surprised? I'd known in my gut what that smell was; I'd smelled it plenty in Vietnam. Wildly, I looked around. It was everywhere. I was standing in it. Choking back nausea, I swung the body so the dim light hit it better. The guard's throat had been slit; judging from his expression, while he was still conscious too. Drip, drip, drip. Around the corpse's neck, Martin had placed a small cardboard sign: I'm Waiting for You. And pinned to that sign was something else.

A Tarot card.

Death.

Old Skinny Bones himself.

It took a few seconds for my stomach to quit churning. I looked back up at this poor kid's carcass with a sigh of anguish. "Martin, Martin, what in the world am I going to do with you, son?" Wiping my hand on my jeans, I brushed past the guard, which started him slowly swinging again. Indicative of nothing, I noticed his shoes had a terrific shine. Not much of an epitaph: the dead man's shoes were well tended.

Side-stepping around the lake of blood, I continued on up. I must have been in better shape than I thought, because I was barely winded as I came to the last door. Penthouse. Turning the knob, I slowly swung it open.

There was no light at all up here, except for that from the city itself coming in the windows. And windows there were, everywhere. This one gigantic area was going to be the dwelling for some lucky, rich son-of-a-gun, and whatever he or she was paying for it, the place was going to be worth every cent. Sure there were room-dividing walls, nailed down and Sheetrocked and spackled, but it was easy to see the penthouse's crowning glory was going to be space.

I walked in, shutting the door quietly behind me. Three steps inside I stopped. Where was he? Where were *they*? On the way down in the Yugo I'd wondered what would happen when this meeting occurred. Was I going to do the gentlemanly thing and give him first crack at me? Forget that. As soon as I saw that freak, I was going to drill him straight through the heart.

"Oh Martin," I sang softly, "I have something for you."

His only answer was a soft chuckle from a far dark corner of the room.

I waved the gun in that direction, but held my fire until I was sure. "You'll like it," I said. "I just bought it today, from a guy named Dave."

Still no response.

My voice grew louder. "We can do this any way you want. Since I'm feeling generous tonight, with Thanksgiving being so close and all, I'll make you a deal: you bring Angela out into the light, and I'll give you a two-minute head start. What the heck, make it three."

Finally he spoke. "I'll pass."

I must have needed to schedule an ear exam, because for some reason his voice now sounded like it was coming from the opposite corner.

"You'll only die quicker with that attitude," I said, looking over there.

His laugh was light. "I don't think I'll die at all. Kill me, and she's lost." Now his voice was back to where it was before. Who was this guy, Senor Wences?

I tried to keep the tightness out of my throat as my banter fell away. "What have you done with her?"

Another soft chuckle, this time coming from above me. "Oh, many things. You'd be surprised."

This was beyond ventriloquism. Another one of Martin's tricks? With a will I banked the fear down as I slowly began moving to my right. If I could get him to do the same, center him in one of the windows, I'd shoot him where he stood. I needed to keep him talking, see if I could make out a pattern in this.

"Did you know Greg is alive?" I said. "I heard it on the news on the way over. The airport police found him in the wreckage. He's in the hospital."

"Oh, I doubt *that*," Martin laughed again. "I finish what I start." Now his voice was coming from *behind* me. It was all I could do not to whip around and stare. He rasped, "I saw that helicopter crash with my third eye. I have one, you know. You can't see it, but it's there all the same." He whispered in my ear. "I'm a spooky old rascal."

That did it. Barely suppressing a scream, I spun around, and if it hadn't been for my training I would have wasted a shot on nothing but air.

"Do you feel me, Joe?" Martin breathed, coming from nowhere and everywhere. "Many men can scare you. But I'm the one who can make you cry."

Sweet Mary, he knew how to slip in the knife. I'd never before been in the presence of such pure, uncut evil. But I couldn't lose control now, not at this point. Silently I said another prayer for protection as I started moving again. I had to swallow before I was able to talk. "You're an interesting dude, Martin. A rare blend of heartlessness and pride. It takes a special kind of guy to kill his own dad."

"Like you wanted to do with yours?" he asked. "Oh yes, Joe, I know. We're not that far apart really."

I didn't trust myself to answer. He'd come closer to the truth than I wanted to acknowledge.

"Dear old Dad," Martin sighed companionably. "He and I had a lot of issues, as they say." He chuckled again. "All of them resolved now."

I'd had enough of this ghoul. Time to finish him and be gone. I gripped the Browning tighter. "*Where's Angela?*"

"I ate her," he said. Then he giggled.

And then the break I'd been praying for occurred. High overhead, the thick overcast parted for just a moment. When it did, the gibbous moon shone down. In the pale, ghastly light washing through the windows, I could barely see an outline in the far corner. I wasn't even sure it was a man until I caught the faint sparkle of light in his weird eyes.

I leveled the Browning at the specter. As soon as I was sure of a clear shot, I'd fire.

Martin must have sensed my thoughts. "Your gun won't avail you, Joe," he said. "But feel free to give it the old college try. Oh, and just in case you're wondering if you really have the wherewithal to kill me, given your recent conversion, let me help you. I'll give you two reasons to shoot me dead, if you can. Your woman had lovely eyes." He paused. "Until I took them."

With a howl of pure grief I started pulling the Browning's trigger just as fast as my finger could move, tracking him as he exploded from his corner in the same instant. But I wasn't the only one armed. Martin fired back as he ran, and from its tinny sound I could tell he was packing some sort of .22 handgun. That sounds like a really light caliber, which it is, but for close-up killing, the .22 is the assassin's gun of choice. A well-placed round can hit a bone and then ricochet around inside the body like a Pachinko game, chewing the insides like a piranha. I'd heard a story once of a .22 striking someone in the collarbone and a second later exiting out his leg.

Luckily the shells Dave had given me were hollow points rather than military ball ammo, which was good. Military ball would have gone straight through Martin, while the hollow points were designed to mushroom out. Martin and I both kept ripping off one shot after another. The noise was tremendous. Neither of us could get a clear shot at the other; trying to shoot at a running target in near darkness is an impossible task, no matter how good you are.

Suddenly I felt a sharp pain in my left shoulder, like someone had punched it with a red-hot ice pick, then it went ominously numb. I kept on shooting.

And then, only seconds after the gun battle had started, it was all over. The eleventh round roared from my gun, the brass tinkling as it hit the floor, and the slide locked open.

He'd vanished again.

Son of a— Now what? Even though my weapon was useless, I still held it out in front of me, my breath coming in gasps as I screamed his name. "Martin! Martin, you sadistic mother, are you dead *yet*?"

I heard him laugh, from everywhere. "Not quite, Joe."

And then I saw him. He was illuminated by a flaring match held in his hand.

Martin was standing in the opposite corner of the room, hard by an item I'd missed: a big, black drum of something. Whatever the stuff was, it was emblazoned with a red diamond and the word "flammable" on its side, and the lid for it was lying on the floor. I could smell its contents, sharp and acrid. That couldn't have been safe. Hey Ange, you missed this in your notes.

Martin took note of the empty, smoking piece in my hand, shaking his head in mock sympathy. "Eleven shots, and I'm still standing tall. That has to be frustrating for you."

"Not really." Most of my rounds I'd fired had missed him. But not all. I lowered the gun, the pain in my shoulder now starting in earnest. "We both got lucky. Look at your shirt."

He did, frowning. "Oh, that's a bother. And I just bought this shirt."

A *bother*? It should have been a shade more than that. In the light of the rapidly dwindling match Martin was holding I could clearly see two holes in him. One of them was nothing, a side wound, glancing. It had probably done nothing worse than crack a rib. But the other one was a different matter altogether: deep, and just to the right of his heart. I'd seen wounds like that back in the war. The shock effect alone should have killed him instantly. So why wasn't he dead?

But I never got the chance to ask.

Martin jiggled the fluttering match at me. "Much as I hate to, it's time to end it, Joe," he grinned. "As I said, I always finish what I start. Now watch. With your fear of burning, you're going to love this."

And with that he savagely kicked the drum over, sending its contents cascading my way.

And in the same motion he dropped the match.

Whatever the stuff was—some sort of cleaning fluid, I guess—it was as volatile as gasoline. The match had barely touched its surface before an immense wall of fire was roaring straight at me.

"JESUS!" I screamed his name as a prayer, jumping aside only at the last second as the heat washed past. But here Martin had made a serious miscalculation. Finally. The floor must have been the tiniest bit off plumb, because just as the fire was on the verge of reaching me, it suddenly stopped and ran back the other way.

Engulfing him.

If I live to be a thousand, what happened next is something I'll never fathom. Martin should have been thrashing on the floor, screaming in agony. Instead, he just stood there grinning, crowned head to foot in flames.

And then ... then he began to laugh. The doomed, crazy fool put his arms out to either side, laughing like burning to death was the funniest thing ever. Lord have mercy, what kind of a creature was this?

Then his laughter stopped. "Do you think I'm a *child*?" he screamed. "Fire can't hurt me. Don't you get it yet? *Nothing* can hurt me!"

Martin should have been hurting. Bad. His clothes were flaming. His hair was a penumbra of fire. I could smell him as he burned.

Just like Yoshi.

But the idiot was oblivious, and his laughter grew even more raucous. "Have you heard the story of Gilgamesh?" he shrieked. "The immortal man, walking the earth forever? I'm that man!"

I could now hear him sizzling, drops of flaming suet falling from his body onto the plywood. Where they fell, smaller fires jumped up. Martin was dead, only the sad, sick, sorry fool didn't know it yet. Mad as a March hare to the end, the devil's payoff. But he was right about one thing. It was time to end it, true enough. The hour had come for me to put paid to his life. But with what? I couldn't begin to get near him.

Martin was still screaming. "Before the world began, I am! The Jesus myth perverted me! But I'm the one they seek!" As he said that last part, one of his eyes popped and began running down his cheek. Man, that was gross. I had to put Martin out of my misery. Then stepping back, my foot brushed something, and I looked down. It was what was left of a five-gallon can of dry-wall mud, lying by my feet. I jammed the Browning into the waistband of my jeans. With my left arm hammering pain, and losing blood with every beat of my heart, seconds counted. I reached down with my right hand and grabbed the can by the handle.

Martin threw back his head, his screams growing even louder. Through the holes in his face, I could see his tongue melting, his words becoming garbled. "I will exalt my throne above the Most High! I will be exalted above the stars of heaven! I am beyond life, beyond death, beyond—"

"*Gravity?*" I yelled, and hurled the can at him just as hard as I could.

Eight pounds of dry-wall mud in a can hitting you in the chest at that speed has to be like taking a haymaker to the heart. Martin blasted back, his remaining eye bulging at me, arms windmilling in spasm as he landed hard against the already bullet-weakened glass. It held for a split second. Then it gave way with a crash, taking Martin's flaming body on through.

I ran over to watch. Sick I know, but I just had to see it for myself.

He fell silently, twisting as he rolled over. And then somewhere in Martin's dying mind what was happening to him must have finally clicked. It had to have been at that point the devil lifted his hand from Martin's life.

Because halfway down he started shrieking in horror.

At the mezzanine level he struck an outstretched girder, landing on it back first with a thud. The crunchy sound of his spine snapping was audible even from where I stood looking down. And then he was draped over both sides of the girder at an impossible angle, head and heels touching, his body swaying gently.

And that was it. Martin was gone. Blown. Barking-in-hell dead.

But there was no time to gloat. I felt heat on my neck,

and I whipped around in panic. The situation with the fire was growing critical. It was spreading, looking for its next meal. I had to get out of here, now. But not without Angela. Regardless of what that freak had done to her, she was my love. And even though it was hopeless, I began screaming out her name.

Nothing. No answer came back but the hungry roar of the fire.

Where *was* she? I looked around wildly, and then the thought hit me: downstairs. She'd made it downstairs, and was safe. That had to be right, because I simply refused to believe Angela was on this floor and was going to burn. Ergo, she was somewhere else. It's amazing how the mind works.

And the heart.

The fire now was only inches away from my feet. In the distance I could hear the wail of approaching sirens. *Burnt out twice in one week,* I thought stupidly; that had be some kind of record. I was lightheaded from blood loss, my skin growing dry, and the smoke now was worse. Across the burning penthouse, dimly seen through the flames, I could make out the stairwell door. It might as well have been on Mars. My choices were stark: stand here and burn with the building, or try to make it to that door. But I knew that even running full tilt, I'd be a human torch before I reached it. I remembered a scene from *The Towering Inferno*, where Robert Wagner had tried just such a stunt. He hadn't made it either. I looked over my shoulder. If I wanted it badly enough, there *was* another way down. Martin had found it. Falling or burning? Either one held terror enough.

But then a thought broke through. No, more: a scripture. I couldn't have told you where it was found, and I only recalled a fragment. But it was enough: *When thou walkest through the fire, thou shalt not be burned.*

Now I understood. Running wouldn't save me. Walking with God would. I gulped. "Thank you for your Word," I whispered, and started moving toward that door.

Don't ask me how it worked, because I can't answer that. All I know is that with every step I took, the flames moved aside. One step after another they moved, and I marveled as I went. Hey, Nebuchadnezzer, take a look. The three Hebrew children and me.

Then I was at the door, then through it, and on my way down. And my clothes didn't even smell of smoke.

I had to have set some kind of a land-speed record as I stumbled my way down all those stairs, bouncing from one side to the other, and then I was at the window opening in the mezzanine. Right at eye level, catty-cornered through the opening on the side of the building, I could see Martin's body as it continued to cook. Burn, baby, burn.

I looked back through the window. Four feet out from me was the crane's leg. I'd just survived getting incinerated. A thirty-foot climb down, even with a bum arm, was going to be a snap. Without a further thought I jumped the gap and began clambering down the steel latticework of the crane, ignoring the pain. Maybe I was a Barbary ape at that. A few seconds later I was on the ground, bent over, sucking in the delicious, freezing November air.

That's when I heard her voice. "Joe?"

I whirled around. It was Angela. And more, she was fine.

"Ange?" My legs gave way, and I found myself on the dirt, looking up at her. "Hey! You're not dead."

She was looking down at me with wide eyes, and no wonder. The guard's blood had to have been all over me, not to mention my own. I must have looked like I'd just been to a hog slaughter. A good analogy. Angela pulled a wad of tissues from her purse, pressing them against my wound. "Somebody get a doctor!" she screamed to no one in particular. "Please!"

She bent back down and kissed me, her eyes now brimming with tears. I heard her praying something unintelligible, then she sobbed, "Don't you die on me, Joe Box. Do you hear? Don't you die on me!"

"I wouldn't think of it," I mumbled. She sounded awfully far away. "But how—?"

She was still mashing those tissues, talking a mile a minute, trying to keep me with her. "I just got here. There was a wreck on 75. A maple syrup truck flipped. Everything was shut down."

"Maple syrup ... ?" So Martin had never had her at all. A deceiver, right to the end. For some reason that struck me as funny, but I couldn't get myself to laugh. "I'll take a short stack ... extra butter ..." The light was fading.

"Oh God, we need an ambulance here!" she screamed again.

A few seconds later her prayer was answered as three cop cars, two engine companies, and a life squad unit came roaring up. The firemen leaped off the truck, the para-medics trotting over with a collapsible stretcher.

"He's been shot!" she said.

One of the medics, a young guy with a kind face, gen-tly pushed her aside. "We've got it, ma'am." The other guy put some kind of IV in my arm, then I felt myself lifted onto the stretcher. As they put me inside the ambulance, I heard Angela say, "Can't I go with him?"

"You can follow," the younger medic said. "We're taking him to Bethesda."

The last thing I saw as the doors were shutting was one of the cops talking with Angela. She was crying.

42

I looked up to see Angela's sweet face hovering over mine.

My tongue felt coated with something vile, my lips bone dry. I licked them once, then said, "Am I dead?"

She bent down and kissed me, her eyes welling up again. "No. But it's not for your lack of trying."

I looked around me. I was in the hospital, not surprisingly. I glanced down at my shoulder. Bandaged. Which meant I'd been in surgery, which meant this was the recovery room. What a detective I am. Behind Angela I noticed five other people standing there: a nurse, a doctor, Olivia Ravine, some other older guy I didn't know, and Jack Mulrooney. Seeing him, I shook my head. "Now I know I'm not in heaven."

The doctor said, "I know you people would all like to

speak with this man, but as his physician I'm going to insist that you to limit your visit to ten minutes." He looked down at me. "Lieutenant Mulrooney wanted me to delay your morphine drip until they've finished, Mr. Box. Of course I wouldn't." He glared at Jack. "But if you're in severe pain, I'd be only too happy to have them leave now." He and Jack were now glaring at each other.

"No, I'm fine," I mumbled. "Let's just get this over with."

The doctor nodded, then turned to the hawk-faced nurse by his side. "Make sure they don't overstay their time, Dorothy."

She nodded grimly at him, as if it would give her immense pleasure throwing them all out. All except Angela, of course. "Yes, doctor," she said as he left. And then she actually pulled up her sleeve to check her watch. Caramba.

The older guy said to me, "I'll bet you don't remember who I am."

I frowned at him, trying to focus. "Not a clue. Sorry."

He gave me a slight smile. "I'm Ken Donnelly."

Ken Donnelly? Good grief, of course I knew him. Donnelly and I had been rookies together during our District Three days over on Warsaw Avenue. I had to stop myself from saying, "Ken, you look like the very devil." Because he did. Ken was no longer the sleek, young, cocky patrolman I'd known. Now he was jowly, paunchy, and red-eyed, redolent of cheap cigarettes and sidetracked dreams. If this was what going a career path with the cops led to, I was glad I'd gotten out when I did.

Donnelly said, "I'm a detective now. Homicide." He flipped

his badge at me, even though he didn't need to. I would have believed him. "We've got some questions for you."

"I'll just bet you do," I smiled weakly. Blood loss will do that.

He cocked his thumb over his shoulder. "Lately Jack's been taking your name in vain, Joe. He's had a standing order at headquarters that if you were found hanging around anything less squeaky clean than a Girl Scout cookie drive, you were to be picked up forthwith and delivered to him personally. I guess this little deal qualifies."

"'Forthwith'?" I muttered. "He must be going for his G.E.D."

Jack just gave me hooded eyes and a slight smile. His look of "I win" said more than words could have.

Donnelly turned to Angela and the nurse. "Okay, ladies, I'm going to have to ask you both to leave while I ask Joe some questions."

The nurse's face grew even harder, if that was possible. "This man is recovering from a gunshot wound, officer. I don't think—"

Donnelly just looked at her. "Ma'm, I'm sorry, but it has to be done now."

The nurse frowned at him, and Angela gripped my hand, her eyes huge. "Can he do that, Joe? Make you be in the room with … him?" That last part was directed to Jack. Regardless of her joke to me the night the Agnes burned, Angela has excellent taste in men. She knows a fool when she sees one.

With pure will I forced my mind to clear. *Let's get this done,* I thought. *I can rest later.* "Jack's vice," I told her. "This is normally out of his jurisdiction, but if he wants to sit in on the questioning, he can probably pull it off." That much said took some starch out of me, so I drew a breath before going on, "Who cares anyway? Once he smelled my blood in the water, he'd have found a way to insert himself in the mix somehow. This way I deal with him now. Let's do it."

Donnelly looked at the women. "Ladies. Please?" He nodded toward the door.

Angela blew out an exasperated breath. "Oh, all right. But we're going to be right out in the hall." She gave me a tender look. "Go easy with him, will you? He's had a rough night."

"Haven't we all?" Donnelly sighed. He waited until the women had left, then he picked up a briefcase from the floor and laid it on my bed. Opening it, he pulled out a large plastic envelope with something inside. My Browning. A small tag was tied to the trigger guard. "This little item here intrigues me," he said. "Make my life easy and tell me you have a permit to carry."

"Sure do, Ken," I answered. And I did. Just not a permit to carry *that* one. They'd find out soon enough the piece wasn't legally mine, since I hadn't paid for it yet, so technically it had only been lent to me by Dave. Maybe that loophole would keep us both out of the pokey.

The rest of the interview went about like I'd thought. Donnelly's questions were fairly straightforward, and Olivia Ravine jumped in only when the question of how the fire started came up. And the more I talked, the stronger I felt. That was weird. Maybe this was that "strength of the Lord" stuff they talked about at church. Jack stalked around while

Donnelly talked. I could tell he was chomping at the bit to have a crack at me, and that was verified when I saw him pull out a cigarette and put a match to it.

"Yo, Jack," I said, "this is a hospital. Don't be lighting up around sick people."

"So call a cop," he said, dragging the smoke deep.

"Yeah, I forgot," I said, "You're already a sick person." He didn't answer but continued his pacing. Olivia just shrugged.

Finally Donnelly was done and stepped aside. "All right, Jack, I'm going to let you finish up here, then I'm shutting this down. Don't go over the line."

"Wait a minute," I said. "Is that kosher? Letting a vice guy grill me?"

"Who cares?" Donnelly answered tiredly. "As long as it gets done. Besides, I owe him. This'll clear it."

"Owe him for what?"

"Never mind," he said, then he stepped back, and now Jack was standing by my bed.

"This won't take long," he said, in his usual insincere way. "I only need to get a few things cleared up."

With that he went into full Jack mode. He pranced and sneered and primped and leered, all the time blowing cigarette smoke in my face. It was pretty clear he'd learned his technique watching Nazis in old war propaganda films. But I pretended like I was a Yank flier shot down and working with the French Resistance, so it helped keep my head clear. Olivia Ravine kept looking at him, and I really think it was her presence that kept Jack from becoming too rabid with me.

Only once did things get dicey, and that's when the

inevitable question came up regarding my knowledge of the barbecue man, and how he'd ended up as Today's Special.

"You're going down for this, Box," Jack growled, "and hard, unless you tell us all we want to know."

I gave him a disbelieving look. "Good grief, Jack, that's awful. Who's your dialogue coach, George Raft?" I looked at the inspector. "Could you do this instead? I think Jack needs more time learning his lines."

That got her. Though she tried to hide it, I saw her laughing behind her hand. Even Donnelly chuckled. Jack spun around and caught her, narrowing his eyes. "You're not helping me here, Olivia."

"Sorry," was all she said, but you could tell she wasn't sorry at all. I think maybe I had an ally of sorts in Olivia Ravine.

Jack leaned down over me. "Let's make this an early evening all around. I'll only ask you three things. Tell me what I want to know the first time, then I'll leave you alone so you can get some rest." He looked up at Donnelly. "Okay with you, Ken?"

"Sure," Donnelly shrugged. You could tell that all he wanted to do was get home.

I doubted Jack would keep his word, but I said, "Okay, shoot."

He held out his right index finger. "One. Who's the victim we found tonight at RiverTower? Two—"

"Which victim?" I broke in. "The guard or the other guy?"

"We already know the guard's name," Jack gritted at me, putting his hand down. "It was in his wallet."

"Then obviously you mean the other guy," I said. I heard Inspector Ravine snort another suppressed laugh.

Jack ignored it. "Yeah," he said. "The other guy. Mister sizzle."

"Him. Well, Jack, that would be one Martin ten Eyck, son of the late, unlamented Senator Henrik ten Eyck, five-time legislator from Ohio and former head of the Senate Appropriations Committee." I smiled at him.

Inspector Ravine quit laughing. "Mr. Box. Is this true?"

"True as anything, inspector," I said. I turned my attention back to Jack. "And to keep you from losing count with your fingers, Lieutenant, the answers to your other two questions are, in order, yes, I killed him, and why? Because he was a murderous, flaming maniac. In his case, literally."

"Maniac?" Donnelly frowned.

I nodded. "Check with Dr. Claude Winter of the Longwood Memorial Hospital in Columbus. He told me all of Martin's sessions at Longwood were recorded, including the threats he made to his father. He'll verify everything I'm telling you. Or should, now that his former patient has become a Yule log."

"His father," Donnelly frowned. "The news has it that he and his chief of staff were killed by spider bites. The bugs came in on some plants he bought."

"Do a little digging and you'll see who sent him those plants," I said.

"This sounds like Sherlock Holmes junk," Jack snarled.

"When the impossible has been eliminated …" I said, but Jack just frowned at me, not getting the quote. What a dullard.

As he was processing all this, Donnelly shook his head. I held up a hand. "Okay, I'm going to give you guys the truth here"—as much as they could handle, anyway—"and since this was a righteous shoot tonight, I'm going to be pleading self-defense at the inquest."

And so I proceeded to tell it: Martin's turncoat activities in Vietnam, his capture and thirty-year incarceration in the nuthouse, and his release and quest for revenge. Of course I left out all the other men's deaths of third squad. No sense trying to prove what was improvable. I made out like the only one Martin was after was me, and he'd used Angela as bait. Which was true, as far as it went.

"So this guy Martin used his cover as a project manager to lure your sweetie down there tonight," Jack said, "for the sole purpose of killing you for what you did to him more than thirty years ago? That's what you're telling me?"

"That's it," I agreed.

He and Donnelly looked at each other, then Jack grinned down at me, "But all we have is your word against his. And he's not talking. Not anymore. I think I—"

"Check the guard's shoes, Jack," I sighed. My lips felt thick. The morphine was kicking in.

"What?"

"His shoes. The guy must have been in the Corps. You don't see them spit-shined like that too much anymore. Then compare the prints you lift off them to the ones Martin ten Eyck had taken when he went into the Marines. You'll find a match."

"You sound awfully sure, Mr. Box," Inspector Ravine said pensively.

"I know," I said. "That's because I am."

"So how do we know you didn't kill that guard, Joe?" Donnelly asked. "And then killed this Martin guy to cover it up?" He shrugged apologetically. "Sorry, but you're going to be asked this again. You know, at the inquest."

"Because I didn't have a motive, and Martin did," I said. My throat was growing tired. "He killed that guard to get him out of the way, and then hung that stuff on him to play with my head. Like that Tarot card thing. My unit used those when I was in-country to intimidate the Cong. Martin knew that. I'll lay even money that if you check Senator ten Eyck's place, you'll find one of those cards there, and that it came in the last day or so. My bet is that it arrived with those plants. And if all that's not enough, there are the phone records that'll bear out Martin's threat to Angela."

"What phone records?" Jack said. "If he called you like you're saying, it wasn't long distance, it was local. There aren't any records of that."

"Check the system on the first floor of RiverTower," I croaked. Now that the interview was winding down, so was my strength. "It's going to be all offices there. Angela told me they got the call system hooked up last week, so they could start keeping records of anything incoming or outgoing. She said it would help keep the personal calls down, and save the future office tenants some money. Not to mention adding another layer of security. So by running the tapes or whatever they're using there, you'll find Martin's call to my office tonight. And his threat to Angela." Blearily I smiled at him, my vision growing dark around the edges. "Satisfied?"

"Not really." Jack's grin was savage. "Tell us again."

I didn't. I passed out on him instead. Jack really was a jerk. Have I said that before?

But I did end up telling Ken Donnelly the whole thing again three more times over the next two days. To my surprise, he'd done as I'd suggested and called the lab, telling them to run the prints off the shoes. As I was telling it to him for the last time on that Tuesday, some uniformed cop brought in the faxed report from there. During that final go-round, Jack was back in the room, and he and Donnelly gathered around the thing, reading it like it was the Rosetta stone. They whispered and muttered and frowned, all the while Jack looking like he'd swallowed a bug. Then cursing me or his luck or something, he stormed out. Sorry, Jack. Skunked again.

And then Donnelly sprung a bombshell.

"We found ten Eyck's car parked a block down the street from RiverTower, Joe," he said, "and we got his address off the registration. Turned out to be some dump apartment over a butcher shop in downtown Columbus." *A butcher shop,* I thought. *That sounded about right.* Donnelly went on, "We had a judge there, a guy named Shanklin, cut a search warrant for it." His lips twisted in a grimace. "You'll never guess what the cops found when they got inside."

"Knowing Martin, it could be anything," I said.

"On the back wall, where his computer and printer were, were news articles," Donnelly said. "Edge to edge, top to bottom. Some from newspapers, some gotten off the Internet and printed off. A lot of them featured his father. In the articles, wherever the senator's picture was shown, Martin had taken something sharp and cut out the eyes. Then he took a red marker and x'd out what was left. There were also Tarot cards lying around. All Death ones. Weird, huh?"

"That's our Marty."

Donnelly fixed me with a gaze. "But that's not all. Besides the stuff on the senator, there were a total of thirty-seven other articles, each one a story about somebody who'd been killed violently in the last month. The date on the first one happened to coincide with the day Martin was released from Longwood. The stories spanned twelve states. So, as a matter of course, all the victims' names were run through CSIS in Washington. Guess what was found?"

"I'll bet you're about to tell me," I said.

"Eight of the victims, including a guy who died in New York a couple of days ago, happened to have been with your unit in Vietnam." Donnelly's placid look belied his words. "And in checking, some of them had been sent Tarot Death cards. How do you figure that, Joe?"

Here we go. "He hated us for capturing him," I said simply. "Mixed in with Martin's rampage were attacks against us. Somehow he made those deaths look like accidents."

Donnelly shook his head. "But that won't wash. Like that article we found about that Haggin guy dying of a stabbing in Boise … unless he was the killer. Or some guy named Przbasky's supposed suicide. And again, what about the cards?"

"Any news of any of third squad dying, from whatever

cause, his own hands or another way, would've made Martin a happy camper," I said, shading the truth again (sorry, Lord). "It must have looked like the fates were on his side. I'd say the bulk of the articles just reflected Martin's simple love of death. The cards, though, I can't explain." And wasn't about to try.

I knew Donnelly wasn't satisfied, but at the end, he slapped his hands down on his thigh with a grunt. "I guess we'll never know the whole story here." *No, I bet not.* Then he spoke the words I'd been waiting to hear: "I'll see what I can do for you, Joe."

It still had to go through channels, but by Wednesday morning the paperwork was done. Donnelly and Jack both came to my room to deliver my exoneration—Jack, I'm sure, hoping for some miracle to negate the thing. And then I got the pleasure of seeing Jack again glaring ropes at me as a male nurse came and wheeled me into the world, a free man —well, released on my own recognizance pending a full hearing, that is. Oh yeah, Donnelly kept the Browning as evidence, no surprise. Dave's turn to be grilled was coming next. I knew that wouldn't be pretty, but he was a big boy and could handle himself. From here on out it was going to be smooth sailing.

Make that skating. The night before, the temperature had plummeted, and now winter had arrived in all its frozen glory at last.

Before they'd sprung me, I'd called Angela from my room for a ride home. As I sat in the wheelchair outside with the nurse standing next to me, waiting for her, my left arm in a sling, I looked up at the sky. The snow was falling at last. *Over the river and through the woods …*

Angela pulled up to the curb, beeping at me. The car, I mean. Not her. She powered down the passenger window. "Hey stranger, need a lift?"

"Are you a woman of good repute?" I asked. "I never ride with women of less than good repute. My Granny always told me to be sure."

"Oh, I try," Angela laughed. "I try."

I levered myself out of the wheelchair, climbed in her car, and shut the door. Both of us grinning like teenagers, with a yip of tires we pulled away then, gone in the swirling flakes.

43

"How about some spuds, ma'am?" Using only my right hand, I dug another large spoonful of mashed potatoes out of the pot, laying a glop of them on her plate.

"Thanks, mister." The toothless old woman smiled at me. Holding her plate with one hand, she tentatively reached over and touched my sling with the other. "Gun or knife?" she asked.

"Gun," I said.

She nodded. "I knew it. I been shot twice and stabbed once. None of 'em was no fun."

"But you're still here," I smiled. "Still standing, when the last dog died. That's the important thing." That was the truth.

"Sometimes standin's all ya got," she nodded again. "Can I have me some gravy with that?"

"Sure can." I picked up the ladle. "You want it just on the spuds or over the whole mess?"

"Cover it," she said. I did, drenching everything on her plate: turkey, yams, dressing, roll, potatoes, everything.

When I finished, the old woman closed her eyes and put the plate up to her nose, inhaling so deeply I thought she was going to vacuum up her food. Grinning at me, she then moved on down the line to get her drink. The next man shuffled up, handing me his plate. I put some spuds on it, and he moved on without even a grunt.

It didn't matter. Just the simple act of filling their Thanksgiving plates bonded me with these homeless folks. I wasn't all that far removed from them myself. John Lennon had said it once: "All you need is love." And Donna Franklin had added, "Then you pass it along."

Angela set a new pot of potatoes down next to me with a thud. Her face was flushed with heat from the kitchen, her hair smeared wetly across her forehead. But as she smiled tiredly at me with those incredible eyes, right at that moment she was the prettiest woman on earth.

"Why don't you take a break?" I said. "I thought I just saw Dempsey Miller bringing in another big jug of iced tea. How about letting me get you a glass?"

"You're the one that ought to be sitting down, Joe," she said. "One day out of the hospital, and you're working the chow line. I'll bet the doctor who took out that bullet wouldn't be happy with you right about now."

I motioned with the mashed potato-encrusted spoon. "No, but they are. I needed to be here today. Doing this." I drew in a breath, looking out over the scene.

The gym floor at the new sanctuary hadn't gotten done—

just as Pastor Franklin thought—so the Pike had instead rented the YMCA meeting hall for the homeless banquet. We were two hours in now, and it was still going great guns. Nearly two dozen members of the church had given up their own holiday meals to cook and serve these people who otherwise would have gone hungry today. The long tables were filled with them; somebody said we'd cooked for and served more than two hundred people so far, and we'd keep doing it until the pots were scraped dry. I saw Nellie Preston, one of the richest ladies in the church, bend down to give a dirty two-year-old a piece of cornbread she'd made herself. Holding it tight with grubby fists, the little kid dug in. Nellie leaned over and softly kissed his head.

I nodded. "This is important," I said.

Angela smiled at me. About then an anorexic-looking teenage boy, the septum of his nose eaten away by cocaine, wordlessly thrust his plate at her. "Hi," she said, taking it. "How are you?"

As I continued to serve, my mind started to drift back to yesterday. After Angela had picked me up at the hospital, I'd asked her if she minded running me over to the office so I could make a few calls.

"I hate to have you do it though, because I'm liable to be there for a while," I said.

"It doesn't matter to me," she shrugged. "The arson people haven't released their findings. Until they and the city inspectors give us the go-ahead, no more work's going to be done on RiverTower."

"I feel bad about that. Like it's my fault."

"Stop it. You didn't ask that maniac to start the fire. If you hadn't thought I was being held there, you wouldn't have been there at all." She smiled. "Macho man."

"Hi-yo, Silver," I said, and she grinned.

Once at the office, I'd started making some calls. The first one was to Melanie Frontenau. Her line rang three times before she picked up. "Hello."

Not knowing what condition she was still in, my words to her were simple. "Mel, it's Joe Box." I paused. "It's done."

I heard her swallow twice. Then she said, "Dat man Little Bit was scared of. Dat man dat killed him. He's dead?"

"Dead as vaudeville," I told her.

She blew out a breath. "Good." She said it again. "Good." Then— "An' the bill?"

I remembered Martin's burning body draped obscenely over that girder. "Paid in full," I said, and we hung up. Somehow I knew we'd never speak of it again.

The next call was to Dave Harrow. "Dave, it's Joe," I said when he picked up.

"Where you at?"

"My office."

He grunted. "Thought you might be locked up for a stay at the Graybar Hotel."

"If Jack Mulrooney had his way I'd have been ordering curtains for my cell by now," I said. "How'd you make out?"

"Not too bad. The cops had me for a while, then they turned me over to the ATF boys." He grunted again. "Pansies. They woulda piddled their drawers in my outfit."

I almost hated to ask the next. "What did they do to you?"

"I had to do some fancy dancing to keep my license. I got off with a stern lecture, a thousand-dollar fine, and a permanent mark on my record." He snorted. "As if I didn't have enough of those already. And it's a good thing you had a conceal-carry ticket. If not, I'd be on my way to Lucasville now." That was the state pen. "Oh yeah," he added, "I heard they kept the Browning. It'll end up in some bureaucrat's collection."

"I'm sorry, Dave."

"I'm the one who insisted you take it," he answered. "Just tell me one thing: is the world short one more bad guy today because of all this?"

"Real short," I told him.

"Good. Then it was worth it." He hung up.

No, what was worth it was what happened next. I hadn't even lifted my hand from the phone when it rang. I picked it up. "Box Investigations."

The voice sounded tired. "Hey, Joe. Just callin' to tell you I'm still alive."

My face lit up in joy. "Marcus!" Angela grinned and pulled her chair closer. "How are you, man?" I said.

"I been better," he allowed. "Feels like I been rode hard and put away wet, you want to know the gospel truth."

"I can imagine."

"Naw, Joe, I betcha can't," Marcus sighed. "Just as soon you didn't." He paused. "You know, as all that grain was thunderin' in on top of me, all I could think of was that time I'd told everybody in the squad that my worst fear was bein' suffocated to death. Durn near happened too." He paused again. "That was Martin's doin', wasn't it." It wasn't a question.

"Yeah," I said. "We'll never be able to prove it, but it was him." I gripped the phone tighter. "Martin's dead, Marcus. I saw it for myself. He'll never bother us again."

There was a silence, and I thought the phone had gone dead. Then I heard Marcus softly sniffle. "God's good, ain't he?" Then, without waiting for an answer, he quietly hung up.

"Hey, mister, can we have some potatoes?"

"Huh?" That was yesterday. Now someone else needed my attention. I looked down. The questioner was a little girl, no more than nine, with an even younger girl—her sister?—in tow. "Sure, hon," I said, reaching for the spoon again. "Here's some for you both. How about gravy?"

An hour later we were finished serving. Now came the cleanup. I was ready to pitch in, reluctantly, when I ran into a phalanx consisting of Nellie Preston, Donna Franklin, and Angela.

"Joe, you've done enough for one day," Donna scolded.

"She's right," Nellie agreed, then she looked at Angela. "Why don't you take this stubborn man on home?"

"Are you sure?" she said. "Joe could go sit down while I—"

"No, shoo." Nellie was making waving motions with the backs of her hands. "There's plenty left here to help clean. You all go on now."

"Well ... okay." Angela took my hand. "Come on, you."

We'd been on the road a few minutes when I turned to her. "Could we stop by where the Agnes used to be? I know it's out of the way, but—"

"But you need to see it one more time." She nodded. "Of course we can."

Angela hadn't balked, sulked, or probed. I almost shook my head. What a marvel she was.

In twenty minutes we were there. We pulled up in front, and I got out. "Do you want to come with me?" Oddly, I really didn't want her to.

"No." She shook her head with a smile. "No, you go on. Do what you need to. I'll be here, waiting."

Walking up to the ruin, I noticed that the same woman who'd spoken harshly to me Sunday was on her porch, sweeping snow. She gazed at me with baleful eyes as I approached my former home.

"I told the cops about you," she called over to me.

"I thought you might."

"They said to let 'em know if you showed up again."

"Well," I said, "now you can." I looked up at the shell. What in the world was I doing here?

"They're tearing it down tomorrow." The woman was holding her broom tightly. "The city sent some men over. I heard 'em talking."

"Is that a fact?" I looked over to my right. All the flattened cars were gone, towed to the scrap heap. It didn't matter. My old car would live on in my heart.

The woman looked like she was going to say something else when suddenly she swung at something with her broom. "Scat, you ugly creature!" I turned to see what had her riled.

Noodles.

I blinked. No. No, it couldn't be. Could it?

It was a cat of some sort, and it was tearing down the woman's porch, making a beeline for the yard like a broken-field runner. Suddenly it saw me. Cutting a sharp ninety-degree turn, the cat charged, jumping the last five feet right up onto my chest. Instinctively I grabbed it, then looked down to see what it was exactly I'd caught.

It was him.

"Noodles! How in the—?" I hugged him close, then thrust him away, peering closely at him for any fresh burns. There weren't any. I hugged him close again, laughing like a loon. I just couldn't believe it. He was alive, in my arms, and purring for all he was worth.

"That mangy cat yours?" the snotty woman frowned.

"He's not mangy," I said, still laughing. "He's disfigured." And some disfigurements you can see, while others are only of the heart. Martin had taught me that.

"That artist fella was over here yesterday," the woman said. "When he saw that cat he said he remembered him tearing out the door between his legs that night. He thought it was a hallucination." She shook her head. "Jerk. Some hallucination, that has to be fed milk."

"You've been feeding him?" As I scratched his ear stump, Noodles groaned in ecstasy.

"That's what I said. But only milk, and he was lucky to get that."

"Thanks, lady," I said, meaning it. "This cat ... he's my friend." The woman rolled her eyes.

I looked down to where Angela sat in the car, and I held Noodles high. When she saw him, she clapped her hands and bounced. I could hear her squealing her joy even through the closed glass.

Tenderly I pulled him down close again. "Come on, buddy. Let's go home."

He looked up at me, blinking. "Naow?"

"Yeah," I said, holding him even closer, the tears squeezing through at last. "Right now."

So we did.

UNTIL THE LAST DOG DIES

Branching Out

A guide for personal reflection or group study.

Joe Box walks the city streets of Cincinnati, helping some, receiving abuse from others. In this way, Joe is very much like Jesus Christ. Jesus, when he walked here on earth, was very human indeed. He felt joy and pain, just like Joe Box, and just like you and I. He endured much to achieve his goal, including the ultimate humiliation and suffering—being nailed to a cross as a criminal when he had done no wrong.

Let us walk for a while with Joe Box through Cincinnati. While doing so, let us look for how we can walk with Jesus on the streets of our city.

Jack Mulrooney has it in for Joe. Do you think this is because Joe left the police force, or could it be a deeper issue—one between Jack and God? Do you meet up with people who take out their internal convictions on you? How would you respond?

Joe says that "Sarge" Tim Mulrooney had a "foxhole conversion" while fighting in Korea. What does he mean by "foxhole conversion?" What triggered your conversion experience?

Joe can sometimes tell when an event is about to happen, or that he needs to get out of his apartment building now. He calls this "being fey." The Bible calls it the gift of discernment (1 Cor. 12:10). Have you experienced this gift working in your life? How did you know it was from God?

Angela, Joe's girlfriend, is referred to as an "intercessor." What are intercessors, and what role do they play in our lives as Christians?

Joe offers to do his investigation into Little Bit's death as *Lagniappe*—an unexpected blessing. How does God give *lagniappe* to you? How do you offer *lagniappe* to others?

Fear was the common denominator among Joe's platoon mates. They each died from what they most feared. What fears haunt and chase you?

Someone has said, "All men are driven either by fear or faith, for they act in the same way. Each is a reaction to an event that has not yet happened." Do you live more by fear, or by faith?

Look up the following verses dealing with fear. How do you respond to each of these?

Exodus 14:13

Joshua 1:9

Isaiah 8:12

Isaiah 41:10

Matthew 14:26

Luke 12:5

John 9:22

Romans 8:15

Hebrews 13:6

1 John 4:18

We are led to believe Martin ten Eyck became the kind of person he was through involvement in the occult—"psychic phenomenon, mind control, Indian fakirs, snake charmers." Are there any occultic influences in your life?

Joe and his pastor, Luke Franklin, are in the pastor's office.

> *Luke's smile was compassion itself. "It's not my church, Joe. You ought to know that by now. It's God's. There's only one standard for membership here, and you made it last August. The man who did those things in Vietnam is more than thirty years gone."*
> *"Then why do I feel like I've still got him strapped to my back, like Martin's rifle?" My throat felt rough, as if I had been crying. Or screaming. "It's like I'm dragging around a dead man. I thought that stuff was supposed to be over with."*

Compare this with what Paul wrote in Romans 7. How do we get rid of the dead man we are carrying? Hint: Look at Romans 8.

Pastor Franklin continues the conversation with Joe:

> *"The Bible talks about working out our salvation," Luke said. "It's a difficult saying, but I take it to mean that we all have issues we're going to have to face in our walk with the Lord."*

What does it mean to "work out our salvation"? Look at Philippians 2:12. How do you work out your salvation in your life?

Luke tells Joe to *"do whatever it takes to shut that madman down."* Is a Christian ever justified in using violence, including lethal actions?

Joe had to call his friends to warn them about Martin. In doing so, he encouraged them to "get right with God." Are there any friends you know who need a similar message from you? How will you handle those calls?

Tim Mulrooney, better known as Sarge, is Joe's spiritual mentor. Joe calls Sarge for advice regarding Martin. Who is your spiritual mentor? When is the last time you talked with him or her?

Angela tells Joe that the spirit world is real—both sides. "The Bible tells us that one of every three unseen spirits is a fallen angel," she says. Do you believe in a literal devil and his demons? What power do they have on earth today? What protection do you have from his devices?

After the Agnes burned down, Joe was a homeless man, with no clothing and no car. The Harvard Pike Church came to his aid, giving this man they hardly knew a place to live, a car (okay, it was a Yugo—but it still beat walking), and clothing. How does this demonstrate the body of Christ at work?

Mr. Sapperstein tells Joe, "In this crazy world, when everything falls, God stands." Do you believe this? How can you apply this to the craziness you are experiencing?

The Word at Work . . .

*W*hat would you do if you wanted to share God's love with children on the streets of your city? That's the dilemma David C. Cook faced in 1870s Chicago. His answer was to create literature that would capture children's hearts.

Out of those humble beginnings grew a worldwide ministry that has used literature to proclaim God's love and disciple generation after generation. Cook Communications Ministries is committed to personal discipleship—to helping people of all ages learn God's Word, embrace his salvation, walk in his ways, and minister in his name.

Opportunities—and Crisis

We live in a land of plenty—including plenty of Christian literature! But what about the rest of the world? Jesus commanded, "Go and make disciples of all nations" (Matt. 28:19) and we want to obey this commandment. But how does a publishing organization "go" into all the world?

There are five times as many Christians around the world as there are in North America. Christian workers in many of these countries have no more than a New Testament, or perhaps a single shared copy of the Bible, from which to learn and teach.

We are committed to sharing what God has given us with such Christians.

A vital part of Cook Communications Ministries is our international out-reach, Cook Communications Ministries International (CCMI). Your purchase of this book, and of other books and Christian-growth products from Cook, enables CCMI to provide Bibles and Christian literature to people in more than 150 languages in 65 countries.

Cook Communications Ministries is a not-for-profit, self-supporting organization. Revenues from sales of our books, Bible curriculum, and other church and home products not only fund our U.S. ministry, but also fund our CCMI ministry around the world. One hundred percent of donations to CCMI go to our international literature programs.

. . . Around the World

CCMI reaches out internationally in three ways:

· Our premier International Christian Publishing Institute (ICPI) trains leaders from nationally led publishing houses around the world to develop evangelism and discipleship materials to transform lives in their countries.

· We provide literature for pastors, evangelists, and Christian workers in their national language. We provide study helps for pastors and lay leaders in many parts of the world, such as China, India, Cuba, Iran, and Vietnam.

· We reach people at risk—refugees, AIDS victims, street children, and famine victims—with God's Word. CCMI puts literature that shares the Good News into the hands of people at spiritual risk—people who might die before they hear the name of Jesus and are transformed by his love.

Word Power—God's Power

Faith Kidz, RiverOak, Honor, Life Journey, Victor, NexGen — every time you purchase a book produced by Cook Communications Ministries, you not only meet a vital personal need in your life or in the life of someone you love, but you're also a part of ministering to José in Colombia, Humberto in Chile, Gousa in India, or Lidiane in Brazil. You help make it possible for a pastor in China, a child in Peru, or a mother in West Africa to enjoy a life-changing book. And because you helped, children and adults around the world are learning God's Word and walking in his ways.

Thank you for your partnership in helping to disciple the world. May God bless you with the power of his Word in your life.

For more information about our international ministries, visit www.ccmi.org.